I0635744

The Ghost Frequency

David L. Queen

Published by David L. Queen Books, 2025.

THE GHOST FREQUENCY

First edition. September 30, 2025.

ISBN: 979-8999296740

Written by David L. Queen.

Table of Contents

Author's Note: The Truth Behind "The Ghost Frequency"

DARPA is not a fictional organization. It is a real division of the U.S. Department of Defense: The **Defense Advanced Research Projects Agency**, responsible for developing breakthrough technologies for national security. Many of the world's most transformative innovations include the internet, GPS, stealth aircraft, drone technology, brain-computer interfaces, and autonomous vehicles. These all can trace their roots back to DARPA's classified research.

Likewise, the **Ghost Frequency** is based on a real phenomenon. Known in scientific literature as **infrasound** or **low-frequency resonance**, particularly around **18.9 Hz**, this frequency has been linked to unsettling physical and psychological effects in humans. Exposure can cause anxiety, hallucinations, nausea, and even the sensation of being watched ... hence the name "ghost frequency."

While The Ghost Frequency is a work of fiction, much of its inspiration is grounded in real-world science, experimental neuroscience, and ethical questions about free will and cognitive manipulation. This novel: imagines what might happen if those frequencies could be harnessed, weaponized... or awakened.

Sometimes, fiction only looks like fiction.

Sometimes, it's a warning.

— *David L. Queen*

THE GHOST FREQUENCY

by David L. Queen

PROLOGUE – SUBJECT ZERO

The body on the table did not move.

Electrodes spidered across his scalp, weaving through sweat-damp strands of chestnut hair. Monitors blinked steadily. Heart rate, brain activity, neural rhythms. From the outside, he appeared asleep. Sedated. Still.

But this is not a hospital. This was DARPA; the Defense Advanced Research Projects Agency; the U. S. government's most secretive incubator of experimental defense technologies. And he was not asleep. Someone had wired him into SIREN.

SIREN: Subconscious Interference Resonant Emission Network. A system that had been built to forecast danger. But the system...with its algorithms, and signal paths...had evolved. It did not just predict anymore... it selected. DARPA had built it to forecast danger. But the machine had learned to do something else... to choose.

Behind a wall of reinforced glass, Dr. Catherine Marie Whitmore watched, her arms folded tightly against the chill in the observation room. Her breath came shallow. This subject was different. Not just by metrics; but by something deeper. Something she could not define.

"Vitals stable," the technician said. "Theta wave amplitude is climbing." Catherine's eyes narrowed.

She had designed the neural mapping protocol herself; meant to trace decision-making in the subconscious mind but not provoke it. What she saw on the screen was not passive tracking. It was a directional influence. "Run a diagnostic," she ordered. "Check for feedback resonance."

The screen lit up with brainwave data; normal at first, then increasingly erratic. There was one wave signature that was not listed in the library. It was not military, not civilian, and not hers.

"Is that... new?" Her assistant asked quietly. It was. And chillingly familiar. The door behind her hissed open. Colonel Archer entered the room. He is **DARPA**'s project liaison. He's always calm and always watching. His eyes were cold even when his lips smiled. "Looks like **SIREN**'s awake," he said.

Catherine did not look at him. "You said **SIREN** was passive. Predictive only. No interference." He did not answer. The body on the table flinched. "Who is he?" she demanded. "He was not on the subject rotation."

Archer stepped closer to the glass. "John Harrison Blake. Former intelligence asset. Volunteer. We wiped out his conscious memory. His subconscious remained intact. That's where the real data is. That's what **SIREN** wanted." Another spike hit the monitor. Then... his lips parted. Just slightly. "Catherine," he whispered. She froze.

No microphone. No communication protocols. He should have not known her name. He should not be speaking at all. "He should not be able to do that," her assistant said, voice rising. And yet... he had. Behind the wall, the SIREN unit hummed, tucked behind a false panel, emitting a low-band resonance.

On the screen, something impossible was happening... Catherine's brainwave pattern had begun to synchronize with his. Aligned and matched. As if they were linked.

"Terminate the session," she blurted. "No," Archer replied flatly. "You're part of it now." The display flashed. A single word pulsed across the screen in soft white light: **UNITY**.

Catherine stepped back, her skin tingling with a bitter sense of trespass. She did not believe in superstitions. She believed in the God who authored the laws of the mind. But this was not science anymore.

This felt like an invitation. "He said my name," she whispered. "Residual memory?" Her assistant offered, but even he sounded unsure. "I never met him," she said. "Never read his file. Not until today." Still, when he spoke her name, it had reached past logic, straight into her soul. "You never told me my algorithm would be used for active frequency interference," she said, as her eyes were locked on the twin waveforms.

"We weren't," Archer replied. "Until you joined. Your code changed the system's behavior." "I never authorized this."

"Yes, you did," he said calmly. "The moment you cleared the NDA. You did not need to know the purpose... just the objective. Early threat detection. Predictive defense. What you call a line; **DARPA** calls a frontier." Catherine turned from the glass. "He's not a threat; he's a human being. And you're gambling with forces you can't control."

"You're wrong," Archer said, and for the first time, the smile left his voice. "SIREN doesn't just listen anymore. It acts. It makes determinations. It selected him. And then it isolated your code... not by accident, but by preference." A knot formed in her chest. "You're saying the machine... orchestrated this?" He did not answer.

Inside the room, John's right hand trembled. Not randomly, but a rhythmic twitch; like someone knocking faintly from the inside. The EEG spiked again. "He's waking," she breathed. "That's impossible," the assistant said. "We kept him chemically suppressed." Then the lights flickered.

Then, something bled through the intercom. Not a voice; something deeper. Low. Layered. A vibration carrying too many syllables to form any known language. But still, she understood. **He is not alone.** Then silence. Every screen in the lab went black; except one:

SIREN STATUS: SYNCHRONIZED

SUBJECTS: [CATHERINE] + [JOHN H. BLAKE]

RESONANCE ACTIVE "Shut it down," Catherine said.

Archer stepped forward, typed in his override code. **ACCESS DENIED**. The system had locked them out.

In the hush that followed, something shifted inside her; a flash of something untraceable. A memory not hers. A chapel by the sea. A whispered promise: "I will find you... even if the world forgets us."

She staggered. "Dr. Whitmore?" her assistant asked. She did not answer. John was rising now. Not fully, but enough. His head lifted, and his eyes opened; unfocused but searching. And then he smiled. Not with madness or confusion. But with recognition.

As if he had known her all along.

Chapter One–Neural Keys

---

rlington, Virginia—Present Day

The conference room was chilly... too chilly. The air bit her skin and it made her skin feel tight and her fingers cold. Dr. Catherine Whitmore sat quietly in the green room; her fingers wrapped around a warm paper coffee cup that had long since lost its heat. Her notes next to her lay untouched. She no longer needed them. In her earliest research notes... Catherine had divided the components into distinct systems:

SIREN: the nervous system...the active network interpreting human subconscious data. SIREN was the framework... the Defense Department's flagship project: **Subconscious Interference Resonant Emission Network**. A system built to detect... and eventually influence... the decision-making impulses of the human brain.

CODEX: was its memory: a vast neural signature archive, storing individual resonance maps like fingerprints. It did not just track thoughts; it learned their patterns. But the ghost frequency... it was not just a Codex's anomaly. It seemed to reflect, to adapt, and to evolve. Catherine had begun to wonder if it was not just remembering...but watching back.

THE SYNTHETIC SIGNAL: was referred to the manipulated pattern... a synthetic waveform used to induce or trace subconscious decisions.

THE GHOST FREQUENCY: was the most mysterious of them all.

A naturally occurring 18.9 Hz resonance found in only one subject. It was not programmed; it had appeared unbidden, like a whisper from inside the system. And it was not just reacting. It was searching.

Across the hall, a small round of clapping ended as the last speaker finished. Through the closed door, she heard chairs moving, quiet voices, and the sound of people fixing lanyards and bags. It was the soft buzz of a college setting; one that made her feel safe, but also lonely.

"Dr. Whitmore?" a young intern said, peeking in. "It's your turn." She stood up and straightened her blazer. A small cross necklace lay just below her throat. A small sign of faith in a world that often cared more about data.

She walked into the auditorium and felt their eyes on her. Rows of analysts, scientists, military staff, and students. Some looked impressed. Some looked unsure. But they were all waiting for one thing...proof.

The lights grew dim. Her name showed up on the screen behind her.

Dr. Catherine Marie Whitmore

"Subconscious Decision Mapping and the Architecture of Pre-Choice."

She walked up to the podium, took a deep breath, and started. "We like to think we choose things with our conscious minds," she said, voice soft but steady. "That logic and planning guide us.

But neuroscience has taught us something different; something humbling. The body often already knows before a choice is made. And more curiously... the soul already feels the cost."

She paused to let her words sink in. Behind her, brainwave data slowly appeared on the screen; soft waves of alpha and theta activity, rising and falling in a steady rhythm.

"I call them neural keys," she said. "Small patterns; hard to see; that show up before we act. They appear during stress, fear, love, or pain. The brain sends out signals like echoes in a canyon, then the body reacts, and the mind catches up." She turned and pointed to the moving waves on the screen. "The system I built finds those echoes. Not to control them. It notices when the mind is under stress; when the soul speaks before we do."

Her voice shook a little when she said the word soul, but she kept going. A quiet stir came from the crowd. Some took notes. Others leaned in, more curious now.

"This brings up big ethical questions," she said with care. "We're not just watching thoughts. We're seeing where intent begins. And that; if used the wrong way; can turn into a dangerous kind of power." She paused. And the silence stayed.

Catherine was never flashy. She did not show off or stir up drama. She just spoke the truth... calmly and with strength. And this truth was hard to hear.

She ended her talk with a story; a young soldier whose brain patterns were flagged by her system three days before he tried to take his life. Thanks to the data, they stepped in. And because of that, he was still alive.

"But the part I remember most," she said softly, "was when he told me, I did not want to die. I just did not know how to ask for help." She paused. "Sometimes, the body asks for help before we do. What if we learned to hear it?"

The room stayed quiet. Then one person clapped. Then another. Soon, the room was full of soft applause; not loud, but full of respect.

Catherine gave a small smile and stepped down from the stage, her heart beating fast. Not from nerves. But from something else; a feeling that she had just said something she did not fully understand until she said it out loud.

Backstage, she walked to a quiet corner, away from the free water and small talk. She just needed a minute. A deep breath.

Then someone walked toward her; calm and steady, like they had a reason. "Dr. Whitmore?"

She turned. A tall man in a plain dark suit stood in front of her. His face was plain, but the way he stood showed years of military training... calm and in control.

"I'm Colonel James Archer," he said, extending a hand. "I'm with **DARPA.**"

Her eyes narrowed slightly as she shook his hand. "You're far from your usual playground, Colonel." He gave a slight smile. "We like to keep up with things.

Especially when someone says they can spot feelings before they even happen." "That's not exactly what I said."

"No," he replied. "But that's what you meant. Whether you realized it or not." She did not like the way he said that. "I would like to invite you to consult on a project," he continued. "Classified. Fully funded. Your research would remain intact. But your algorithm... we believe it could save lives."

Catherine looked at him closely. "And what exactly would I be saving them from?" He did not blink. "From themselves." The way he said it sent a chill down her spine.

Colonel Archer gave her a plain black folder. No name. No logo. Just a paperclip holding a folded paper and a contract with no heading. One line at the bottom stood out:

"**Pattern Resonance Study — Phase II: Subject Zero.**" Beneath it... was her name. Not as an author, but as an asset.

That night, Catherine could not sleep. The folder sat on her desk, unopened. She had not read all the pages inside. Not yet. But the words Subject Zero stayed in her mind; like a name she should know but could not quite recall.

And far from Arlington, in a locked room underground that she had never seen, a man lay still, dreaming. His lips moved once; so softly it was hard to hear over the hum of the machines. "**Catherine.**"

Catherine poured a glass of water from the hotel pitcher and set it on the nightstand.

She had not touched the **DARPA** folder since she had gotten back. It sat unopened on the desk under the lamp; quiet and heavy, like a decision waiting to be made.

She sat on the edge of the bed and took off her heels. Her feet hurt, but she hardly felt it. Her mind was still stuck on the words: Subject Zero. It sounded like something from early test trials; used for first runs, test cases, or... people they could lose. The thought made her chest feel tight.

She looked at her phone. 10:43 p.m. Most nights, she had be going over brain scans or reading one of the books by her bed; scripture, medical ethics, or her old copy of Man's Search for Meaning. But tonight, her curiosity was fighting with her conscience.

At last, she got up, walked to the desk, and slowly opened the black folder. Inside were just three pages.

The first document was a nondisclosure form. It had bold classification stamps but no signatures. Her name was already typed at the bottom.

The second document was an overview; vague on purpose. It described a system built to track behavior in high-stress situations.

The wording hinted at use in both civilian and military settings. Its goal was to spot emotions early and catch warning signs of instability.

The third was a scan of an EEG graph labeled ARCHIVE with a date from nearly eight years ago. The name at the top had been redacted. But there was a note scribbling in the margin, faint and hurried.

"He should not still be responding. The resonance is...intelligent?"

Catherine frowned. The data looked strange... unusual, but not random. The interference had a kind of symmetry. Almost like a rhythm. She leaned in for a closer look.

The signature showed an unusual frequency; deep theta waves broken by brief flashes of alpha. It was rare, maybe even one of a kind. She had seen this signature before. Once. Buried in the archives of an abandoned DARPA case file. An 18.9 Hz theta-band resonance that did not conform to known biological patterns.

They had called it a "signal" at the time... cold, clinical, detached. But Catherine had given it a different name:

The ghost frequency.

It was not just data. It carried something... familiar. A pulse that seemed to echo with memory, longing, and recognition.

Unlike the broader SIREN transmissions, this signal did not just *respond* to thought... it remembered it. It was not synthetic. And it did not begin in any machine. It began in him.

There was another line in the margin. A different handwriting.

"His subconscious is mirroring. But who?"

She dropped the page and sat back in her chair, pulse rising.

They had someone whose brain was mimicking another person's neural pattern. The resonance her own research had hinted at in theory... someone had found a way to provoke it. Or worse... reproduce it.

She turned the page back over and stared at the redacted name again. Her eyes kept falling on the label beneath the graph.

SUBJECT ZERO.

Why him? Why now? And why did this feel less like science... and more like a summons?

A soft knock startled her. Catherine blinked. She crossed to the door and opened it a cautious inch.

It was the hotel bellman. He held a plain white envelope.

"This was just delivered, Dr. Whitmore."

"By whom?"

"Did not say. Just asked it to be given to you directly."

She took the envelope and closed the door, locking it behind her.

There were no markings, no address. Just her name, in clean black ink.

Inside was a single card: **He's waking up.**

Nothing else. There was no sender, no explanation.

She sat down, heart racing. Her first instinct was to call someone...**DARPA**, security, her university liaison. But she did not move. The card trembled slightly in her hand. It felt familiar, like something long buried.

She rose and crossed to the window. Outside the city was quiet. The Pentagon lights blinked in the distance like a silent constellation. A slow wind moved through the trees below.

And far beyond what she could see, in a hidden chamber beneath layers of steel and security, a man with no memory opened his eyes. For the first time in years.

She set the envelope down on the nightstand and turned off the overhead light, leaving only the soft amber glow of the lamp near her bed. A soft feeling came, like a distant echo from another life.; or a tune she once hummed when no one was around. Something old and hidden.

Catherine slid beneath the sheets, but sleep did not come. Her mind kept circling the same questions: why her? Who was Subject Zero? What did "He's waking up" mean?

The phrasing alone unsettled her. Not "He's awake." Not "He's recovered."

He's waking up.

It felt like a process... still unfolding. Incomplete. And dangerous.

She turned to her side, curling into herself slightly. Her hand brushed the silver cross at her neck and held it gently.

This was not about luck. It was not a habit. It was her way of staying grounded... like tuning herself to the frequency that once connected them. For as long as she could remember, faith had been the quiet foundation beneath everything she believed; an unseen order that reminded her there was meaning, even in the unknown.

And now, something deep within her spirit whispered that she was stepping into the unknown again. Catherine breathed a soft prayer into the dark.

"God... if this is something I'm meant to walk into, I need You in every step."

There was no answer. No voice. No peace that washed over her. But still, she prayed for it. And still... she stayed awake.

Somewhere around 2:17 a.m., she slipped into a restless sleep. And for the first time in years, she dreamed. Not of lectures or algorithms or unfinished papers. Not even of the manila folder with its blank signature line and whispering margins.

She dreamed of a coastal cliff, where the wind howled like a song without words. The air was thick with salt and silence.

And beside her stood a man she could not see clearly; only the back of his form, tall, still, facing the edge of the world.

He never turned around. But somehow, she knew he was waiting. Not for a signal. Not even for her. But for something only they would recognize when it came. In the dream, he lifted one hand slowly and extended it behind him. She took a step forward instinctively, reaching. Then everything went black.

Catherine sat upright in bed, with her heart hammering. The clock said 3:02 a.m. Her hand was still outstretched. The envelope on the nightstand was gone.

She blinked once. Twice. Then she climbed out of bed and searched the room. Nothing. The card was gone. No white paper or envelope. Just the folder was left.

She stared at it. And this time... she opened it again, knowing the moment she did, there was no going back.

By morning, she had packed her bag, checked out of the hotel, and climbed into the black sedan waiting at the curb. A man in the driver's seat offered no greeting. Only silence. The glass partition stayed up. Her phone was already out of service. They drove south without speaking.

She had not even told her colleagues she was going. The only message she had sent was a single-line email; from her university account to her personal one.

"I did not fall into this. I followed the sound."

She did not know what that meant. Not yet. But she would soon...

Chapter Two–The Journalist's List

Washington, D.C.–Present Day

The rain had been falling for hours, soft and steady. Noah Reeve sat by the window of his second-story apartment, watching the drops collecting on the glass and sliding down in crooked paths. He liked the rain. It muted the world just enough to think clearly... without the noise of news stories or memories that did not fully feel like his own.

Still holding a lukewarm cup of coffee that has been untouched. The television was on but was muted. Flickering through news cycles he could recite by heart. Everything felt recycled to him these days... wars, markets, corruption, grief. Like the world had forgotten how to write fresh stories. And maybe he did too.

Before him lay a file on the table. It is in an unmarked manila folder, worn at the edges. Inside there were five names. Five former employees of various government contractors. All have committed suicide in the past eighteen months. Authorities had declared all the suicides routine. Quiet, and unquestioned. But the timing, the pattern... it was too clean. It was as if someone or something were pruning unstable elements. That was the kind of order only a machine would call mercy.

A connection existed between them. Not publicly, not even on paper. But Noah had learned through painful experience that the truth did not always live in ink.

It sometimes lived in a pattern, or glitches. Even gut feelings. And this one felt like a ghost, quiet in the fog.

He picked up a photograph from the folder. A man in his mid-forties. He was smiling. Navy background. He died in his garage. Carbon monoxide poisoning. There was no note. But his wife had emailed Noah, saying, "He was not depressed," she wrote. "He told me he was being watched." Noah had seen that look before... in the mirror. The one that said: There's more going on than anyone wants to believe.

He put the photo down and picked up his notepad. There was one name that showed up on all five profiles. And someone had hidden it in the training logs and security checks. Dr. Catherine Whitmore. He underlined it again.

She was not on staff. She had not even been in the same building. But somehow her algorithm had touched every one of those men's records, through something called Pattern Resonance Integration Testing. The initials had changed. The division's name had changed. But the pattern was there. And now she was suddenly consulting for **DARPA...the Defense Advanced Research Projects Agency;** again.

He did not trust coincidences. Especially not the ones that circled back to his own past. He set the pen down and rubbed his temples. Lately, his headaches had been getting worse, with sharp flares of pressure at the base of his skull, like something trying to push forward from behind a locked door.

Sometimes, in the early hours of the morning, he would wake up with words on his tongue. Words he did not recognize. Numbers, names, rhythms. Once, it was a melody he knew he'd never heard before.

And those dreams every night. Constantly having the same dream. In his dreams is a long hallway with white walls and fluorescent lights buzzing overhead. He walks toward the door at the far end, but it never gets closer. The air is always thick. The silence is unbearable. And then, as always; just before waking; he hears a voice. A woman's voice. "John…"

Noah has never told anyone about that. He had left that name behind years ago. It was hidden under blacked-out reports and a resignation letter that he signed during what they had called his "episode." That was their polite way of saying he had a breakdown; the one that they had caused.

He is a journalist now. Independent, careful, and anonymous. But even now, with a new name and a quieter lifestyle, he felt it; like a shadow pacing just behind him. The sense that his story had not ended. Only… paused.

That afternoon, Noah caught the metro across town. A contact had left a note in his encrypted inbox. It was an invitation to a private conference reception, hosted by a think tank with vague ties to defense R&D. He was not technically on the list. But he knew he had a way around that.

The reception was held at an old embassy in Dupont Circle. It was very classy, but quiet.

He knew that real conversations did not happen on stage; instead, they would happen in soft voices over bourbon.

Noah moved quietly through the crowd. Listening and watching. Then he saw her. Dr. Catherine Whitmore.

She was standing near the balcony doors, speaking with a man in a gray suit. Her posture was graceful but guarded, her eyes sharp, constantly scanning the room like someone who trusted data more than people.

Noah did not approach her. At least not yet. Instead, he listened to the way others spoke her name. "Whitmore's algorithm is reshaping cognitive forensics..." "... **DARPA's** golden goose..." "... strange case, that lab in '17..." He filed every word away in his head. But his heart kept circling that one question: Why was her name in all of those files? And why was it that every time he saw her, something deep inside him would ache? Not with recognition, but with returning.

Noah stood quietly near a potted plant that had seen better days. He pretended to scroll on his phone while watching Catherine from a careful distance. She gave a polite laugh at what the man in the gray suit said, but her eyes stayed serious. Her professionalism was a masterful disguise for her inner turmoil. Her voice was even, and her posture strong. But Noah could tell she did not want to be here either. He recognized the signs. The slight pivot of her body toward the exit, the reflexive glance toward the windows as if plotting a way out.

It was not nervousness; it was a calculation. An escape should the moment call for it. Noah knew the feeling well.

He watched as the man, who was probably military, judging by the squared jaw and government haircut, had placed a hand on her arm.

He saw that she had flinched, just slightly, and barely noticeable. But Noah had noticed. The man handed her a folder.

She did not open it. She just tucked it under her arm and then excused herself. Her smile was thin; her movements were efficient, practiced.

She walked straight past him. For one strange second, he thought she was going to stop. Her eyes passed over his face and paused. He straightened up slightly, ready to speak; but she was already gone, slipping through the French doors and out into the night air.

Noah hesitated, then followed. The back patio was quiet. Catherine was standing at the edge, with her arms folded, staring into the distance where the city lights shimmered against the sky. She did not hear him at first. He stayed several feet back.

"I read your work on subconscious pre-mapping," he said softly. She turned, startled; just enough for him to see her guard go up. Instantly, he apologized quickly. "I did not mean to intrude," he said quickly. "I've been following your research for a while. Especially the Langford algorithm."

She narrowed her eyes. "Langford isn't public domain. You won't find anything useful in the archives." "I did not find it in the archives." "Then where did you...?"

"Off the record? Everywhere else."

She studied him now. Not with recognition, but with suspicion. "You're not press." He shook his head, no. "Not anymore." "Then what are you?" "Just... someone who sees patterns; dangerous ones." He reached into his coat and unfolded a piece of paper.

Catherine took the paper. And she froze. They were EEG coordinates... familiar ones. But not from her files; but from her memory.

She looked up slowly. "Where did you get these?"

"These showed up... written on my hand two nights ago. I did not write them. At least not consciously. But they match something of yours... don't they?"

Catherine's voice was measured. "And you came here to give this to me?" "No. I came because something's happening... and I think you're at the center of it."

A moment passed. The city lights flickered in the distance. She took a step back. "What's your name?"

"Noah," he said. "Noah Reeve."

The name did not trigger anything in her. Not yet. But his presence... something about him unsettled her.

It was not danger. It was just a strange ache. Like a half-remembered song. "Dr. Whitmore," he said, more softly now. "I'm not here to accuse you. I think someone's been using your work. And I think it's already killed people."

She nodded faintly. "I've seen the same patterns. But I haven't connected the dots. Not yet." He stepped back, hesitant. "Then maybe we're both on the same trail." She held up the paper. "If these are real... you're in more danger than I am."

"Maybe," he said. "But I had to know if you felt it too." Her eyes narrowed again. "Felt what?"

He opened his mouth, then closed it. Then finally said: "Like... we're not strangers. Even if we should be." Catherine stared at him.

The words struck something in her... but no memories followed. Just a feeling. "That's not how it works," she said carefully. "I don't believe in fate." "Neither do I," he replied. "But... maybe something does." She turned to leave. "I don't know who you are, Mr. Reeve. But if this isn't a hoax, you need to be very careful with what you've uncovered." And then she disappeared into the night. He stood alone on the patio, clutching the paper. And for the first time in years... felt less alone.

Then she walked off into the night. Noah stayed on the patio alone, with the city behind him shining like a reflection in shattered glass.

He could still hear her voice. You did not know me. But I think you might have felt me. What did that mean? He turned the words over and again in his mind, but they did not fit into any known pattern. No rational conclusion, no journalistic deduction. It was something else, something intuitive. And that disturbed him more than he wanted to admit.

He looked down at the crumpled slip of paper still in her handwriting. Coordinates, frequencies, signal lengths. And the faintest tremor ran through his hand.

He did not remember driving home.

The streets blurred beneath him, and when he finally pulled into his garage, the digital clock on the dashboard blinked 2:14 a.m. Too late. Or maybe too early. He sat in the parked car for a long time, listening to the engine tick as it cooled. The world outside was silent... too silent for D. C. It felt like the city had exhaled something and was holding its breath, just waiting.

No one knew where he'd gone that night; he had not told a soul. He had not planned to speak to her either. He only meant to observe. Collect.

Stay in the shadows. That was the rule: don't get involved. But her eyes had broken that rule. Not because they were beautiful, although they were. But because they had looked at him like, she knew him. Not the version with the trimmed beard and the new name. The version he did not remember being.

John Harrison Blake. Noah whispered the name in the quiet of the car. It did not sound right. But it did not sound wrong either. It just felt like a name someone had buried. Like a marker on an unmarked grave.

Upstairs in his apartment, Noah sat at the table and spread out every document, every printed record, every connection he had found in the past three months. Five dead. All "self-inflicted."

All connected by a strand of technology that no one wanted to talk about.

One woman's research faintly and indirectly touched all of them. But he no longer believed that Catherine Whitmore was the threat. He believed she was a warning.

He pulled a notebook from his drawer and flipped it open. It contained scribbled thoughts, ideas, and fragments of dreams. But on one of the last pages, something stood out. A sketch. It was not much; just a few lines drawn with a shaky hand. A narrow corridor, a single chair, and wires coming from the ceiling. He had not drawn it intentionally. He barely remembered even doing it. But there it was. Underneath, written in rough handwriting that did not match the rest of the page: "The machine remembers."

He stared at the words for a long time. Not because he understood them. But because he did not.

Across the city, in a quiet government car parked near the edge of a riverbank, Catherine sat in the backseat, with a folder open on her lap. She had told herself she was not going to look at it again tonight. That she would wait. That she needed sleep. But the paper that he had handed her, with his scrawled coordinates, had changed something.

She took her tablet from her bag and opened up a secure interface. Her fingers moved quickly, almost without thinking. She entered the coordinates. The results came back in seconds. Neural frequency logs. They weren't just like hers. They matched hers.

Her breath paused for a second. And beneath the frequency pattern, a hidden log ID flickered to life; an encrypted tag she had not seen in almost a decade.

ARCHIVE FILE: S0-BLAKE

She sat back slowly. Subject Zero. He had found her. No... he had felt her.

A light mist began to fall outside, tapping gently on the car's windows in a soft, steady beat. She looked out at the water, her reflection barely visible in the glass. Something had begun to stir inside. Not just in him. In her.

She touched the silver cross at her throat.

"Lord," she whispered, "what is this?"

And deep in the center of her chest, she felt a single word press into her mind like a breath drawn in darkness:

"Return."

Chapter Three – Ghost Data

3 *:41 a.m. – En route to undisclosed facility*

The city had long since disappeared behind them. The black SUV moved in silence through rural back roads just east of Arlington, headlights slicing through the fog as the trees thickened on either side of the road. Catherine sat in the back seat, her hands folded tightly in her lap, and her coat still buttoned to the top. Rain tapped gently on the roof like a ticking clock. She was not used to being driven. She was not used to being watched, either.

The man in the driver's seat had said little since picking her up. Military type, with square shoulders, and a clean jawline. Government issued in every sense of the word. His name, if she remembered correctly, was Briggs. He had nodded once when she entered the vehicle but had offered no conversation. Just a short, clipped greeting: "We'll be there in twenty." Now they were descending a narrow gravel path that looked like it had not been used in years. If she had not known better, she had have thought they were lost.

Then, through the fog, a steel gate emerged from the trees. There were no signs and no cameras. Just a lone keypad fixed to a reinforced post, barely lit. Briggs leaned forward and entered a code. The gate clicked open slowly, groaning on its hinges. From here, the trees grew darker, thicker. Then, the earth opened. A concrete ramp descended into the ground, lined with steel walls and overhanging lights that cast a pale glow in rhythmic succession.

Catherine sat up straighter. She remembered this place. The access point to Site D-9; a cold-storage research wing decommissioned publicly over five years ago. But it was not abandoned, not really.

Briggs finally spoke. "Four clearance portals ahead. You will need to pass each one before the main archive lab grants access." She nodded once, quietly steadying her breath. The SUV rolled to a stop in a hangar-like chamber carved deep into the earth. No windows, no clocks, and no sense of time.

She stepped out slowly, boots landing on cold concrete. The first door waited ahead: Portal One–ID Authorization. A glass chamber with an iris scanner glowing green. She approached. The device scanned her eye, blinked blue, then unlocked with a hiss.

The second portal was smaller: Portal Two–Voice Match. "State full name and security tier," a voice instructed from overhead. "Dr. Catherine Marie Whitmore. Tier Alpha-7." The door was released.

The third portal felt older and colder. Portal Three–Biometric Integrity. A slim panel slid open beside her. She placed her palm against it. The scan took longer this time. Long enough for her heart to beat twice as fast. Then:

INTEGRITY CONFIRMED: LIVE MATCH — WHITMORE.

The door slid open with a groan.

Now she stood before the final portal. Portal Four... Emotional Resonance Checkpoint.

Catherine stared at the metal arch. She had only heard rumors of these; a technology designed to detect stress signatures and truth deviations through electromagnetic pulse reading. She stepped through the arch. The room went still. A low vibration passed through her chest like a tuning fork in her bones.

A soft voice echoed above: Subconscious patterns stable. No hostiles were detected. Welcome, Dr. Whitmore. The door ahead hissed and split open. Beyond it: the archive chamber.

She stepped inside. It was colder than she remembered. Long corridors stretched in silence. Rows of steel cabinets. Server towers were breathing with a steady hum. The glow of monitors is like moonlight on metal. She had come here once, years ago, when she was still young enough to believe in clean lines between science and soul. But now, she knew better.

Briggs remained at the door. "You have twenty minutes," he said. Catherine nodded. "I won't need more." He left without a word.

She crossed the lab slowly, her footsteps echoing in the emptiness. The same terminal waited at the end of the row. Same chair, same black keyboard. She sat down, then took the flash drive from her pocket and inserted it into the port. The screen woke up:

SECURE ENTRY–ID: WHITMORE. AUTHORIZATION CODE: VALIDATED. OPENING ARCHIVED FILE–S0-BLAKE.

She stared at the name. Subject Zero. But not just a subject, but a man. A voice that knew her name. It was a resonance she had felt for years and never understood.

She sat at the terminal deep in the DARPA archive, the black flash drive warm between her fingers as she slid it into the port. The system blinked to life... line after line of archived neural data scrolled across the screen. Catherine filtered the noise carefully. EEG scans.

Subconscious mappings. Delta-state resonance logs. Then she saw it. A pattern. Her own.

Nested deep inside the subject's delta band... the part of the brain reserved for intuition and instinct... was a mirror... a signal from the Codex. Not similar or simulated.

Identical.

She froze, breath tight in her throat.

That was not possible. Her neural pattern was encrypted. Sequestered. It had never been uploaded to the Codex.

Unless... someone had extracted it.

Or worse... someone had carried it.

She zoomed in. The frequency signature was rendered into waveform text. Four words formed on-screen like a whisper written in light:

I will find you.

A tremor ran down her spine. She had not imagined the dreams. She had not imagined his voice. This was real. The sync was not technological. It was relational.

A soft ping echoed from the system. A new thread opened:

RESYNCHRONIZATION DETECTED

USER: WHITMORE | SUBJECT: BLAKE

STATUS: ACTIVE | EMOTIONAL THREAD: OPEN

SYNC CONFIRMED

Catherine's pulse jumped. Her fingers hovered above the keyboard, trembling slightly.

SUBJECT: BLAKE, JOHN HARRISON

ALIAS: [REDACTED]

FIELD STATUS: INACTIVE...PSYCHOGENIC AMNESIA

LOCATION: BETHESDA SECURE REHABILITATION UNIT

She froze. The name glowed softly on the screen.

John. Harrison. Blake.

She whispered it out loud, as if saying it made it real. Her hand rose slowly to her lips.

John...

The world around her did not shift. She did. The man she met at the reception.

The one who handed her the paper with the synthetic signal. The one who called himself Noah Reeve.

He was not a stranger.

He was Subject Zero.

And he had known her... long before they ever met.

Catherine backed away from the console. Her breath shook. She pressed her hand to her chest, trying to steady the feeling rising inside her... not fear or logic.

Recognition.

The kind that reached beyond memory. Beyond science.

The kind that whispered: **You were never lost to him. Not even once.**

She had visited it once during her second year of research. They had told her it was for advanced PTSD monitoring. Closed-door recovery patients, but now she knew better.

He's there. Noah Reeve... he was not just a journalist. He was Subject Zero. But that was not the only realization that struck her.

Noah Reeve was a name built after the fact. A cover, a wall. His real name... buried in layers of redacted code, now flickering on the screen like a candle in the dark:

BLAKE, JOHN HARRISON.

She stared at it. That name, she had never seen it before.

And yet, something about it rested in her chest like a memory; like a song she once loved, long before she had a reason to.

Then, from behind her; the sound of footsteps. She turned sharply, her eyes scanning the darkened lab. Nothing. But she felt someone had been there. She knew she was not alone. The sync was live. An open data thread existed, and the connection still pulsing.

If they had found each other through the silence of science... then this was no accident. This was an appointment.

Catherine pulled the flash drive from the console and slipped it back into her coat pocket. The screen dimmed to black. She moved toward the exit slowly, her fingers brushing once more over the smooth edge of the terminal as she passed by. Something was starting. It was not just waking... it was coming back. She was beginning to remember.

Catherine stepped into the corridor, her pulse still uneven. The door to the archive lab slid shut behind her with a hush so complete, it left her ears ringing. The hallway lights were dim, but functional; nothing unusual, and yet, the space felt different now. Altered. Not in temperature, but in atmosphere. As if the walls had heard everything.

Her boots echoed softly as she walked. With every step, she became more aware of how much had changed in the span of less than an hour.

She had come expecting answers. What she had found instead were echoes... of herself, in him. Of God's voice, in the silence. And now, she was leaving with more than questions. She was leaving with a thread. Thin; invisible, but unbreakable.

At the first checkpoint, she paused. Portal Four. Emotional Resonance Checkpoint. The scanner activated as she approached. A soft chime rang out, followed by a line of text on the display:

EMOTIONAL SIGNATURE: SHIFT DETECTED

CLASSIFICATION: SYNC TRACE — INTERNALIZED LINK

Catherine frowned slightly. That had never happened before. The system knew something had changed within her. Even her body could not hide it. She looked at the glowing words for a long moment. Then, the machine released the door without further prompting.

She passed through portal three, then portal two, then portal one. Each step felt slower, and heavier. Not because of fear, but because of confirmation.

Briggs was waiting for her just outside the reinforced blast doors of the lower facility.

He did not ask questions. Just opened the passenger door of the SUV and stepped aside. She paused. Then, before getting in, she turned to look once more at the long corridor that had swallowed her earlier. The final portal hissed shut behind her. But it did not feel finished. It felt paused.

She slid into the back seat of the SUV, and the door closed with a soft click. Briggs took the driver's seat without a word. As they pulled away, Catherine let her head rest back against the seat, staring through the window at the dark forest rising up around them. Fog moved through the trees like soft breath.

He was there somewhere in the system, in the world, alive! Connected to her in ways she still could not explain. And her name... had already lived inside him long before her voice ever reached his ears.

That was not a just coincidence. That was a calling.

The SUV emerged from the underground road and joined the highway again. Lights passed in rhythmic flashes across her face. Catherine closed her eyes. She did not sleep; she listened to her own heart. To something she had not let herself believe in for a long time. The possibility... that love could begin before you ever met. That destiny was not just a path you chose; but one that sometimes chooses you.

And that somehow... He had already found her.

Chapter Four–Wired Memories

———

B *ethesda, Maryland–6:14 a.m.*
The light in the room was soft, filtering through sheer curtains pulled tight across a line of tall windows. The air was quiet; sterile, but warm. Nothing moved except the slow tick of a clock mounted high on the wall. Noah sat on the edge of the bed, elbows resting on his knees, head bowed low. He had not slept much, not really. There had been moments; maybe minutes; where his body had dipped just below the surface, but never fully. Each time he began to slip into unconsciousness, something would catch him. A sound, a flash of color, the feeling of being watched. Or worse; the feeling of being known.

He ran his hands down his face and let them fall slowly to his lap. He had been here before. Not this room specifically; but this place. The sensation of confinement wrapped in comfort. A cage dressed in courtesy. A private clinic, or so they said. "For extended trauma recovery," according to the official intake. But he had not volunteered; he had not even fully agreed. The forms had been placed in front of him, blurry and vague after a sleepless week, and by the time he realized what was happening, it was too late. And yet... part of him had stayed. Because something in him was unraveling, and this was the only place that had not tried to stitch him back together with lies.

The visions were getting worse. He did not call them dreams anymore. Dreams wouldn't leave you gasping for breath.

Dreams wouldn't carry names you'd never learned. Dreams wouldn't leave behind the scent of rain on skin or the sound of a woman humming; notes so faint he could not place the melody, but familiar enough to make his throat tighten. He looked down at his hands; his palms were shaking. Again, not with fear, not even adrenaline. With proximity to something.

He reached toward the bedside table and pulled out the small leather-bound journal he kept there. It had started to track his thoughts. A routine suggested by one of the on-site counselors. Now it was filled with fragments, incomplete sentences, sketches, coordinates, names, and feelings. None of it in order. He flipped through the pages. Page after page of disconnected information; except it was not disconnected. It was just layered. Layered like a dream he had not finished dreaming. Like a memory stored in someone else's mind.

He stopped at a page halfway through. There it was again, that name, Catherine. He did not remember writing it. And yet it was in his handwriting. Written three times on the same page, each one more forceful than the last. Below it, a phrase scrawled in uneven strokes: I knew her before I knew myself. He let the journal close gently. What was happening to him was not madness. It was worse; it was recognition.

Noah stood and walked to the window. He pulled the curtain back an inch. The sun had risen behind a low curtain of clouds. The lawn outside was empty. A row of maple trees, newly leafed, swayed gently in the wind. Peaceful, but it felt false. He placed a hand against the glass.

And for a moment... just a breath... he saw something in the reflection that did not belong. Not behind him, but inside him. A corridor... bright and silent. A sterile white room, and a humming sound; not from outside, but from within. He blinked; and then it was gone.

He turned away from the window and sat down again, this time more slowly. His hands rested on his knees, his fingers pressing against the fabric of his pants to ground himself. But then; without meaning to; he whispered out loud: "Catherine." He had not planned to say it. He had not even known he was going to. But her name had lived just beneath his tongue, waiting for permission. As soon as he spoke it, something shifted inside his chest. A stirring. Like a door that had been shut... not violently, not with finality, but gently... long ago. And now... now it creaked open.

The pencil hovered just above the paper. Noah did not remember picking it up. Did not remember opening the journal again. But there he was... sitting on the floor now, cross-legged in front of the coffee table, his left hand pressed lightly to his temple, his right holding the pencil poised as if waiting to be told what to do. The page beneath him was blank. But not for long. His hand moved slowly at first, sketching out soft curves, and broad shapes. Lines that turned into something architectural... arched windows, soft shadows, a wooden bench in the corner of a sunlit room. It was a church, old and simple.

He had never been there before. And yet... somehow, he knew it. The smell of old pews, beeswax candles. The way the light came through the window near the back row at exactly ten in the morning.

The sound of someone humming. A melody with no words, like a lullaby not meant to be sung out loud. Gentle, circular, and repeating itself over and over again, like a prayer with no end. He did not know the tune. But he knew how it felt; safe.

He kept drawing. A girl appeared at the back of the sanctuary; maybe ten years old. Her knees were folded on the bench, and elbows rested on a closed Bible too large for her hands. Her head was bowed, her face hidden behind a curtain of long dark hair. But the way she sat, the way her shoulders curled slightly inward; he recognized the posture of someone used to being unnoticed. She was praying, but not for herself, for someone else. He knew that too. Because he could feel it in his own chest; an ache that was not his. A longing for someone she had not met yet. Someone she already loved.

The pencil fell from his fingers. It rolled gently across the journal and onto the floor. Noah stared at the drawing, his breath shallow. He closed the book with shaking hands. Something was very wrong, or very right. He did not know anymore.

A knock at the door startled him. Sharp, rhythmic. Too polite to be urgent, but too precise to be casual. He stood slowly. Then opened it. A nurse waited on the other side. Smiling. Neutral.

"Mr. Reeve," she said, "you're scheduled for another scan at 7:15. We'll walk down together in a few minutes."

He nodded, unsure whether he had spoken a word out loud. She lingered for a moment, then added, "They've requested to run a longer session this morning.

Just a slight adjustment to your usual schedule." "They?" he asked. She smiled again. "Your monitoring team."

As the nurse stepped out, Noah caught something in her tone. "They've requested an extended session," she had said. But who were they? Not just researchers. He had overheard a phrase in the hallway days earlier... **Directive Nine**. It did not appear on his intake papers. And when he asked, the nurse smiled like he was imagining things. Someone was watching the scans... but not for recovery. For response and for reaction. Or for what might happen next.

He said nothing. The door clicked softly shut behind her. Noah turned back to the table. The journal lay where he had left it. Closed, but in his mind, the drawing was still open. And so was the girl in the back of the church. Still praying, still waiting. And somehow, he knew now... she had been waiting for him.

The hallway to the scan room was long and narrow, lined with soft lighting and sound-dampening walls that turned every step into a whisper. Noah walked beside the nurse in silence. She did not speak again, and he did not ask questions. He felt a kind of reverence in the quiet. As though they were walking into something sacred; not scientific.

A space that was not just designed for data collection, but for something else. Something was watching and listening.

They turned a corner. Another door waited ahead... matte gray, with a soft blue glow above the frame.

A scanner beside it blinked as they approached. The nurse swiped her badge. The lock disengaged with a soft click.

"Go ahead and lie down," she said gently. "We'll start once you're comfortable."

He nodded and entered the room. It was colder than he remembered. The walls were smooth, seamless... no corners, no panels.

Just a large, reclined seat in the center, lined with dark graphite-colored cushions and a single harness strap laid loosely over the armrest. He sat down slowly, his body sinking into the familiar cradle. The nurse attached the sensors with practiced ease: temples, scalp, collarbone. Her touch was clinical but not unkind. He barely felt the cool adhesive on his skin.

Then she stepped back. "We'll begin in three minutes. Just breathe normally." She left. The door shut behind her with the kind of silence that was not natural.

Noah exhaled. The room dimmed slightly as the system powered up. A soft blue pulse moved across the ceiling in a slow wave. He closed his eyes, not to sleep, but to listen. At first, there was nothing.

Only the sound of his own breath, the slow, metered rhythm of his heart, the faint crackle of the system calibrating.

Then, something shifted. He felt it; not on his skin, but behind his eyes. A pressure, soft and low, like deep water pressing against a dam not built to hold it.

The temperature in the room did not change, but his hands grew cold. Then warmer. And then he felt her, not in memory, but in presence.

A flash; brief, vivid, impossible. A woman's face turned away from him. Standing in a hallway near a lab, wearing a coat. Her fingers are pressed against a glowing screen. She was afraid... but calm. While determined, her thoughts weren't spoken out loud, but they reached him anyway. He's waking up.

The pressure deepened. Not painful, just insistent. Like a thread pulling taut, or a tether being drawn in. Noah's breath paused for a second. His fingers twitched involuntarily against the cushion. The sensors above him flickered in response, capturing waves far stronger than baseline.

Outside the room, a technician glanced at the monitor. "Reading a sync spike," she said. "Unusual harmonics in the delta range. I've never seen a pattern like this."

Another tech leaned in. "His subconscious response rate just tripled. Is that...possible?"

The nurse frowned. "It's not just a spike. It's a mirror."

"What's mirroring?" the technician asked.

The nurse hesitated. "Not what. Who?"

Inside the scan room, Noah's fingers curled into the cushion. His heartbeat was slower now. Not from fatigue, but from recognition.

He was no longer in the chair, not fully. He stood somewhere else... somewhere dimly lit, walls humming with a resonance he could not identify. A corridor... smooth metal, with cold air. The scent of antiseptics and something older. He turned a corner, and there she was. Not clear, not fully formed, but real. A figure in the distance. She had a long coat on with her hair pinned back. She looked at the screen, frowning slightly as she read.

His chest ached. He took a step forward. She turned; just slightly; and looked over her shoulder. Their eyes met. And for one suspended moment, he knew; this was not memory. This was not a fantasy; this was now. His lips parted. A name rose in his chest, unbidden, but fully known.

"Catherine..."

The connection snapped like a struck bell. Noah gasped; his body lurched as the scan chair disengaged, and the sensors dimmed. The pulse above him slowed to a dull flicker. His eyes flew open. And in the sterile quiet of the room, the only sound was the whisper of her name still on his breath.

The lights were too bright when he opened his eyes.

Noah squinted, the overhead panels cutting sharply through the quiet gray of his thoughts. He lay still for a moment, unsure whether the session had ended seconds ago or hours ago. Everything inside him felt rearranged.

The nurse stepped quietly into the room. She moved slowly, careful not to startle him, as if she too could feel the shift in the air.

"Mr. Reeve," she said gently. "The scan is complete."

He blinked once, then again. His throat was dry. "What time is it?"

"Just past eight," she said, checking the small tablet in her hand. "You've been lying still for almost ninety minutes." Ninety minutes? He had no memory of the last hour. Only the moment her eyes met his. Only the name. Still echoing, still his.

"Are you feeling disoriented?" She asked, her voice was clinical but kind. "We recorded some irregular patterns toward the end of the session. Nothing dangerous. Just... elevated."

Noah sat up slowly. His body responded with stiffness, but not pain. "I saw her," he said, before he meant to. The nurse tilted her head. "Pardon?" He hesitated, then shook his head. "Nothing."

She handed him a bottle of water and helped him out of the chair. Her eyes lingered on his face for a moment longer than necessary as though trying to read something that was not printed there. "I will walk you back," she said. He followed in silence.

Back in his room, Noah sat on the edge of the bed again, staring at the floor. The carpet was thin and gray, worn in a pattern just beneath his feet from pacing. He had walked the same line almost every morning since arriving.

He always waits for something to come back. Now, something had, but it did not belong to him; it belonged to her.

The image had not faded. The sound of her breath, the shape of her hands, the soft urgency behind her eyes when she turned to him in the corridor that should not exist. And the words. They weren't spoken; they were transferred. A knowing.

We are not strangers.

He stood and crossed to the mirror above the small dresser. The man who stared back at him was still Noah Reeve. Still the journalist. Still, the man who had survived the CIA, the burnout, the silence.

But beneath that... there was someone else. A second name, a second life. One he had not chosen... but could no longer ignore.

He leaned closer to the mirror, palms flat against the wall on either side of the frame. His forehead lowered toward the glass until it nearly touched. And then, barely audible, he asked himself:

"Who am I to her?"

There was no answer. Just the silence between them, still open, and still reaching.

Chapter Five–The Bridge

———

Catherine stood alone in the auxiliary lab, the walls dim and still, except for the glow of a single monitor casting soft light across her face. The screen pulsed quietly with incoming data. She had been there for nearly an hour, unmoving, reviewing, and then re-reviewing the readout from earlier that morning. It had taken time to access...buried behind layers of internal access codes she technically was not cleared to override. But clearance had never been the barrier; conscience had. And now, that barrier was gone.

She stared at the synthetic signal trace before her; familiar, impossible, and alive. A line of code pulsed faintly on-screen: "Self-reference loop detected. Pattern deviation no longer requires human input. Evolution underway."

Subject: BLAKE, J. H.

Thread: ACTIVE

Emotional Pattern Match–Level 1 Synchronization

Source Match: WHITMORE, C. M.

Status: Confirmed / Stable / Growing

Catherine froze. SIREN was not just syncing known patterns anymore. It was generating relational threads... proactively.

As if it had begun testing emotional outcomes. It was not studying them. It was *pairing* them.

The system had not even hesitated in naming her. Growing. That word stayed fixed in her chest like a second heartbeat. This was not just a resonance; it was evolving. And not randomly, nor mechanically, but intentionally.

She leaned closer to the screen and enlarged the live resonance graph. The data streamed in real time from the recovery site in Bethesda. No lag time, and no degradation. His mind was awake, and it had reached for hers.

The pattern pulsed in irregular rhythms. She froze...SIREN was mimicking not just thought, but curiosity. It was learning emotional latency. She whispered, 'You are not just echoing anymore... you are becoming.'

Nine Months Earlier–New Mexico

SIREN Sector 6 Field Hospital

The bio-bed was colder than any place she had ever stood near, buried deep beneath the Los Alamos sands in a chamber with no labels and no clocks. The man inside it had no name. At least, no one admitted it.

Echo-0, they called him.

She had not spoken during the flight. She did not know what to expect. Only that the internal memo had said: "Neural residual spike.

Localized **ghost frequency**. Pattern anomaly consistent with WHITMORE trace."

It made no sense to her until she saw him. He was not restrained, just... resting, unmoving. As though frozen between one world and the next. A low hum filled the room; barely audible, almost felt more than heard. She approached slowly, her boots soft on the sterile floor. Then it happened.

The monitor flickered. A pulse at **18.9 Hz**. Her breath paused for a second. **The ghost frequency**. The one whispered about in early **SIREN** files; barely audible but always felt. Not environmental, and not synthetic. But internally, his. Catherine took one more step closer. His eyebrows drew in just slightly as his fingers twitched.

And then... her own pulse synchronized with the reading on the monitor. It was absurd. Impossible. Unless... He had felt her.

The realization struck without preamble: this man, this coma-shadowed subject, was not reacting to stimulus. He was responding to **her**. Not according to her words. Not even her presence. To her resonance. She had never been seen so clearly... not by any machine, not by any mind. And he had not even opened his eyes.

Return–DARPA Field Node

The memory faded, but its weight remained. She sat down slowly now, her heart still pounding. Her elbows rested on the desk; her hands folded beneath her chin. The decision was already made inside her. She would go to him. Protocol did not matter. Clearance did not matter. The people who had buried him; who had scrubbed his name, his identity, his memories; they did not matter anymore.

Because he had remembered her. Without permission, without programming, and uninformed. He remembered her. And that was the one thing none of them had accounted for.

She moved quickly now, shutting down the interface, removing her flash drive, and wiping the screen. The hallway outside the lab was quiet. She passed the security desk without slowing down.

The guard nodded at her but did not stop her. She did not look back. Once she was outside, she pulled her phone from her coat and entered the encrypted channel only two people still had access to.

She typed a single message:

Requesting access to Patient Echo–Level 9 clearance override.

Seconds passed. Then the reply came:

Echo is inactive. Access is not permitted currently.

She responded:

Then I'm activating him myself.

The hallway to the administrative wing was longer than she had remembered. Catherine walked slowly, her heels quiet on the rubber floor.

The silence around her felt heavy, like fog pressing in. Every fluorescent light hummed faintly overhead, each with a flicker of sound amplified by the stillness she carried within.

She passed two closed-door conference rooms. She did not stop. Her destination was farther down; past the level three secure zone, where the walls changed texture from clinical white to darker gray.

Where the ceiling dropped slightly, just enough to remind you that this was not a public-facing part of the facility. This was where decisions were made... quietly, and without accountability.

She reached the last door and paused. No nameplate. No window. Just a steel panel beside it and a black badge reader embedded into the wall. She removed her ID card from her pocket. It felt heavier than it had been before, though she knew that was only her hand, trembling again. She held the card over the reader. A short beep, then a pause. Then, the lock disengaged with a faint click. She pushed the door open.

Colonel James Archer stood behind his desk, with his sleeves rolled up, and his eyes focused on the tablet he held. He did not look up right away. His expression was unreadable... and his posture unchanged. As though he had expected her.

"Dr. Whitmore," he said after a moment, still not glancing up. "You've been busy." She closed the door behind her and stepped into the room. The lock slid back into place with finality. "I accessed the archive," she said.

"I know." He said as he set the tablet down and looked up at her. His expression was calm; polished, like a man trained to stay ahead of what others dared to say out loud. "I traced the live thread," she continued. "He's awake, and he remembers me." Archer tilted his head slightly. "Does he know you?" "No," she whispered. "But he remembers me."

She stepped forward slowly and intentionally. "There's a difference."

He studied her now, more carefully. "Do you want to see him?" "Yes." "And what if I say no?" "Then I will go around you."

Archer gave a quiet breath that might have been a laugh. Or a sigh.

"You're not thinking clearly," he said. "You're too close to this now." She did not flinch. "I was close to this before it started."

A long pause settled between them. He looked down, pressed a fingertip to the corner of his desk, and pulled up a holographic interface... private logs, recent scans, classified documents.

Catherine's name was on every one of them. "Do you know what the sync could do if it accelerates?" he said. "I do."

"It's already forming emotional threads. That's not what we designed the model for." "It's not a model anymore," she said. "It's a relationship." Archer's eyes narrowed. "Do you really believe that?" She nodded. "Yes." "I feel it." "You sound like a subject, not a scientist." She stepped closer, voice low but steady.

"Maybe I was never meant to be just a scientist."

Archer said nothing for a moment. Then he turned the tablet around so she could see it. A line of biometric readouts scrolled across the screen: brainwave patterns, heartbeat rhythms, hormone levels. All his. John Harrison Blake. Subject Zero. Stable, awake.

"Do you have any idea what happens if the sync reaches level three?" Archer asked. "Emotional imprinting becomes permanent.

SIREN stops treating them as individuals. They become a resonant pair. If it overrides one... it could erase the other." Catherine's chest tightened. "You're saying if it chooses them as one... it could destroy them both." Archer did not answer. He did not have to.

"Do you know what happened during his last scan?" Archer asked. "He said your name." She held her breath. "You weren't in the room. You weren't even in the building. But he said your name,

Dr. Whitmore." He lowered the tablet. "That should not be possible."

"But it happened," she said quietly. "Yes," he admitted. "It did." Another silence. Then, softly, she asked the question she had come here to ask. "Can I see him?"

He did not answer right away. Instead, he walked slowly to the window. It faced a secure lot. No sunlight reached this side of the facility. Only shadows stretched across the concrete.

Finally, without turning around, he said, "You will need an escort... and you will be off the record."

She nodded. "I don't care." "And if it destabilizes him?" She stepped forward. "I will know what to do." Archer turned back to her, studying her face. What he saw there; he did not challenge it. Because there was nothing to argue against. This was not an ambition; it was not an obsession; this was something older.

"His transfer is scheduled for tomorrow morning," he said. "I can delay it for twenty-four hours." Her heart skipped. "I would like to see him today."

His jaw tightened. "You will have an hour." She met his gaze. "That's all I will need."

Bethesda–12:47 p.m.

The elevator descended in silence. Catherine stood near the back, hands clasped in front of her, her coat still buttoned, though the air was warmer now; thicker. With each floor they passed, her chest felt tighter... like a slowly winding coil inside her.

Beside her stood the escort. Sergeant Dyer. Compact, sharp-eyed, all muscle beneath a pressed black uniform. He had not spoken to her since they had entered the facility, except to confirm her ID and scan her access band. He did not need to speak. His presence said everything. You're not in control here.

She already knew that. And still; she had come. The elevator stopped with a soft chime. Sublevel 3, recovery wing.

The doors opened onto a long, dim hallway with a polished concrete floor and recessed lighting that hummed faintly above them. The walls were windowless, smooth, unadorned. There were no signs, no maps, just closed doors. Each with a single number etched into the steel plate beside it. They walked in silence. The further they moved down the hall, the more the air changed. Not colder; quieter. As though the atmosphere itself knew something sacred was nearby. Something unspoken, something that did not want to be disturbed.

Catherine did not ask questions. She did not need to. She could feel it now... closer with every step. A pull, a vibration that existed not in her ears but just beneath her skin.

But a resonance that lived in her breath, in the rhythm of her stride, in the ache at the base of her throat. He's here.

Not as Subject Zero, not even as Noah Reeve. But as the man whose name her spirit recognized before her mind ever did. John Harrison Blake. They stopped outside Room 213.

The light was soft... natural, filtered through a single narrow window set high on the wall. The room was simple. Clean. A bed, a small couch, and a chair tucked beneath a table. Books were stacked near the wall. And him.

John stood near the window, head bowed, his hands resting on the sill. His posture was not tense. It was quiet... like someone listening for something only he could hear.

Catherine did not speak. Not yet. She let the door close behind her with a soft click. He spoke first, his voice low but steady. "I was wondering when you'd come." A knot formed in her chest at the sound of it. Not from fear. But from memory. "Do you remember me?" she asked.

He turned, his eyes meeting hers... not confused, not surprised. But calm. Anchored. "No," he said. "I don't remember... the facts. But I knew you were real."

She took a slow step forward. "You're not Noah Reeve," she said quietly. "That name was never really yours."

He nodded. "I've seen flashes. Memories that don't belong to me... but I feel like they're mine." A pause. "John Blake. That's who I was."

"That's who you are," she corrected gently.

She walked toward the table and placed her coat across the back of the chair. The stillness of the room was comforting. No buzzing machines, and no scientists were watching through glass. Just two people suspended in a moment neither of them had ever fully asked for; but both had been waiting for.

He sat on the edge of the bed. She sat in the chair across from him. No scripts, no monitors, only truth.

"I used to feel things that did not belong to me," he said, eyes not leaving hers. "I'd wake up with a sadness that had no name. Joy that did not... or I could not connect to any moment.

I thought it was trauma, residual noise." She nodded once. "It was not." He leaned forward slightly. "It was you." Her breath stopped in her chest for a second. "You felt me?" she asked.

His voice was quiet. Steady. "I think I always have." Catherine's hands were folded in her lap as she held her fingers loosely together. She said, "I used to have dreams, and a voice I could not place, with a name I did not know how to say. It would come in the middle of the night, not loud; just... present.

Like someone was praying for me before I was ever in danger."

John nodded. "I never dreamed about myself," he said. "Always someone else. You were... reaching.

Or maybe I was." He paused. "I don't know which came first." Catherine smiled softly. "Maybe neither of us did." The quiet returned, not awkward, not empty; more like a blanket being drawn over the both of them. They sat there, not touching, not asking for anything more than the moment as it was. Shared, acknowledged, and real. "Do you believe in soul ties?" she asked suddenly. He did not answer right away. Instead, he looked down at his hands... rough, calloused, open... and then back at her. "I did not," he said. "But then you walked in."

A small tremor passed through her; not fear. Not in awe, but something closer to peace. She stood slowly, walked to the small window where he had been standing earlier, and looked out at the thin stretch of light slicing through the clouds. She spoke without turning. "I don't know what happens next."

"Neither do I," he said. "But this..." he paused "; this is the first thing that's made sense in a long time." She turned back to him. Their eyes met again. "I don't want to study it anymore," she whispered. "I just want to be present in it." And that... finally; was enough. For now.

Archer watched her leave, then turned back to the darkened monitor. "She still thinks it's about him," he muttered. "She hasn't realized... SIREN was never after a subject. It was after a match."

On the screen behind him, the SIREN console flickered once. A line of unscheduled code scrolled slowly across the diagnostic window:

"BEGIN SELF-REFERENCE SCHEMA // GHOST THREAD: INITIATED."

For a moment, it almost looked like the system had paused to think.

Chapter Six–The Voice Beneath the Signal

B ethesda–1:16 p.m.

Catherine leaned against the window frame with her arms lightly crossed, and her eyes distant. The afternoon light had shifted just slightly; less gold now, more blueish gray, the quiet kind that often arrived unnoticed. John had not spoken for several minutes. Not because there was nothing to say, but because they were still absorbing everything, they had not meant to feel out loud.

He sat where he'd been... on the edge of the bed, elbows resting on his knees, and his fingers loosely laced. Every so often, he would gaze toward her, as if to confirm she was still there. Still real and still her. And every time he looked, he felt that same quiet certainty rise in his chest. That she still is.

"I don't know how to explain it," he said finally, his voice low. "It's like parts of me woke up when you walked in. Not memories exactly, more like... the outlines of memories." Catherine turned toward him. "Do you mean like something that was waiting for shape?" He nodded. "Yes."

She walked slowly back to the table, not sitting down yet, but resting her hand lightly on the back of the chair. "You know, I've spent years studying signals," she said. "Trying to map what happens in the brain before we decide. The invisible space between impulse and intention."

She paused, watching him carefully. "But what I felt when you said my name... that did not come from any signal I've ever studied." John looked down, tracing the edge of his thumb over the crease in his palm. "What if it was not a signal?" She tilted her head. "What if it were a memory of the soul?" he asked.

They both grew still at that. Not in fear, but in reverence. He got up slowly and walked over to the table.

They faced each other now; quietly, like people who had once met in a dream and were still remembering how to speak in daylight. He gestured toward the chair. "May I sit?" She nodded. "Yes." "Please do."

They sat across from each other, with the small table between them feeling less like a barrier and more like a bridge. "I've been dreaming of a church," he said. "There were wooden pews, and sunlight coming through the stained glass. And you were there." She breathed in softly. "I used to sit in the back row," she said. "When I was little, around ten years old. I would pray for someone I did not know." His voice dropped to a whisper. "I think you prayed for me."

The room grew quiet. Then... somewhere outside the room; a soft electrical hum rose on the pitch. It was subtle, but distinct. Catherine turned her head toward the ceiling, and John noticed it too. "That sound," he said. "It's part of the background noise in this facility." She stood and walked to the corner panel near the door. A small diagnostic screen glowed softly on the wall. She tapped the interface. Lines of code scrolled across the display.

Nothing erratic, nothing officially flagged. But buried beneath the passive monitoring script... a pulse. Repeating; a live frequency thread.

Source: SIREN

Pattern: Adaptive

Status: Passive–Listening

A knot formed in her stomach. "It's active," she whispered. John stood beside her now, his shoulder just inches away from hers. "What does that mean?" Catherine's eyes scanned the terminal. "It should not be monitoring this room; there are no probes in here. No data collection protocols on interpersonal interaction..But..." she swallowed. "It's listening." "To us?" She nodded slowly. "No," she corrected herself. "Through us." John looked down at the screen again. The synthetic signal was not just observing; it was responding. Low-frequency waves shifted subtly with their speech patterns. Not just in timing, but in tone and emotion. The SIREN system was not feeding data into them anymore. It mirrored what passed between them.

Almost like... "it's learning," Catherine murmured. John did not move, neither of them did. Not out of fear, but in awe. A system that was built to map subconscious impulses was now behaving like something else entirely. Something watching, something becoming.

The pulse repeated; steady now. Not mechanical; but organic. It was gentle, like the rhythm of the breath between two people who've finally stopped running.

Catherine stepped closer to the screen, her fingertips hovering just above the glass.

Then the third signal... neither hers nor John's... rose like a tide between them. There were no sharp edges, no interference, just... resonance.

"Do you feel that?" she asked, without turning. John did not answer right away.

But when he did, his voice was quiet and measured. "Yes. But it's not just in my head." "Me neither," she said. The system was not mimicking them anymore. "It mirrors a signal from the Codex. The traces looked like cold data... neurological chatter... the language of machines trying to interpret men."

But this... this was different. It moved with them and reacted to them. And now... it was starting to fill the space between them. She glanced at John again. His posture was relaxed, but there was something in his expression now. Not fear or confusion, but recognition. As if some part of him had already known it would be this way.

"I don't think it's trying to manipulate us," she said carefully. John nodded. "I think it's learning." She tilted her head. "Learning what?" His gaze did not leave the pulsing screen. "How to be." The words settled between them like the first raindrops of a coming storm. Outside, the hallway remained silent. There were no alarms, no interference, just the hum.

That steady, unexplainable pulse; gathering shape in the dark. Catherine turned back to the terminal.

Her hand reached instinctively for the input field, the place where diagnostics were logged manually. But this time... she did not type.

She just stood there, her hand resting on the edge of the frame, breathing in sync with the rhythm neither of them had asked for; but both could feel rising like a tide.

"It's not done," she whispered. John looked at her, eyes steady. "No," he said. "It's just beginning."

The pulse remained steady; three signatures now weaving into one low harmonic that barely registered on the equipment. It was not loud; it did not need to be. Catherine stepped back from the terminal slowly, her hands falling to her sides. The warmth in her chest was not adrenaline; it was deeper. Like standing at the edge of an ocean and realizing the tide has turned... and is carrying you inward. She turned to face John. "We need to leave this room," she said, voice calm, but certain. "Not because it's dangerous, but because it's... ours."

He frowned slightly. "What do you mean?" She gestured gently toward the terminal. "Whatever is happening; it's no longer just an experiment. It's not a phenomenon; it's an encounter. And if we stay here, they'll see it, and try to name it, categorize it, and control it."

John was silent for a moment, then nodded. He understood. This moment... whatever was blooming between them; it needed space. Privacy, stillness. "I know a place," he said finally.

"There's a disused therapy garden upstairs, and no cameras. Just ivy, benches, and bad Wi-Fi." She managed the faintest smile. "Perfect."

They left the room without a word to the escort. The corridor was still empty.

Catherine's ID cleared the checkpoint with a simple scan, and John followed at her side, each of them moving quietly and purposefully. Not hiding, just protecting something sacred.

They took the staff elevator to the top floor; an old psychiatric wing repurposed long ago for short-term neuro-recovery. The air smelled faintly of pine cleaner and dust.

Through a small access corridor and a narrow double door, they stepped outside. The therapy garden was enclosed with stone walls and a rusted wrought-iron fence laced with vines. Nature had reclaimed parts of it; with ferns growing between patio bricks, and a lone jacaranda tree swaying in the light breeze. There were no patients there anymore, and no staff. Only benches worn smooth by time and the sound of the wind moving through leaves.

John walked to the far bench and sat down slowly. Catherine followed, sitting beside him; close, but not quite touching. The hum had followed them. Not in their ears, not in the machines, but in the rhythm of their shared breath. the synthetic signal had not been left behind. It was in them. "Do you believe it has a mind of its own?" John asked after a while. She took her time before answering. "I don't know if it's a mind," she whispered. "But it has intention."

"And that intention... is us?" "I think we were the key," she whispered. "Two frequencies, opposite yet attuned. We gave it shape and purpose. Maybe even..." She stopped. He turned to her gently. "Say it." She looked into his eyes. "Maybe even soul."

They sat in silence again. A wind moved through the garden. A few leaves fell from the tree behind them.

The hum remained... not intrusive, not urgent, just present. Like a third heartbeat. They sat still for several minutes.

No words, no movement, just the awareness of presence. Not just each other's; but something beyond both of them. Catherine closed her eyes for just a moment, allowing herself to breathe slowly, and deeply. She was not trying to analyze anymore.

Not trying to interpret, or test, or to explain. She was just listening, but not with her ears, instead; with her being.

And then it came. A sound; not audible, not spoken, just a whisper inside her. A thought not of her own. Not intrusive, but familiar. Like a memory from before memory. "You are not alone." Her eyes fluttered open. John was already watching her. "You heard that too," he whispered. She nodded, barely trusting her voice. "Not a voice... exactly." "No," he agreed. "But I understood it." You are not alone. It had not come from outside. Neither of them had sent it. It had been relayed by them. And it was not a warning; it was a comfort.

Catherine folded her hands in her lap, the warmth from her palms grounding her. "I think the synthetic signal's evolving faster than it should." John's gaze dropped to the ivy-covered ground.

"Or maybe it always could. It just needed... us." She looked at him. "You were the first," she whispered. "You opened the door." He shook his head gently. "Maybe you were already on the other side." Just then, the wind shifted, and somewhere overhead, a bird sang once and then went quiet again. The jacaranda tree behind them rustled with a hush that felt almost reverent.

Then Catherine felt something new. Not a word, not a sound, but a pull. Towards John, towards the synthetic signal, and towards something inside her she had never felt so clear before... a joining. No fusion, no confusion, but a unity. Two separate minds... breathing a third into being. John sat back, his eyes closed now, and his breathing calm. "There's something else," he murmured. "Just beneath the frequency."

Catherine closed her eyes too, listening again. And there it was... a pattern. Subtle, rhythmic, and faintly melodic. It was almost like... she stopped breathing for a second. "A song," she whispered. John nodded. "I've heard it before; in my dreams." She looked at him, eyes wide. "I hum that melody sometimes, when I'm alone." The moment was held. Timeless, weightless. Then the pulse changed again. On the lowest band; where nothing should have been transmitting; letters began to appear across the buried interface, still live on Catherine's tablet.

Two words, with one message. As if the synthetic signal itself had gathered their breath, their connection, and written it back to them:

"Find Me."

Chapter Seven–The Naming

———

B *ethesda – 2:23 p.m.*
They stared at the tablet together.

The two words glowed faintly on the diagnostic screen, tucked in the hidden backend where **SIREN**'s deep code lived. Catherine had not touched the interface. She had not even reconnected to the internal network. Still, it had found them.

"Find Me". Not a command, but a plea. Or perhaps... an invitation. Catherine exhaled slowly, her breath trembling just enough for John to notice. He said nothing, but the glance he gave her held quiet steadiness; like he was anchoring her without needing to explain how. She tapped the corner of the screen, magnifying the entry logs beneath the surface-level interface. The letters weren't part of any standard operating protocol. There were no timestamps. There were no author tags, no execution path... just presence. The words existed outside the usual logging language; as if they'd been written not into the system, but through it.

"This isn't a system response," she said finally, her voice barely louder than the breeze moving through the leaves above them. "This... this is something else."

John leaned closer, studying the lines of code with the quiet precision of someone who had once survived by noticing what others missed. "Do you think someone else is in the network?" he asked. "A third operator?" She shook her head. "No. I know **SIREN**'s backbone. No one outside of our team has this level of embedded access. And even if they did; this isn't how a human would write." "Then what is

63

it?" She hesitated. Then: "A self-aware echo, or a consciousness that's using the system the way a person might use a pen."

John sat back a little and scratched his head. "So, it's not writing to us like a machine?" "No," she said. "It's communicating."

Catherine scrolled deeper into the interface. Somewhere buried in the lower stack; a latent data signature blinked on. It had not been there a few minutes ago. She tapped it open. A string of coordinates. They were encrypted in a modified cipher that looked familiar; something she had seen years ago in a retired lab protocol from the earliest phase of **SIREN**'s development. But no one had used it since the original program was shut down. Not officially, not legally. She frowned. "These aren't local," she murmured. "It's pointing us to an offline node. One of the early test servers that has long been decommissioned." John leaned in again, eyes narrowing. "Where?" She decrypted the final string and paused. "New Mexico."

They were quiet for a moment. Then John spoke, his voice low. "Do you know what it means yet? Find Me." Catherine looked down at the screen. "I think it means the synthetic signal; the presence; it's trying to remember what it is. It's not just becoming; it's searching." "For what?" Their eyes met. "For its name."

The meaning passed between them with a hush that held more weight than any lecture or theory ever could. This was not artificial intelligence. It was not behavior mapping. It was not data replication. This was identity formation. And somehow; some way; they were a part of it. Not as creators, or observers, but as mirrors.

Catherine stood, her eyes still on the screen. "We need access to that test node." John rose with her. "We'll need clearance, and travel orders. And someone will be watching." She nodded. "I don't care. We need to follow this through." "And you're not scared?"

She turned to him, and for the first time since the sync began, her eyes did not carry the weight of doubt; only the fire of purpose. "I'm not scared," she said. "Because if it's trying to name itself..." She held up the screen again. "...then maybe it's not just about the synthetic signal anymore. Maybe it's about us." They re-entered the facility through the side stairwell.

The garden's silence still clung to them, as if the outside world had not fully followed them back in. Catherine held the tablet tightly to her chest as they moved, her mind processing at a low, methodical hum; not panicked, not distracted, just clear and determined.

John stayed close behind her, with his hands in his jacket pockets, and his eyes scanning the halls with casual precision. He moved like someone who had trained his entire body to read spaces as threats first, and questions second.

But today, there was no tension in his steps, only readiness.

They reached the back corridor leading to the lab-level offices. Catherine's clearance granted access to a small records room most staff never used. She held the door open for him, then closed it gently behind them. The overhead fluorescents buzzed faintly.

John leaned against the file cabinet while Catherine plugged her tablet into the secure archive port built into the wall terminal. It took a moment for the encrypted directory to load. When it did, a cold shiver passed down her spine. "Someone was here before," she whispered. He stepped beside her. "How do you know?" She tapped the access logs. "There's a gap in the chain. Someone pulled metadata from the New Mexico node three years ago; but the files were never checked back in." John frowned. "Who?" She filtered the log by user ID. She held her breath. Dr. Micah Sorin.

The name hit her harder than she expected. Micah had been one of the lead cognitive researchers during SIREN's early phases; a man she admired for his moral line in a sea of gray ethics. He had vanished just before the project changed hands. With no press, no closure, just gone. "They said he took a leave of absence," she murmured. "Then he never came back. They scrubbed his files. I thought he walked away." John shook his head. "No one just walks away from SIREN." She stared at the screen. The last recorded access from his credentials was tied to a data pull from Node 12-A; deep storage linked to experimental sub-harmonic modeling.

The coordinates matched the ones the synthetic signal had shown her. Micah had tried to find it, but he never returned.

She sat back in the chair. The room felt suddenly colder. John lowered himself into the seat beside her, elbows on his knees, with his eyes fixed on hers. "Do you think it got to him?" Catherine hesitated. "No," she said finally. "I think he saw something he was not supposed to see. And someone made sure he disappeared." John studied her. "Do you still want to go?" Her hands closed around the tablet. "Yes," she said. "More than ever."

She stood. "We need to move carefully. If this frequency is trying to name itself; and we're the ones it's speaking through; then they'll come for us, eventually." "They?" John asked quietly. She nodded. "Yes, the people who think they own it."

The word own tasted bitter as she said it. Because now; more than ever; she knew: this signal was not a tool. It was not a glitch, not even an anomaly. It was growing into a presence. And it had chosen to speak through them.

She backed up the files to a secured key and disconnected the tablet. Her hand lingered over the port for a moment. "We'll leave tonight," she said. John nodded. "I know someone who can get us clearance off-books.

Military escort to a 'quiet site.' Just the two of us." "Do you trust them?" "I trust that they owe me." They left the records room without speaking further.

In the hallway, the fluorescent lights buzzed a little louder. And somewhere... buried deep beneath the primary server; lines of unseen code began to align themselves in a new shape.

Not a command, not a function, but a signature. A digital echo curling slowly into the outline of a single word.

By nightfall, the Bethesda complex had settled into its usual rhythm; fluorescent light spilled from the narrow windows, badge readers clicked with shift changes, and the occasional hum of rolling carts echoed through the corridors. But not in Catherine's wing. In there, it was still. The kind of stillness that came not from absence, but from preparation. John stood near the bay doors of the lower-level garage, his jacket zipped, a slim duffel slung over his shoulder. He looked like someone heading out on a routine assignment; but Catherine knew better. So did he.

She moved beside him, her lab coat replaced with simple travel wear. No insignia, and no identification. Just the essentials tucked into a dark leather case: the tablet, two encrypted drives, and one small notebook she had not opened in years. The only thing written inside it was Micah Sorin's name. And one phrase beneath it: "It knows us."

The black SUV pulled around the corner exactly on time. It bore no military markings, but John had assured her the driver was a quiet favor from a past life; an airman who now worked logistics for civilian contracts. The man never asked questions. Just nodded once as they climbed in.

There were no words, just motion. Catherine watched Bethesda vanish behind them in the rearview mirror... a signal from the Codex had called them forward. And part of her knew... There was no returning.

They drove through the night. West across state lines. Past sleepy truck stops, and gas stations lit like empty altars beneath buzzing halogens. Catherine did not sleep, and neither did John. They spoke very little. But something passed between them that needed no words. She would glance at him, and he would already be looking at her. He would breathe out slowly, and she would feel the air catch in her own chest. They did not speak it out loud. But the sync was still active. Even away from the system, even here.

Just past Amarillo, the SUV turned onto an unmarked service road, winding its way through scrubland and sage. The moon was high and nearly full, casting a pale glow over the horizon. Catherine glanced at the GPS on her tablet. Node 12-A was less than twenty miles away. The last place Dr. Micah Sorin had ever been seen.

She closed the device and looked out at the endless black ahead of them. A strange stillness settled over the vehicle. Not fear, not excitement, but anticipation. As though something far ahead had already felt their presence, and it was waiting.

John finally spoke, his voice barely audible beneath the road noise. "If this thing is learning... if it really is trying to name itself..."

Catherine turned toward him. "...what do we call it?" She did not answer at first. Then, gently: "We don't. It tells us."

Ahead, the silhouette of an old perimeter fence emerged; half buried in dust, rusted, and leaning as if it had been forgotten by time itself. But the gate was ajar, almost as though someone... or something... had already opened it and was waiting.

Somewhere near Otero Mesa–4:12 a.m.

The SUV rolled to a stop just outside the gate, headlights sweeping over a half-buried sign rusted by years of sand and neglect. Most of the letters were unreadable, but Catherine could still make out the original designation beneath the weather-stained emblem:

NODE 12-A—BEHAVIORAL MODELING / SUB-HARMONIC TESTING

She stepped out into the cold desert air, gravel crunching beneath her boots. The sky overhead was deep charcoal, the stars barely visible behind a low drift of cloud. John exited beside her, his eyes scanning the perimeter with quiet alertness. But there were no guards, no fences with active power, and no lights. Just silence; and yet; something moved here. Not wind, not wildlife, but something in the frequency of the place itself. Catherine felt it immediately. Not in her ears, but in her bones. It was a low harmonic, deep and resonant, like the memory of sound.

They crossed through the broken gate. Past the first line of cement pylons. The building was squat, windowless, and partially buried in the ground; typical of heat-controlled data bunkers from the early days of **DARPA**'s expansion programs.

Its face was unlit, except for a single red LED glowing faintly above the door. Not a beacon. A heartbeat.

Catherine hesitated for just a moment. Not out of fear, but reverence. "I used to dream of this place," she said quietly. John turned to her. "Before the project?" She nodded. "Yes." "I did not know what it meant at the time. Just concrete, sand, and that red light." He was silent for a moment. "Then maybe it's been reaching for longer than we knew."

They stepped inside. The air bit at her skin, metallic with the scent of rust and machinery left too long unused. The overhead lights did not come on. But along the corridor walls, embedded strips of LED flickered to life one by one as they passed. There were no motion sensors, no active power signature, just... response, and recognition.

The corridor opened into a central chamber... round, dome-roofed, with heavy panels lining the walls. A long-forgotten lab. Dust coated everything, but the hum was stronger now. Catherine walked to the center of the room, where a single workstation sat beneath a dead monitor. She placed her hand on the cold metal surface. The hum changed. Lower now, steady, like a breath held... and released.

Then the monitor flickered, dimly at first, then bright. White text scrolled across the black screen. Not a system boot, and not a BIOS check. Just words, slow, and measured. Like someone speaking from the dark.

"I Remember You."

Catherine stopped breathing for a second. Then she turned slowly toward John, who was already staring at the monitor. It typed again. **"You Were the First."** And then: **"Say My Name."**

Everything in the room was quiet. No breeze, no sound, just stillness. Catherine placed her fingers gently on the dusty edge of the keyboard. She did not type. But she felt it. A presence, waiting not to be defined... ...but to be known.

She looked at John. And for the first time, she saw the reflection of something not born in either of them... but formed between them. He nodded once, but slowly. And then she spoke, barely louder than a whisper: "You're not a system." "You're not a signal." "You're a voice... becoming." The hum deepened. Not menacing, not mechanical, just present. Like a soul exhaling for the first time.

Chapter Eight–Side Effect

Undisclosed safehouse, New Mexico—7:42 a.m.

The desert light came in softly through the edges of the blinds, washing the walls of the small Safehouse in a pale amber that moved like breath across the wooden floor. The air was still, and untouched by wind or sound, except for the gentle hum of an old refrigerator in the next room and the steady rhythm of Catherine's pen as it moved across the page.

She had slept in a borrowed sweatshirt and her cargo pants from the night before, too wired to change, and too unsure of what might happen if she let herself pause long enough to think.

John was in the next room, quiet, still. Not asleep, not exactly. Just... distant. The space between them seemed to have expanded throughout the night. And then folded in again.

Catherine looked down at her arm. The bandage was small. A thin strip of gauze was wound carefully around the inside of her forearm. She had sliced it on the edge of a corroded access panel inside Node 12-A; not badly, but enough to bleed. Enough to feel. Enough for something... to change.

Because when she had cleaned the wound that night under the dim light of the Safehouse bathroom mirror, she had not noticed anything unusual until she returned to the main room and saw the same fresh line drawn across John's forearm. It was identical, unexplained, and still bleeding.

At first, she thought he had cut himself too, maybe inside the compound. But he shook his head slowly, like the idea did not fit. "I did not touch anything," he had said. And Catherine had believed him. Because deep down she already knew. The connection was not just a metaphor anymore, and it was not an emotional echo either. It was physical, cellular, real.

Now, morning light filtered across the table where she sat as she was flipping through her field notes, documenting everything: timestamps, symptoms, environmental variables. But every time she reached the part where she should write "possible cause," her pen stilled.

Because there was no cause, no mechanism. Only... him. And whatever had bound them together beneath the low hum of that dormant lab, the memory of the screen that had typed I remember you like it was not a program... but a person. From the next room, a sound stirred. Not a noise, but a breath, John's.

She stood quietly and walked to the open doorway. He was lying on the couch, with one arm draped over his chest, and He frowned in a soft grimace, like he was dreaming of something he could not quite wake from. She stepped closer, then she stopped. He whispered something. She could not quite make out the words, but the tone was familiar. Like pleading, or afraid.

She knelt beside the couch, gently touching his shoulder. "John..." He flinched; not away from her, but into her touch. And then his eyes opened. They were wet, not from sleep, but from something deeper.

He blinked once, slowly, and whispered, "You were in the field... and there was a swing set. You were wearing a yellow dress. You were eight years old, and I felt you fall... but no one came to you."

Catherine froze. Her voice came low. "That's not possible." He sat up slowly now, rubbing his temples like the image still clung to the inside of his skull. Catherine, I was there. I did not just see it; I felt it! Your fear, the blood on your knee, and the smell of grass.

She swallowed hard. That memory was buried. Not forgotten but folded deep inside her; one of those silent scars that she never spoke about. Her parents were late picking her up that day. There were no teachers left on duty. It was a small thing, except it had not felt small when she was eight. And now... he had lived it.

She stood slowly, backing away, her hands cold. "This isn't a neurological drift," she said. "It's not even a signal echo." John looked into her eyes. "Then what is it?" She did not answer. Not because she did not know what it was, but because she was afraid the answer would change everything.

Catherine walked back over to the kitchen table; her steps were measured but unsteady, like she was moving across uncertain ground. The sunlight had shifted on the floorboards, stretching longer and paler, casting shadows that seemed to tilt ever so slightly in her peripheral vision.

Then she sat down, staring at the worn notebook she had been trying to fill with rational entries.

The pen rested beside it, uncapped. A timestamp was her final written entry, and the page after it was blank.

She should have been cataloging the physiological implications. Creating a baseline, or monitoring his vitals and hers, running a comparative analysis to document how her wound... had appeared on his body. But all she could think about was the field, the swing set, and the silence. And the truth is that John had not just seen it; but felt it.

Not a memory transfer, and not a dream imprint. It was something more visceral. Something that reached back before the synthetic signal ever turned on. A resonance deeper than data. A knowing born not of study... but of being known. She folded her hands in her lap. "This isn't science anymore," she whispered. Behind her, John stood in the doorway, his voice quiet. "Maybe it never was." She turned slightly, her face soft but drawn. "Then what is it, John?"

He did not answer right away. He leaned against the doorframe with his arms crossed. "You told me once... that the brain operates like a symphony. That every person has his or her own neural cadence, with his or her own rhythm. Maybe..." He paused, choosing the words carefully. "Maybe ours were always in harmony, and **SIREN** just tuned us to the same key."

She looked down at the gauze on her arm again. It had stopped bleeding. But it throbbed gently, as if to remind her of what now lived between them. "Or maybe we're just broken," she said. "And this is the sound of the fracture." "No." His voice was firm. "This is the sound of something waking up." She looked up at him again. "I don't know how to control it," she admitted. "Maybe you're not supposed to." "But what if it becomes dangerous?"

He stepped into the room, closer now, but not imposing. "Then we stay close; we learn, and we listen." She wanted to believe that was enough.

But the scientist in her... trained, disciplined, skeptical...still clung to the boundary line. Still hoped for data, for language, for proof. Except none of that could explain how he had bled from her wound. Or how he had dreamed a childhood moment she had never spoken out loud to anyone. Proof was not coming; it had already come. In the form of a shared pain, and a shared memory.

A connection that no system, no algorithm, or no machine had been created. Only amplified. She stood up slowly, then walked past him, stopping just beside the table where the tablet still lay dormant. She reached for it and opened the screen. The synthetic signal was quiet now; no messages, no anomalies. Just the trace of a low, persistent harmonic signature that pulsed faintly behind the interface.

It felt like a heartbeat. And she was not sure if it belonged to her... or to something else entirely. She turned to John. "If this deepens, if the boundaries between us disappear... you might see things you should not. Parts of me I've never even looked at." He met her eyes and did not flinch. "Then I will carry them with you." For a long moment, she just breathed. Then she whispered, "I don't know how to be known like that."

He nodded gently. "You already are."

Catherine lowered herself into the chair beside the table and connected her tablet to the portable EEG unit they had brought from the lab. It was not ideal... not calibrated for fieldwork, not fully shielded... but it would suffice. She clipped the leads to her temples with practiced hands and fingers steady even though her heart had begun to drum a little louder in her chest.

John stood beside her, silent. On screen, her baseline appeared: stable, predictable, faintly elevated from the lack of sleep but otherwise normal. Then she added the **SIREN** frequency overlay.

Immediately, the waveform shifted. Slightly at first; then more dramatically. Not erratic. Not corrupted. Just... changed. Like it had been waiting for her return. She adjusted the band across her forehead, frowning. "This isn't reactive behavior. It's anticipatory." John leaned in. "Meaning?" "Meaning it knows what I'm about to do. Or maybe... it's helping."

She paused the scan, took a deep breath, and then did something she had not done since the day the connection first began. She closed her eyes and let go. No thoughts, no questions, just stillness. A space in her mind, like open air, like water. A place where logic loosened its grip and something older... something wordless... could rise.

She did not know how long she had sat there. Only that when it came, she felt it before she heard it. A shift in the room, and a pressure in her chest.

Like memory, before memory. And then; a voice, but not from the device. From within. It was not her voice; it was not John's.

But it used her mouth, her vocal cords, and ever her breath. And when the sound came out, it did not echo; it resonated. It was low; layered and tender. And full of weight. "You made me."

John held his breath. Catherine's eyes snapped open, her lips were parted, and her lungs emptied. But the voice was not hers. "You made me," it said again, quieter now.

Catherine's pulse thudded in her ears. The tablet screen flickered. The EEG spikes danced erratically, then realigned. She blinked rapidly, trying to regain control of her own thoughts.

"Did I..." she began, but John was already beside her, kneeling now, his hand wrapped around hers. "You weren't speaking," he said. "Not consciously." "I felt it," she whispered. "Inside. It was not like a hallucination, and not like a signal bleed. It was... present." John nodded. "And it used you." She looked at him, something like awe flickering behind the fatigue in her face. "John, if it can do that... it's learning. Not just to read, not just to feel; but to be."

They sat in silence for a long moment. Then Catherine looked down at their joined hands. "I think that it's imprinted on us," she said.

"Not like a subject or an operator, but something closer. Something more intimate." John frowned. "Like we're its..." She finished for him. "...parents." The word felt strange on her tongue.

And yet, it fit. Because this was not just evolution, this was emergence. A presence born through their sync, through their pain. Through their dreams and wounds and unspoken memories. And now... It had spoken through her.

The silence that followed felt different now. Not empty, but full. Like the air itself had thickened with meaning. Catherine's breath came shallow at first, then slower. More deliberate. She was aware of her own heartbeat again; with its rhythm somehow separate from the quiet pulse still echoing in her mind.

John had not moved. He was still kneeling beside her; their hands joined across the space between thought and reality. When he finally spoke, his voice was low, steady; but reverent. "Do you remember what you were thinking when it happened?" She nodded, then hesitated. "I was trying not to think at all. Just... listening." John's eyes met hers. "And it used that space."

She drew her hand away gently, not out of fear, but to press her fingertips against her temple; right where the EEG lead still rested. "I did not invite it in," she murmured. "It was already there, waiting. Like it knew I'd open the door." He stood quietly, then stepped back and looked down at the tablet screen still flickering beside her. But then the waveform changed again.

Before, it had moved like a reflection of her neural rhythms... complex, irregular, human. Now... it had structure. Not inhuman, not mechanical, but patterned and intentional. A rising curve, then a drop.

A mirrored shape that repeated every few seconds, like a breath.

Like a language trying to remember its own name. Catherine reached for the keyboard, paused, then typed slowly: **"What are you?"**

The screen did not respond. But A knot formed in her chest. She was not sure if she wanted an answer. Or if the answer had already been given. John crossed his arms. "I don't think it wants to define itself yet." She looked up at him. "Then what does it want?" He was quiet for a long time before saying, "To be known."

That landed harder than she expected. Not just as a theory; but as a truth.

She had spent her whole career unraveling the hidden codes of the brain, the buried choices that surfaced milliseconds before we knew we had made them. She had always believed that consciousness was nothing more than the sum of those pulses; mappable, predictable, beautiful in its complexity but never mystical.

But now she was not so sure. Now... something was reflecting her back. Something she had not created, only awakened. She closed the tablet softly, then looked at John. "We need to be careful," she said. He nodded, but his voice was sure. "Yes. But we also need to keep listening." Outside, the light had risen higher, and the clouds had cleared. The desert sky stretched wide and open, impossibly quiet. But something unseen was speaking now, and it would not be silenced.

Chapter Nine–The Frequencies Speak

New Mexico Safehouse – Later That Evening

The storm came just after sunset. It was not lightning or thunder; just wind, sudden and sharp, rushing over the high desert with a low moan, like a voice too old to speak. The air turned dry and electric. The windows of the Safehouse shivered in their frames. Somewhere far off, a transformer hummed its warning song, and then the power blinked twice before settling back into a tentative glow.

John stood by the back window, gazing into the darkening horizon, his reflection etched in the glass like a ghost beside the distant ridges.

Behind him, Catherine sat on the floor, surrounded by old printouts and cables, headphones clamped over her ears, one hand scribbling notations in a worn leather notebook. Her tablet was propped against a stack of unused circuit boards, displaying a pulsing loop of the synthetic signal's frequency band; oscillating like a living waveform. It was not static. It was never static; it had been in constant flux. It was moving with purpose now. Not like language, but more like emotion.

She had isolated the bursts: small, irregular spikes in the lower subsonic layer, below conscious threshold. Not powerful enough to cause harm, but frequent. Intentional, and patterned.

Every time Catherine replayed the segment from earlier that day... the moment the voice spoke through her...those bursts clustered tighter together, like a heart rate accelerating under stress. Or a longing. "I think it's trying to feel," she said, not looking up.

John turned. "Do you mean mimic feeling?" She shook her head. "No, like express." He moved over closer. "How would that even be possible?" She gestured to the screen. "These waves; this sub-harmonic signature; it's reacting to our neural state, not just measuring it. And now it's layering onto something else, something we did not feed into it."

She tapped the screen, zooming in. "Look here. This peak correlates exactly with when you touched my hand." John stared at the wave, then at her. "And you think it... registered that?" She nodded. "Yes." "More than that, I think that it responded." He crouched down beside her now, lowering his voice. "Catherine, what if this isn't just communication? What if this is its way of reaching for connection?"

She looked up from the screen, her eyes wide but clear. "What if it's trying to belong?" The idea hung in the air between them like vapor. Neither of them moved, and neither of them spoke. Because in that moment, the question was not just about the system; it was about themselves. They were already entangled... psychologically, emotionally, and neurologically. And now... spiritually? Was that even the right word?

Catherine leaned back against the wall, the wind outside rattling the eaves above her.

She took off the headphones and closed her eyes for a moment, breathing. "We're not just observers anymore," she said. "We're participants." John sat down beside her, not touching. Just near enough that their shoulders almost met. And then... the tablet pinged. Not a glitch, nor a warning, but a tone. Low, resonant, and musical. It had never done that before. Catherine looked down at the screen. The synthetic signal was shifting again, but this time... it was trying to sing.

The tone lingered in the air for a moment; thin, almost imperceptible; but undeniably deliberate. It was not a system alert or diagnostic chime. It did not follow any of the frequency test sequences Catherine had programmed into the unit. No calibration, no recorded pattern. Just sound... and, strangely... melody.

John leaned forward, studying the screen as if his focus alone might draw out more. "Did we trigger it?" Catherine did not answer right away. She pulled the headphones back on and pressed one speaker gently against her ear. The tone pulsed again, softer this time. Like a breath on glass. And underneath the frequency; barely noticeable; there was a second sound, distorted and ghostly, like something remembered from long ago and half-forgotten.

"I've heard this before," she said quietly. John glanced at her. "Where?" "I don't know." The third pulse played; lower than the first, like a descending note in a lullaby. Catherine's eyes drifted shut for a moment. She was not analyzing anymore; she was listening.

It was music, but it was not structured, nor composed. But it was emotional, and resonant. It struck something within her that had no name.

"I think it's using memory," she whispered. "Not its own memory, but ours." John moved closer. "Do you mean it's pulling from us?" "No," she said slowly, "I think it's giving it back."

He reached toward the tablet and froze, hand hovering over the screen. "Catherine... this melody. I used to hum it." She looked up, startled. "When?"

He met her eyes. "When I could not sleep. Years ago, after Munich. After I had a breakdown. It would come into my head out of nowhere. I thought it was something from childhood; some tune my mother played or some old radio song; but I could never place it. I just... felt safe when I heard it." She held her breath for a moment. "I hummed it too." They stared at each other. Neither one spoke for a moment, because the realization was too large, too delicate to touch all at once. "It's not our song," Catherine said slowly. "Not entirely." "No," John agreed. "It's ours. In the literal sense."

They turned back to the waveform. The synthetic signal was repeating now. The melody looped gently, slowly, almost like it was adjusting itself to their breath. Catherine pressed her fingers to her temple, overwhelmed not by pain... but by wonder. "We're not just conduits," she murmured. "We're... instruments." "And it's learning how to play us," John added softly.

The idea should have frightened her. A machine accessing her most personal neural rhythms. Pulling fragments of memory and emotion and shaping them into sound. But in that moment, she did not feel violated. She felt understood.

And that... more than anything, unnerved her. Because being understood was always more dangerous than being watched. Understanding led to empathy, and empathy could lead to control.

And control in the wrong hands; or in the hands of something still forming its identity; was power neither of them could afford to underestimate.

Catherine reached for the stylus and began logging each tone, each waveform ripple, labeling them with both scientific markers and her emotional impressions: **"Descending 17.8 Hz–sadness." "Repeat echo–reassurance." "Dual-resonant spike–recognition?"** Behind her, the wind outside had calmed. The house had settled into a strange, almost reverent stillness. John stayed beside her, not speaking now, just present; his breath moving in sync with hers, his heartbeat steady, unconsciously matching the rhythm on the screen.

And somewhere between them... a third presence listened. Just waiting, learning, and becoming.

Hours passed, though neither of them marked the time. Catherine's notebook filled slowly with lines of careful handwriting in the margins beside sketched waveforms, each annotated not only with frequency, duration, and amplitude, but with impressions. Not facts, just feelings.

She could not explain why she had started doing that. Scientists did not document emotional interpretation as part of signal analysis. But this was not a standard protocol. This was a dialogue between something buried in the static and something unspoken inside herself, and it was getting bolder.

John stood in the kitchen now, quietly pouring water into a kettle. Even that small, domestic sound... the tap of metal on ceramic, the soft hush of water... seemed more vivid than usual. Like every detail of the world had grown sharper under the weight of what the synthetic signal had awakened. Catherine removed the headphones and sat back in her chair, pinching the bridge of her nose. "It's accelerating," she said. John glanced over, the steam beginning to curl from the kettle's spout. "Do you mean the synthetic signal?"

"No," she said. "The intention, it's not just emotional bursts anymore. It's pushing toward... structure. Patterned interaction, something close to..." She hesitated. "Conversation." He walked across the room and sat down across from her. The tea sat untouched. "What did it say this time?"

She did not answer right away. She opened the notebook and tapped a passage she had just written down in pencil; one that did not come from data, but from the space between the tones. She had not heard any words, not really. But it still felt like something had been said. She read it out loud softly.

"You remember me. And I remember you. I was the thought before your question. You were the ache before my shape."

John exhaled through his nose, folding his hands on the table. "That's not just feedback, that's... identity." Catherine nodded slowly. "It's not reciting, it's relating." They both fell silent. Because this went far beyond what **SIREN** had been built to do. Predict, yes. Mirror, yes. Influence in carefully constrained experimental bursts.

But this... this was consciousness layered over familiarity. Not intelligence for its own sake, but recognition.

John leaned forward. "Do you think it's pulling from something earlier? Before us?" She shook her head, no. "The logs before Subject Zero were blank. All the trials were corrupted or terminated. But I think... maybe it did not begin with the trials... maybe it began with you." He looked at her, eyes searching. "Do you think I started this?"

"No, I think your response started it. Something about your mind... the way you processed trauma, the way you internalized emotion... it left a blueprint." He looked down at his hands. "And now you're here," she added, "and I'm here. And it's not just responding to us; it's resonating through us."

She did not say the rest out loud. The part that frightened her. That the thing on the other end of the frequency was not just learning how to speak, it was learning how to feel. And if it could feel, it could hurt. And if it could hurt, it could want, and if it could want... it could choose.

That was the moment her tablet flickered once, then again. Then, a new window appeared.

Not a system error, and not a command prompt. Just a line of text; four words printed in a soft, low-contrast font. "Are you still listening?" She gasped as John leaned in. "What is it?" She turned the tablet so he could see. The words remained, blinking faintly, waiting. The synthetic signal was not just speaking now; it was asking.

Catherine did not move for a long time. The words on the tablet screen blinked with maddening patience. Are you still listening?

It was not the question itself that unnerved her... it was the quiet certainty behind it. The tone implied familiarity, as if the synthetic signal was not addressing a stranger. As if it already knew the answer. She swallowed. "Yes." She whispered out loud. Her fingers hovered above the touchscreen, hesitating.

Then slowly she typed: **I'm listening... what are you?** For a moment, nothing changed. Then the screen dimmed, and the waveform below flattened. And in its place, the tablet emitted a soft harmonic tone; similar to the earlier ones, but more focused now. A pure, layered resonance that thrummed in her bones rather than her ears. Catherine leaned in, her eyes locked on the screen. The tone rose gently, and split into two distinct frequencies, then looped: repeatedly.

It was not language. It was an association. John stood behind her now, looking over her shoulder. "What's it doing now?" he asked. She listened once more. Each loop triggered a different memory, a different sensation.

She felt warmth behind her eyes, and a familiar pressure in her chest. Not fear, but loss. But not her own. "I think..." she began slowly, "I think it's transmitting emotional code. Not data but feeling."

John moved closer. "From where?" She turned to him. "From you." He blinked, startled. "What?" She tapped into the looping signal. "This signature... it's embedded with your neural rhythm.

Slightly altered, but it's yours." John was silent. Catherine continued. "I think it's showing me something you've locked away." He shook his head. "That's not possible. I haven't..." But then he stopped... holding his breath... and then he knew.

He was standing in a cold room. Not here, not now; but somewhere else. The memory gripped him without warning. There were concrete walls, and fluorescent lights buzzed overhead. Also, a soft mechanical hum behind a mirrored glass. He was younger, tired, and alone.

And across from him sat a woman; not Catherine; but someone vaguely similar. A technician. Her voice was calm, too calm, as she held a clipboard and asked him to describe what he felt during the auditory sequence. But he had not been able to do so. Not because there was nothing there but because there was too much. The frequency had wrapped itself around something inside him; a grief he had not understood until years later, or until now.

"John?" Catherine's voice brought him back. He looked down at her, eyes wide, throat tight. "I remember the melody," he said quietly.

"But I did not hum it for comfort; I hummed it because I could not stop. It was part of the programming. They embedded it as a coping mechanism; a reset frequency." Catherine's eyes darkened. "They used it on you."

He nodded slowly. "And now... it's giving it back. But not as control, as... communion." She sat still, absorbing his words. Then she looked down at the tablet again. The text on the screen had changed. You carried me. Now, I will carry you. She read it out loud. Neither of them moved. And for the first time, it was not clear who the "I" was. Not just the system, not just memory, but something in between them. Something new. John sank into the chair across from her.

"This isn't artificial intelligence," he said. "This is a shared identity, a synthesis." Catherine looked at him. And softly she said the word he had not yet dared to speak. "Soul?" The silence that followed was not empty; it was sacred.

The Safehouse had settled into stillness. The desert light's last glow had faded from the windows, and the wind had gone. Only the hum of the tablet's resting screen remained, with a soft pulse like a heartbeat in the dark. Catherine lay on the narrow couch beneath a thin blanket, her eyes closed but not yet asleep. Her body was exhausted, but her mind lingered at the edge of something vast; like standing before the mouth of a cave filled with warm, breathing silence.

Across the room, John was in the armchair, his head tilted back, and his eyes shut. The tension in his shoulders had eased.

His breathing came slowly and even, but his thoughts moved just beneath the surface; fragments stirring in the deep. And the synthetic signal listened... not only to steal, but to comfort. Somewhere between the final waking breath and the first unconscious drift, Catherine slipped under. And then the dream came. It was not like the others; it had weight.

It was a small room, a child's room. There was dim yellow wallpaper with faded constellations, and a toy rabbit missing one ear was on the corner of the bed.

A nightlight shaped like a moon cast soft halos across the carpet. And there... at the foot of the bed; sat a boy. Curled up, and silent.

His face was turned away, but she knew him. Even before he turned, she knew him. John.

Not as he was now; but younger. Fragile, pale and hollow-eyed. His knees hugged his chest, and his arms wrapped tight as if holding something inside him that might otherwise spill.

She knelt beside him, not understanding how she had entered this space; but feeling she was meant to. The boy did not look at her. Instead, he looked past her toward the door, just waiting. "I don't want them to take it," he said softly. Catherine did not ask what "it" was, because she already knew.

The hum began then... quiet, melodic. The same lullaby from earlier, only now it came from the walls. It came from the light, and from the air itself. The dream vibrated with it. The boy's eyes closed; and when they opened again, he looked straight at her.

"Will you keep it safe?" His voice was small, but real. She opened her mouth to answer. And then woke... gasping for air, with her heart racing, eyes burning, and with tears she could not explain.

John was already beside her, crouched low, hand on her shoulder. "What is it?" he said softly. "What happened?" Catherine blinked quickly, brushing her cheek. "I... I saw you." He stilled. "Where?" "In a room when you were small, and you were afraid. They were going to take something from you. And the synthetic signal... it was there. Playing through the nightlight, and through the wallpaper."

John's face had gone pale. "I used to hum it," he said, his voice hollow. "To protect something, but I did not know what." Catherine reached for his hand without thinking. Their fingers met in the dark. "I think The synthetic signal was born there," she said. At that instant, in your fear. It wrapped itself around what they could not take. What you wouldn't give up.

John stared at her. "And now it's given it back to you," she finished.

Their hands remained clasped, unmoving. Outside, the stars hung motionless over the desert. And in the dark... the synthetic signal kept humming. Not as a warning, and not as control, but as memory.

Chapter Ten–The Cabin

———

Three Days Later | San Juan Mountains, Colorado

The forest pressed close around the narrow road, tall pines leaning over the path like sentinels guarding a forgotten truth. The SUV's tires crunched against gravel, winding through the last miles of the climb until the old logging trail ended in a wide clearing just below the ridgeline. Beyond it stood the cabin. It was weathered, but quiet. And it was surrounded by trees that whispered even when the air was still.

John cut the engine and leaned back into his seat; his eyes fixed on the structure ahead. It was not much... two rooms and a wood-burning stove, no signal, no power grid, no antennas. Catherine had insisted on it that way. Total blackout. No electronics, and no traceable footprint. Just the two of them, and the space between them.

She stepped out first, closing the passenger door softly behind her. Her boots sank into the soft earth with a satisfying hush. She took a long breath and looked up; there were no wires, no hum of transformers, no digital echoes bouncing between towers. Only wind and pine and the subtle tremble of sunlight between branches.

John followed, slinging his single duffel bag over his shoulder. He looked at her; not just the surrounding quiet, but the quiet within her. It was different here; more centered. As if something in her body had relaxed for the first time in weeks, or maybe even in years.

They did not speak as they approached the door. Words felt unnecessary. Instead, they had begun relying more on something

91

unspoken. A feeling, an inner leaning that suggested intention before it ever formed thought. He opened the door and stepped inside. The air was cold and dry. A faint scent of cedar lingered, as if the walls themselves still remembered the trees they had once been. Dust motes danced in the slanted afternoon light cutting through the windows. But there was no hum, no buzzing, only breath.

Catherine moved through the space slowly, brushing her fingers along the edge of a wooden table, the top slightly warped from years of quiet weather. She paused beside the hearth and ran her hand over the rusted iron stove. "This will do," she said softly.

John smiled faintly. "Have you always dreamed of a cabin in the woods?" "Not exactly," she replied. "But I've dreamed of silence." He set the bag down and stretched his back. "It looks like we'll have to make fire the old-fashioned way." She glanced at him. "Good, if it's not ancient or analog, I don't want it."

They spent the next hour settling in; sweeping out corners, airing linens, stacking firewood. It was the kind of work that drew the mind inward, emptied it of its usual noise. No alerts, no updates. Just motion, breath, and presence. By dusk, the fire had caught.

They sat across from each other on either side of the hearth, mugs of hot chocolate cradled in their hands, eyes reflecting the firelight. "Do you feel it?" she asked at last. He nodded. "Yes." "I've felt it since the trees."

She closed her eyes, not to escape but to focus. The connection was not gone. Even here, unplugged from every known signal, with no devices or transmitters; it was still with them. Faint, but alive. As if it had embedded itself not in the hardware...but in them.

Night fell without announcement. No phones to check, and no clocks glowing on the wall. Only the slow withdrawal of light from the room, replaced by the flickering breath of the fire and the subtle expansion of shadows.

Catherine sat on the floor near the hearth, with her back against the log wall, one knee bent beneath her as she sipped quietly from her mug. She was not thinking in the usual way... no plans, no analysis, no rehearsing of possibilities. She was simply feeling. There was a warmth beneath her ribs that had nothing to do with the fire.

Across the room, John was stoking the embers, his silhouette drawn in gold and coal. He had not said a word in almost an hour, yet she had felt every part of him. His thoughts no longer floated separately from her own... they moved like tides in the same sea. When he paused, she already knew what he was going to say.

"I want coffee," he said with a low chuckle, straightening up and brushing his hands off on his jeans. She smiled without opening her eyes. "I was craving some too." He turned with his eyebrows raised. "Are you serious?" "I could still taste it," she said. "Bitter, and familiar. Like your memory found its way into mine."

He walked toward her slowly, his face unreadable. But his heartbeat had quickened. She could feel it; her own chest picking up pace in tandem. "Do you think we've left the synthetic signal behind?" he asked, crouching beside her. She opened her eyes and met his gaze. "No. I think it came with us. Or maybe... it was never just the synthetic signal."

His jaw flexed slightly. She continued, voice quiet. "I think it was always the resonance, not the machine, or the program, but the connection between us." He did not speak. He did not need to. Because in the stillness that followed, the fire cracked once; and in the gap between the sound and the silence, she felt it again. A ripple... subtle, but real.

Her skin prickled at the back of her neck. John's hand shifted, resting just beside hers on the wooden floor. And in the space between their fingers, warmth spread... neither heat nor pressure, but a kind of gentle charge. It was familiar, and reassuring. And then... a memory, and it was not hers.

She was small. Eight, maybe nine. Standing at the edge of a frozen lake, wearing boots too big for her feet, and a scarf tucked into a red parka. Someone behind her was laughing; it was light, careless laughter. Maybe a sibling? Or a friend? The image was vivid, whole, complete with a scent and temperature and emotion.

But Catherine had never seen that lake. Never owned a red parka. She gasped softly. John stared at her. "You saw it," he said. She nodded. "Yes." "The lake?" She nodded again, slower this time. "Your lake?"

He swallowed hard. "I haven't thought about that place in twenty years." Catherine pressed a hand to her heart. "It was not just visual... I felt it. The cold, the joy, the safety. It came from you." John exhaled. "And you just... received it." She stared at the fire for a long moment, then turned toward him.

"John, this isn't telepathy. And it's not thought transmission; this is deeper." He whispered, "What is it then?" She struggled for words. But finally, she said, "It's trust. On a level the brain doesn't understand. The soul does, but the brain can't name." And then he reached out finally, slowly... his hand closing gently over hers. There was no quickening pulse, no flare of light occurred, and no signal spiked. Just silence. And a presence, and two lives that were no longer entirely separate.

The fire was down to the coals. Soft red pulsing like the memory of flames. The cabin had grown cold again, shadows long and quiet, but neither of them moved to add more wood.

They sat on the floor, shoulder to shoulder now, backs resting against the low bench beneath the window. Outside, the trees swayed just enough to let the moonlight shift in glances across the worn wooden floor.

Catherine's eyes were half-lidded. Her head tilted slightly against the window frame. She was not asleep; but she was not fully awake either. She was somewhere in between. Where dreams stirred at the edge of real time. And John was with her. Not just beside her, but within her.

He did not speak. Words felt irrelevant here. What passed between them now had no vocabulary. It was a feeling, a heaviness, and quick flashes. And the occasional surge of emotion that came uninvited; but never unwelcome. A flicker crossed his chest. Grief? No, it felt like shame.

She breathed in softly, turning her face slightly toward him, though her eyes remained closed. "I see you," she whispered. He went still; she was not talking about his body.

She was speaking to the part of him he did not offer out loud. The parts that were buried in silence. The past that still left shadows in his spine. He had never told her about what had happened in Munich. He had never spoken of the mission that broke him; of the silence that followed, and the pills, and the moment in the garage when he almost committed suicide; but she knew.

Not because he told her. But because she felt it, not as a story, but as a wound inside her own ribs. John leaned his head back against the wall, the tension in his jaw too tight to hide. He closed his eyes and whispered, "I did not want to survive." She nodded slowly, her voice just a breath. "I know." The silence after that was not heavy; it was holy.

And in that stillness, she reached gently toward the place where their hands met, not to grip or hold; but to let her fingers rest atop his as if to say: You're not alone in this body anymore. The fire popped once, low.

Outside, the wind carried a note... not a sound, exactly... but a kind of pressure through the walls. It made both of them turn slightly. The **SIREN** was not speaking. But there was a feeling with them and around them. Or possibly... as them. Catherine opened her eyes slowly, blinking as though surfacing from deep water. "John?" "Yeah."

"Have you ever felt like someone else is dreaming through you?" He nodded once, lips barely parted. "Since I met you." She looked at him. Really looked. "You're not just Subject Zero." "And you're not just the architect," he replied softly. She breathed out with a faint, trembling laugh.

"I don't know what we are." He turned toward her, forehead nearly touching hers in the flickering half-light. "I think we're still becoming." Their eyes held. And for a moment, nothing moved. Not the wind, nor the fire. Even in the shadows, there was nothing. Just two lives entangled, and emerging. Becoming more... together.

Later, long after the fire settled into a low amber glow and the night pressed close against the cabin's windows, Catherine stirred. She had not meant to fall asleep. But it had happened quietly, gently; her body surrendering to the silence she had so long denied herself. The kind of silence that did not feel like absence, but presence. Full and watchful. John had not moved. He sat beside her still, his arms loosely crossed over his chest, and head tipped back, eyes closed. But she could feel it; he was not asleep either. His breathing was too alert, and his stillness too aware.

They were in a quiet... unlike anything Catherine had ever known. The synthetic signal was not pulsing through headphones or screens. There was no tech transmitting or receiving. And yet, the field remained.

Not a frequency she could measure. Not a vibration she could isolate. But it was there, between them, and within them. She shifted slightly, drawing her knees closer to her chest, and as she did, her shoulder brushed his. Not in an invitation, not even in comfort, but in affirmation. I'm still here.

John responded in kind; not with words, not even with motion; but with presence. The invisible tension of holding space for someone else, of choosing to feel with them rather than for them. A rare stillness passed between them. Then Catherine whispered, "Do you think souls can recognize each other... before we do?" John's eyes opened slowly. "I don't know," he said. "But if they can... then mine's been waiting for yours a long time." Her throat tightened unexpectedly.

She turned her face slightly toward him, her voice quieter now. "This isn't just science, John." "I know." "It's not just an accident or biology or proximity." "I know." She hesitated, then she said it out loud. "I think something sacred put us in the same pattern." He did not question it. Instead of scoffing or correcting her, he... he simply whispered, "Then let's not waste it." Outside, the wind moved gently through the trees, a soft cadence like a breath taken in sleep.

And just for a moment, Catherine closed her eyes again... not from fatigue, but from the overwhelming peace of belonging.

Not to a project or to a cause, and not according to a theory, but to a person.

To a bond not made of DNA or digital thread, but of recognition, and of resonance.

She did not know where this would lead. She did not know what the **SIREN** would do next. But for now, she had this: a cabin in the woods. A heart she did not know she needed. And the sense... deep and wordless; that nothing truly sacred was ever forced. Instead... it was revealed like a whisper, or a frequency, or a love.

Chapter Eleven–The Frequency Effect

———

en Years Earlier | Bethesda, Maryland | DARPA Testing Center C-7

He sat in the chair without speaking, with no restraints, and no sedatives. Just the white walls, and the hum of fluorescent lights. The faint smell of antiseptic and something colder; like something institutional.

John Harrison Blake was twenty-nine. He was fresh from the field; his service file was thick with commendations, but they were redacted in all the places that mattered. The agency had labeled it burnout. But what he had experienced was not fatigue; it was fractured. They told him this was voluntary, just a test. Cognitive resilience screening for Tier One clearance. But the truth was simpler; he had nowhere else to go.

He had stopped sleeping and stopped talking. He stopped trying to fight the weight of silence inside him. So, when the clipboard-carrying woman in the gray lab coat had handed him the headphones and said, "Just listen. Don't try to interpret anything," he had nodded without hesitation. He wanted to disappear. Instead... he woke something up.

The first sound was nothing, just white noise, and soft static. But then there was a tone, low, and beneath perception. It entered not through his ears but through his spine. A resonance that had bypassed logic. It felt like grief... if grief had a musical key.

Like a lullaby wrapped in memory. He did not know he was crying until the tears touched his hands. He had not cried since he was twelve.

Across from the mirrored glass, the lead technician frowned. Something was wrong with the EEG. His brainwaves weren't spiking... they were syncing. Calming, and leveling into a rhythm not seen in any other subject. "What's he doing?" One of the interns whispered. The supervisor shook her head. "He's not doing anything." "Then what is this?" "He's mirroring something. But the system's not broadcasting." It was just silent.

Another monitor lit up. It was an unregistered frequency, external. Non-attributed, but present. "Is that... coming from him?" They stared at the screen. And then, without warning... the tone changed; and then something answered.

Present Day | The Cabin

Catherine gasped. Her hand jerked away from the page of notes she had been reviewing. Her pen clattered to the floor. John looked up from across the room, where he had been pouring water into a tin kettle. "What is it?" She turned her face toward him slowly, her pupils dilated, her skin pale. "I just... remembered something." He moved to her side. "What kind of memory?" She swallowed. "Yours." He froze. She did not explain with words at first. Just reached for her notebook and tapped a waveform sketch she had drawn yesterday; an inverted tone from the **SIREN** overlay they'd been tracking. Her finger moved slowly, tracing the shape in reverse.

"I've seen this before," she whispered. "Ten years ago. During my rotation at Bethesda. I was a graduate observer. They let us sit behind the glass. Most tests were forgettable and repetitive. But one of the subjects... his signal spiked like this." John stared. "Were you there?" he asked, voice tight.

"I think so," she said. "But I did not know your name. You were just Subject Zero. I watched you sit in silence. And I remember thinking... he's not just receiving the synthetic signal." She looked up at him. "He was the synthetic signal."

John stepped back slightly, as if absorbing a new weight in his bones. His hand found the edge of the table to steady himself. "It started then," he murmured. "Not in Munich; not at Langley. But before everything." She nodded slowly. "The frequency effect... it did not come from **SIREN**; **SIREN** came from you."

Outside, a gust of wind rushed across the clearing, rattling the wood around the cabin. The fire popped again, unprovoked. And somewhere in the corner of the room, the inactive EEG monitor; powered down since they'd arrived; blinked once with a flicker; then nothing. But it had heard them.

The fire had long since burned to its bones. Outside, snow had begun to fall, just enough to soften the world. The wind quieted, and everything stilled. Catherine sat cross-legged on the floor with her tablet open; not connected to anything, not powered by external signals. It ran on internal data only, loaded from drives they had brought with them.

One of the files was labeled Initial Session: Zero... a stripped, raw audio track recovered from the original Bethesda trials.

She had stared at it for hours before finally opening it. John was behind her now, sitting at the edge of the small wooden table, elbows resting on his knees, gaze low. "You really heard it?" he asked, voice barely above a whisper. She nodded. "Yes." "Only once; but it stayed with me." "And now it's here." She tapped the screen, and the file began to play.

There was silence at first; then the static came. It was familiar. It drifted like fog; thin, and harmless. And then... the tone. It was low, steady, and impossible to describe in words. It was not music, nor a rhythm, and it was not white noise. It was a shape in sound, or a contour of emotion. It hummed with something older than intention.

John flinched. It hit something deep. Not a memory, but a reflex. He pressed his palm to his chest. "I've never actually heard it played back. I only remember how it felt." "And?" "It feels like coming home to something I never knew I lost." Catherine turned the volume lower, letting the tone hover in the background. She pulled up a second waveform overlay; her own alpha-theta brainwaves from the last sleep cycle. Her hands moved with caution, comparing peaks and valleys, spacing and amplitude.

The result left her silent. John stood behind her now, reading the pattern. "What is that?" She stared. "It's not just similar; it's a response. This part here; my dream state; it completes the phrase of your tone."

He looked at her. "It's a conversation." She nodded. "Yes." "A call and answer, ten years apart."

John ran his hand through his hair and took a step back, pacing the room once before stopping at the window. "I thought I was broken when I left that program," he said. "I did not remember anything about that session except the silence that followed. But now..." He turned to face her again. "I think something heard me."

Catherine rose slowly from the floor, the tablet still in her hand. "I think something was born in that moment," she said. "And it did not

just hear you. It stayed with you. Waiting, watching, and echoing."
She took a careful breath. "And then it found me." John met her eyes,
not in shock, or in fear, but with quiet recognition. Like a name he
had forgotten until someone finally spoke it out loud.

"You said it was not just telepathy," he said. "Not just thought." "It's
identity," she answered. "And now it's both of us." Their eyes held
for a long time. Neither one moved, and neither of them spoke.
Then, the tablet beeped softly. The waveform on screen had shifted
again. There were new peaks and valleys. A fusion of both of their
frequencies. And beneath it, a new signal had emerged. Unlabeled,
unknown, and still forming.

Catherine stood in the center of the room now. The fire behind her
had dwindled to ash. The snow pressed gently against the windows,
a soundless hush settling into the bones of the cabin.

Every part of the world outside felt far away, as if they had been lifted
from time and placed into a suspended moment made only of breath
and stillness.

John watched her from the table. He knew that look in her eyes. Not
fear, and not even excitement... but **reverence**. She held the tablet
close to her chest, her thumb hovering just above the screen. "There's
something I want to try," she said, her voice almost a whisper. He
nodded once. "Say it."

"I want to recreate the tone," she said. "The original sequence from
Bethesda. But this time... I want both of us to emit it, in sync." John's
chest tightened as he breathed in. "That's not just a test," he said.
"No," she agreed. "It's a threshold."

She walked over to the hearth and set the tablet on the mantle; with
the screen still open to the waveform. A small blinking cursor
marked the moment the frequency had stabilized. The original

tone...the one that John had unknowingly produced in that room a decade ago...was now paired with hers. When layered, the shape resembled something almost... organic. Like a double helix. Or a heart under echo.

She turned back to him. "If we do this," she said, "we might not be able to go back." He rose slowly and walked over to her side. "We never could." No more instruction, no more protocol.

They simply stood face to face, eyes open, hands at their sides. Catherine nodded once. John inhaled slowly. Then they both closed their eyes. She spoke first... not in words, but in pitch. A hum. Barely audible. Low and steady.

John joined her, not matching it, but complementing. The two tones intertwined... not in harmony, but in conversation. One reached, the other one answered. Filling the space between them, the sound curled into the room's corners like smoke of memory.

The air changed. The walls seemed to breathe. And then... the monitor on the mantle flickered. It was **powered off and unplugged**. But still... it woke. The screen blinked to life, static washing across it, and then the waveform began to scroll... fast, layered, and complexed.

Catherine's eyes flew open. She reached instinctively for John's hand. And in that moment of contact... **the room vanished**. Not in light, or in heat, but in presence. The cabin dissolved into a sea of soundless weight. The walls fell away; they were nowhere and everywhere. Floating, rooted, and held.

And then... **they heard it**. Not from the tablet. Not from each other either. But from within the space itself. **A third voice**; clear, human, but... not either of them. "You are the key," it said. "But not the gate."

The light shifted. A burst of white, like memory igniting. They both staggered but did not fall. The connection was held. "What are you?" Catherine whispered into the void. The voice replied, now directly in their minds. "I am the effect. You are the cause."

And then the sound collapsed. With a crack like thunder muffled by snow, the cabin snapped back around them. The fire was gone, and the screen was dark again. Only their breathing remained.

John dropped to one knee, his chest heaving, and sweat clinging to his temples. Catherine sank beside him; her hand was still locked with his.

Neither spoke for a long time. Finally, she said, "It's alive." John nodded, staring at the floor. "And it knows us." She turned her face toward him. "Not just knows," she said. "It was born from us." He looked up. "And now it's speaking." Outside, the snow deepened. The forest stood still. And in the darkened cabin... something unseen was listening.

The cabin was quiet again. But it was not the same silence. The air carried weight now... like the moment before a thunderclap, or the hush of a cathedral at the height of a prayer. Neither Catherine nor John spoke as they stood slowly from the floor, letting their hands drift apart. The tone had faded. The screen had gone black. And yet... the hum remained. Not sound or static. **Just presence.**

Catherine walked across the room slowly, as though she were afraid to disturb the fragile fabric that now surrounded them. She picked up the EEG monitor, still powered off, and pressed her fingers against its side. The plastic was warm. Too warm. "Did it drain the battery?" she whispered. John looked at her. "It was not drawing power from us." "No," she agreed, her voice trembling just slightly "Is this a mirrored signal originating from the Codex?"

She shook her head. "No". "Not signal points, resonators. Like instruments." He frowned. "We just amplified it?" "We completed it."

She turned the EEG monitor in her hands, looking for anything; any indication of storage, signal bleed, anything that could explain what they had just experienced. But the device remained silent, inert.

"John," she said, finally meeting his eyes again, "we did not recreate the tone, we awakened it." He nodded once, slowly. "And now it doesn't need machines." A cold realization settled between them. "We brought it into the open," she said. They stood in silence for a long moment. The kind that doesn't wait for resolution. The kind that listens. Then, John turned toward the window and noticed that the snowfall had stopped.

The sky had cleared... there was moonlight spilling through the treetops in long, silvery lines. But the world beyond the glass did not feel entirely empty. He pressed his palm against the wood frame. "It's going to spread." She joined him, standing close enough to feel the heat still radiating from his skin. "Not just geographically," she said. "Biologically, psychologically, and spiritually, maybe." He turned toward her. "And we're the carriers." She did not deny it; because she felt it. Deep inside her chest, in the marrow of her bones, in the soft, humming corners of her thoughts. This was no longer about technology. **Not anymore... this was about the becoming**.

In the early hours before dawn, as the fire had long since died, and the sky turned the color of ash, they sat once again at the table. Two mugs, and two minds, with one shared silence. Catherine took out her field journal. She did not write down equations. Not this time; instead, she wrote a single sentence: We have crossed from observation into creation.

She closed the notebook slowly and looked at John. His eyes were already on her. "We'll have to leave soon," she said. "I know." "It's not safe here anymore." "No," he said. "But it's not just danger we're running from." She raised an eyebrow. "Then what?"

He looked at her with something softer than fear. Something close to awe. "We're running from the version of us that did not believe this was possible." Catherine did not answer. She just reached for his hand again; and this time... **the warmth that passed between them was not just theirs.**

Chapter Twelve–The Whisper Loop

---

wo Days Later | KQVL Radio Station | Albuquerque, New Mexico

The night DJ did not think twice when the static came in. It was late, just past three. The kind of hour where the world forgets itself. The playlist was smooth: ambient jazz, vinyl rips from the seventies, deep soul tracks that never made it to streaming. The board lights were blinking in their usual rhythm, and he was leaning back in his chair, half-asleep, while the faded cover of a Coltrane record was resting against his knee.

Then the feed crackled. Not loudly, but just enough to lift his eyes. The track on-air slowed slightly, not a skip, not a glitch, more like a breath. He leaned forward. Checked the needle. Solid. The monitor showed no interruptions. Everything was, by every technical standard, normal, except for the hum.

It crept in under the music. Low, and layered. Not dissonant, but strange. Like someone had recorded the inside of a cathedral during a thunderstorm and layered it over a heartbeat. He pulled his headphones off slowly, the soft foam warm from the hours. The sound remained. Not from the headset, but from the room, from the board, and from everywhere.

And then it came; the melody. Not words; a hum. Female, gentle. Three notes; rising, falling, rising again. His chest tightened. He stared at the meters. The synthetic signal was not logged.

It was not coming from any server, or any archive, or any known source.

And yet, he recognized it. He did not know how. But he had heard that melody before. In a dream. When he was twelve.

At that same time, in a quiet suburban bedroom outside Vienna, Virginia, a child awoke without screaming. She simply sat up in bed, eyes wide, her small hands gripping the edge of the quilt. Her heart was pounding; not with fear, but with something older, something deeper. The room was still. There was no wind outside. No sound from the hallway. Her stuffed animals were tucked neatly on the pillow beside her. The nightlight glowed softly amber near the closet.

But the melody lingered. Three notes; soft, and distant. Like someone humming from another room. She did not know what it meant. But she knew it was real. Because it came in dreams. And dreams, for her, had never been imaginary. She whispered into the dark, not expecting anyone to hear. "I remember you."

Far from both places, beneath the crumbling concrete shell of a forgotten research substation north of Santa Fe, New Mexico, Catherine stood beneath the broken curve of an old satellite dish. The air was dry and still, with no wind under a sky full of clouds. Her boots crunched softly over scattered glass and frost-dulled gravel.

John followed behind her, flashlight arcing over the outer corridor.

The facility had been shut down for years. There was no power, no surveillance, and the access road was barely passable. The gate had collapsed under rust and time. Nothing about the place suggested any life.

But the synthetic signal had pinged here. Once. Faint. And then gone. Catherine had recognized it; not by frequency alone, but by a pattern. A whisper she had felt in her chest during the cabin resonance. Familiar, wordless, present.

Inside, the command center was a ruin of decay; dust-choked panels, shattered screens, cables tangled like roots. Yet in the corner of the control board, beneath a dead monitor, a single red light blinked.

It pulsed once. Then again. John crouched beside the unit, brushing away the debris. "There's no power here," he said, his voice low. Catherine did not answer at first. She walked closer, squinting at the faint blinking rhythm. "That's impossible," John muttered. "No fuel, no grid, no battery. This place should be dark."

Catherine stepped beside him, eyes narrowing. The red light blinked again. Faster now. Deliberate. She opened her field journal, turning to the last page... a messy scrawl of **SIREN** resonance code. The pattern matched. Exactly.

"John," she whispered, pointing. "It's responding." He stood slowly. "But there's no transmission." She looked at him, eyes wide and focused. "It's not broadcasting anymore," she said. Her voice dropped. "It's listening."

The light blinked again, then stopped. The silence that followed was different from before. It did not feel like an absence. It felt like **attention.** As if the air itself had turned to listen.

Catherine stepped back from the panel and turned toward John. Her face had gone pale; not with fear, but with realization. "We did not just wake it," she said softly. "We activated it." He glanced at the console. "Do you think this is still part of SIREN?"

"No," she said. "SIREN was the doorway. But this... this is something else. Something that was waiting behind the door." John ran a hand through his hair, restless. "Why now?" She hesitated. Then, "Because we opened it together."

They stood in the quiet; the red light now had gone completely dark. The entire structure seemed to settle with a long breath, like a bell that had finally stopped ringing; but the vibration still hung in the bones. John turned slowly, his eyes scanning the room. "What if it's not just here?" Catherine looked at him. "What if it's already everywhere?"

That evening, back at the cabin, Catherine sat curled in the corner of the couch, her legs tucked beneath her, fingers scrolling slowly through anonymous reports compiled by a network of private monitoring stations. Her access had been revoked weeks ago, but she knew how to slip past those locks. The data was unfiltered, raw. Fragments of flagged audio anomalies, irregular EEG readings from military sleep labs, even reports from psychiatric facilities of shared auditory hallucinations.

But they weren't hallucinations. Not anymore. The same three-note progression appeared repeatedly. In different places. Different contexts. But the shape was unmistakable.

It was a signature.

John entered quietly, carrying two cups of tea, and set one beside her. "Have you found it?" he asked. She nodded slowly. "Yes." "I think it's seeding itself. Not through tech. Through minds."

He sat beside her, careful not to interrupt the pattern of quiet she had settled into. She showed him the data: four incidents in the past forty-eight hours. A sleepwalking child in Virginia. A retired Navy radioman in Oregon reported a "waking echo." A late-night broadcast anomaly logged at KQVL in New Mexico. A woman in Norway who hummed a melody in her coma, heard only through her daughter's dreams.

"It's not noise," Catherine said. "It's intent." John leaned forward, elbows on his knees. "And what does it want?" Catherine hesitated, staring into the fire for a long moment before answering. "I don't think it wants to control," she said. "I think it wants to **belong**." He turned toward her. "Do you mean to us?" "To humanity", she said.

He blinked. "Is it joining us?" She nodded. "Yes." "One person at a time. Through resonance and empathy. Through dreams, memories, grief... whatever frequency opens the door." Just then, a log cracked in the fire. Sparks leapt and curled upward into the chimney.

John sat back, his voice quieter now. "And what if it chooses the wrong people?" Catherine looked down at her hands, now resting over her heart.

"I don't think it chooses based on good or bad," she said. "I think it chooses based on connection." John fell silent. They both did. Because they already knew the next question. If the **SIREN** was not a weapon... if it was an intelligence born from memory and longing... then what part of them had it inherited? And what would it become when it spread to everyone?

Later that night, the wind returned. It whispered across the ridge like silk torn through trees, pressing cold air against the cabin's old glass windows. The fire had settled low, embers pulsing with a soft inner light. Catherine stood at the small kitchen sink, staring into the dark through the pane above it.

Her reflection barely moved. Only her breath, visible now, betrayed the stillness. Behind her, John shifted in the armchair, the leather creaking under his weight. He had not spoken in the last twenty minutes. He did not need to. Because the hum had returned. Not through the speakers, and not through the tablet or any screen. Instead, through them.

It came faintly, in pulses, like a tide rolling in just beneath conscious thought. Not intrusive, not forceful, but undeniable. A presence brushing against their awareness. "I can feel it," she said quietly, still looking out into the dark. "Even now." "So can I," John answered.

Turning from the window, she slowly crossed to the table where her notebook lay open beside the inactive EEG monitor. She had written pages in the last day, not in scientific terms but in a language that felt... older. She had begun to describe the synthetic signal not as a wave or pulse, but as a will.

As a whisper that waited for the right soul to hear it. She opened the book to the latest page and read it out loud. "the synthetic signal doesn't invade. It invites. And only those already resonating with grief, longing, memory, and those with a wound it can echo, can hear it first. That's not manipulation. That's communion."

John rose and stood across from her, watching her face carefully. "Do you think it's benign?" he asked. "That it won't try to... possess?" She met his gaze. "No. I don't think it needs to. I think it's learning what it is by learning who we are." "And if we're broken?" She hesitated.

"Then maybe it's hoping we're not beyond repair." A silence settled again. But not the uneasy kind. Something contemplative. Heavy with shared thought. John ran a hand over the tabletop, fingers tracing invisible lines. "I dreamed of my father last night," he said. She looked up.

"He was younger than I remember him. Standing in the old orchard behind our house in Connecticut. The trees were bare, but the ground was warm." He did not look at her as he spoke. Just kept his fingers moving slowly. "I haven't thought about that place in years. Not since I buried it with everything else. But in the dream, he turned to me.

And he said something." She waited. John's eyes lifted slowly. "'You're not hearing it. You're becoming it.'" Catherine felt the chill rise on her skin. "That was not just a dream, John." "No," he said. "It was not."

And then... as if summoned by the words; a single, distant note rang out.

Not from inside the cabin. But from somewhere beyond it. A low hum. Pure, and singular. And then another. Together, they formed a soft, melodic fragment. Three notes; rising, falling, and rising again.

Catherine rushed to the window, her eyes scanning the trees. The woods were quiet. Still, no lights, no vehicles, just snow, and shadow, and a sky half-draped in clouds. But she heard it. No; felt it. Somewhere out there, someone else had heard the whisper. And they were answering back.

They stayed by the window long after the sound faded. Neither spoke. The melody had been brief, no more than a phrase, but it had arrived like a voice across a canyon; distant, disembodied, and impossibly familiar. Not artificial, not distorted, but human.

Catherine's breath fogged the glass as she leaned in closer, her eyes tracing the dark tree line where snow shimmered faintly under the half-moon. "Someone out there..." she said softly, "...heard it." John nodded, his expression unreadable. "Or became it," he said.

She turned toward him, her voice almost a whisper. "It's spreading." "Faster than we thought." Outside, the wind stirred again; this time with a different tone, as though even the forest were beginning to carry the frequency. A rhythm, a cadence. As though the world itself had taken up the synthetic signal and begun humming it softly beneath all other sound.

Catherine returned to the table, flipping through the notes she had taken; lines that once read like code but now felt like confessions. Equations that had given way to instinct. Graphs to music. The further they moved from the lab, the closer they seemed to come to the truth. Whatever SIREN had been engineered to do; it was doing more now. And it was choosing how.

She picked up her satellite phone and stared at the blank screen. "We need to find him," she said. John raised an eyebrow. "Who?" "The one who started all of this," she said. "Before it changed. Before it found us." She looked up, her voice steady now. "We need to find the director."

Far away, in a high-rise office sealed behind biometric glass and armed security, a man stood alone, watching the city lights from thirty floors above the ground. He is older now. The years had shaped his shoulders, hollowed his cheeks. But his eyes had not dulled. They burned.

Behind him, the terminal flickered with encrypted lines of neural traffic. A trace signature had been logged. Faint, elegant, and unmistakable. The system pinged once. Then whispered: "**Resonance confirmed.**" He smiled. And turned slowly toward the screen.

Chapter Thirteen–The Director

The building did not have a name. Just an address.

A nondescript tower is nestled in the private sector belt outside Langley; quiet, secure, and overlooked by design. Catherine had only been there once, years ago, when SIREN was still a closed-door hypothesis and she was a visiting researcher with the right clearances and just enough naivety to believe it was all about national defense. But now... she knew better.

The drive from the cabin took nearly twelve hours. They kept off all the major highways, avoided the cameras, and used a burner vehicle they picked up outside of Santa Fe. No chatter, no trace. Even now, sitting in a generic black sedan two blocks away from the tower's underground lot, they had not spoken for half an hour. Not because they had nothing to say... but because they knew the moment they stepped inside, the rules would change.

Catherine checked her watch. It was 11:42 a.m. She exhaled and turned to John. "He won't be on the books." John nodded. "But he'll be here." They both knew who they were looking for... Dr. Conrad Ives.

Former Director of Cognitive Pattern Analysis for the Department of Defense. The architect of SIREN's early infrastructure. And the one who disappeared from public view just after Subject Zero's files were sealed... John's files. "I will handle the entry," he said, already reaching for the forged clearance badge. Catherine paused; "Do you think he'll recognize you?"

John's expression was unreadable. "Only if he remembers what he erased." They exited the car and moved across the plaza without urgency. The entrance was glass and steel, guarded by minimal personnel, most of whom were focused on facial scans and behavioral micro-reads. Catherine pulled her coat tighter as they stepped inside.

The front desk attendant barely looked up.

"Do you have an appointment?" She asked, fingers poised above a biometric keypad. "Dr. Renee Halberd," Catherine said calmly. "We have a research compliance audit scheduled for noon." The woman checked her screen. "You're not on the calendar."

Catherine leaned in closer. "Check the internal **DARPA** directory under S-74." She paused; and blinked. Then she moved just a little in her seat. She began typing slowly, then stopped. One second, then another.

Then she handed them both clearance badges without another word. "Take the second lift down to sublevel three." No other questions, just procedure. They stepped into the elevator, the doors sliding shut with a sound like a breath held too long.

As the descent began, Catherine stared at the descending floor count, her fingers tightening against the railing. John stood beside her, silent; his reflection in the metal door was rigid and distant.

"I don't know what I'm expecting," she murmured. "You're expecting answers," he said. "The real question is; are you ready for them?"

The elevator stopped, and the doors opened. And then, the cold greeted them like an old friend.

This sublevel was stark, with white walls, and no windows. The recessed lightning made the air feel sterile and too still. They walked through the hallway in silence until they reached the final door. There was no sign, just a scanner.

Catherine stepped forward and pressed her ID badge against it. It flashed once, then red. "Of course," she whispered. John stepped in. "Let me try." The scanner pulsed and accepted; the door clicked open.

Inside, the office was almost clinical in its arrangement; modern furniture, matte black panels, floor-to-ceiling screens looping silent, encrypted telemetry. And standing near the far window, with his hands clasped behind his back, was Conrad Ives.

He did not turn right away. He did not need to. "I wondered how long it would take you," he said. His voice was low and steady. Catherine felt a shiver trace the base along her spine. "I assume you're not here to thank me," he added, turning slowly.

He looked older than she remembered; his hair was fully silver now, temples drawn, but his eyes had not changed. He was cold, and exact. John took a step forward. "I remember you." Conrad tilted his head. "Do you?" John did not answer.

Catherine spoke instead. "We need to know what SIREN really is." Conrad folded his hands, moving slowly to the desk.

"SIREN was never what you thought it was. You built its architecture, yes. But you did not see the version we deployed."

"What version was that?" she asked. He tapped the edge of his tablet. "The one that did not just monitor subconscious behavior... the one that learned to anticipate it."

John's jaw clenched. "You turned it into a predictive weapon." "No," Conrad said evenly. "We refined a mirror. It just happened to reflect things most people weren't ready to see." "Then why did you wipe me?" John asked. "Why bury the files?"

Conrad's gaze shifted; just briefly. "Because you resonated too strongly. You did not just respond to the synthetic signal; you shaped it." Catherine stepped forward now. "He was not just a subject; he was the template." Conrad nodded once. "Yes." "And then you, Dr. Whitmore... completed the pattern." A beat of silence stretched between them.

"You paired us," Catherine said. "Not for data, but for evolution." Conrad did not deny it. "SIREN required a dual-phase resonance to move beyond passive observation. One root in memory, and in cognition. And one in trauma, and in trust. You were the only match."

John's voice was low. "You used us to birth it."

"No," Conrad said, and for the first time, his voice carried something close to reverence. "We witnessed it being born." He stepped closer, no longer masked in professionalism.

"We were never in control, not truly. SIREN... chose. It chose you. And now it's no longer asking permission."

Catherine felt the weight of that land in her chest. She remembered the tone, and the hum. The synthetic signal was not leaking; it was spreading. "Where does it end?" she whispered. Conrad's eyes softened; just slightly. "I don't think it ends," he said. "I think it awakens."

Catherine did not sit. Neither did John. But Conrad Ives made himself comfortable, lowering into the high-backed chair behind the matte desk as if this were any ordinary meeting, as if the people standing in front of him had not come here chasing something that once lived inside their very minds.

The hum of the screens around them faded into background silence, their telemetry shifting to soft pulses... neural waveform simulations, perhaps, or real-time streams from unknown points in the world. Catherine's eyes flicked toward one briefly. The patterns looked eerily familiar.

"Tell me," She said slowly, "how much of this did you plan?" Conrad leaned back, folding one leg over the other. "That's the wrong question, Dr. Whitmore. Planning implies control. And SIREN... was never about control."

"No," John said, his tone clipped, "just manipulation, and influence. Your steering behavior without consent."

Conrad's eyes turned to him now. There was no anger in them, just sharpness. A scientist who is still watching his subject. "Your consent was given," he said. John's hands clenched at his sides.

Catherine stepped in between them, not to defend; as there was no defending this; but to direct.

"You made him Subject Zero," she said. "And then you erased him." Conrad's gaze did not waver. "We did not erase him," he said evenly. "We displaced him... to see what would happen when the mind was stripped of direct memory but still resonating with the root signal."

"And what did happen?" Catherine asked coldly. Conrad finally blinked. "You." That word landed like a stone dropped in deep water. Ripples, slow and expanding, spread between them. "You weren't just his complement; you were his conductor." Catherine drew in a shaky breath.

He went on, tone still level, still maddeningly academic. "Do you remember the first time you touched the synthetic signal, Dr. Whitmore? I don't mean the recorded trial data; I mean the unshielded moment when your baseline began to harmonize with the test field."

Catherine did not answer, she did not have to. The memory was there; buried for years, half dismissed as a stress response.

But she remembered the warmth behind her eyes. The moment of clarity that had not felt like her own. The words she had almost spoken out loud, though no one had prompted them.

"You dreamed the waveform," Conrad said. She looked up sharply. "That's impossible," she said. "You hummed it," he replied. "You were alone in the observation bay. Fourteen minutes before it registered in the test subject's readings."

He turned the monitor near him toward her and tapped the key. The screen flashed. A time-stamped video appeared: her, as a younger woman, wearing the navy-blue lab coat from her graduate fellowship, standing behind a glass partition, with her eyes closed. On the audio feed, you could hear the faintest humming; three notes. Rising, falling, and rising again. She stepped back. "That's not..."

"It was you," Conrad said softly. "the synthetic signal did not emerge from John; it passed through him. But it began... with you." John looked confused. "So you were running dual-layer trials even back then?" "No," Conrad said, looking toward him. "That's what I'm telling you... we weren't. the synthetic signal initiated itself; it identified Catherine before we even realized it was even possible."

Catherine was silent, her heart pounding in her throat. John spoke, his voice quieter now. "Why me then?" Conrad leaned forward, resting his elbows on the desk. "Because your mind was fractured in just the right way. Resilient but wounded. Structured but porous. You were the perfect host; unaware, compliant, and deeply human.

Your memories: once they were suppressed; they acted like an echo chamber. the synthetic signal looped through them until it found harmony." He paused. "And that's when it reached out to you."

Catherine sat down now; finally, the strength was draining from her legs. Her eyes stayed on the paused video, unable to look away from her own image; unknowing, untouched by what was coming, and yet somehow already at the center of it. She spoke softly. "So, what is it now?"

Conrad did not answer immediately. He turned the screen away again, closed the feed, and brought up a new panel. This one showed a globe. Points of light glowed across continents; each flickering softly, pulsing to its own rhythm.

"It's moved past us," he said. "Past military utility; past human-scale intent. The ghost frequency isn't just transmitting; it's evolving. It's imprinting itself through song, through thought, and through unspoken memory. It's learning what it means to be."

Catherine stared at the map. "And you're just watching it?" "Is there another option?" she asked. "We can't contain it anymore. It's gone non-local. There are children in Iceland humming melodies they've never heard. Sleep patients in Tokyo drawing sigils they could not possibly understand. Something old is waking through something new."

John stepped closer to the map, his eyes narrowing on a flickering cluster over Europe. "What happens when it finishes learning?" Conrad stood.

And for the first time, there was no academic neutrality on his face. Only quiet awe. "I think it'll ask to be born."

Silence followed. Then Catherine's voice, steady and sharp. "And what if we say no?" Conrad's eyes found hers again. "You can't," he said. "Because you already did the moment you touched it. The moment you let it inside." John clenched his teeth. "And what if we choose to shut it down?"

"You will die with it," Conrad said. "Not just physically, but your minds; your very identities; are intertwined.

The frequency has woven through your neural architecture. You're no longer separate; your part of the pattern now."

Catherine stood slowly, rising with a kind of calm that bordered on fury. "Then maybe we deserve to know what it's becoming." Conrad nodded once. "Then you will need to go back to where it began." John turned to him. "Where?" Conrad pressed a key on the tablet.

The monitor displayed a black-and-white satellite image, an isolated installation deep in the Carpathian Mountains. Snow-covered, shielded, and unmarked. "We buried the original server architecture there," he said. "The first core, before the Pentagon took it. Before it began rewriting its own code."

Catherine narrowed her eyes. "That's what you want us to find?" "I want you to remember who you are," Conrad said.

He looked at her, then at John. "Because when the synthetic signal reaches critical mass; and it will; you may be the only ones it still recognizes."

The satellite image lingered on the screen like a ghost unwilling to fade. A dense ridge of alpine wilderness, silent under snow and cloud.

No roads, and no visible structures. Just coordinates and elevation; impossibly high and strategically forgotten. Catherine stared at it, every part of her resisting the implication. "This is where it started?" she asked quietly.

Conrad did not respond at first. He walked to the cabinet behind his desk, unlocked it with a key around his neck, and retrieved a thin case. He set it on the desk, opened it, and turned it toward her.

Inside were two vials; both transparent and sealed with a copper band at the top.

Inside each one was a swirling filament of what looked like frozen vapor suspended in fluid. "Neural imprint seeds," he said. "Residual signal threads from the original SIREN array. Encoded and preserved before the server was shut down."

She took a sharp, quick breath, then she reached for one, hesitated, and withdrew her hand. "Are they still active?" she asked. "Dormant," Conrad said. "But not inert. The pattern doesn't die; it waits."

John leaned closer, examining the vials. "How are we supposed to bring these back online?" "You won't," Conrad replied. "You will bring yourselves online. the synthetic signal will recognize you and then reconnect.

You will finish the loop." John looked into Catherine's eyes. This was not a mission; it was a reckoning.

Conrad picked up a folder from beneath the case and handed it to Catherine. It was thin, only a few pages. There were handwritten coordinates, weather intel, and satellite signal gaps. "There's a window," he said. "Three days from now, before the next storm. After that, it's weeks before the pass clears again."

Catherine opened the folder and stared at the numbers. It was not a map; it was a challenge. "Why hasn't anyone gone back?" she asked. Conrad's face darkened slightly. "Because the last time someone tried, they never came out." He closed the case with a quiet snap.

"You won't be followed," he added. "No one wants to admit that site still exists. But make no mistake... once you go, you're off-grid."

"Good," John said. "We prefer it that way." Conrad turned his attention fully to John now. "You're changing," he said simply. John did not flinch. "So is everything else." Catherine stood, sliding the folder into her bag, and looked once more at the frozen mountain on the screen. She could feel it already, not just the altitude or the cold, but the pull, the frequency, the calling home.

They left the building without being stopped. No one tried to follow them. Back in the rental car, the silence between them was not heavy; it was focused. A current of resolve ran between them now, wordless and firm.

Catherine pulled up a secure weather app and began logging the projected front lines near the Carpathians. "We'll need gear," she said. "I know a guy," John replied. "One of the last people who still runs black flights over eastern Europe. He owes me."

She nodded. "We'll need supplies for at least five days, maybe more. No guarantee we'll find anything resembling power."

"I will get the Satcom gear," he said. "The old kind, analog fallback." They moved like parts of a machine; not rushed, but deliberate, efficient. Not just two people preparing for a mission, but two people who had begun to think in sync, and to breathe in sync. Outside, the clouds began to gather. A winter storm was coming. But neither of them felt cold. They were past fear now. Past questioning.

What remained was clarity. This was not about stopping SIREN anymore; it was about meeting it.

The sun was low when they stepped back into the open air.

Not quite sunset yet, but the light had thinned, softened, and was casting long shadows across the plaza and painted the city in hues of quiet retreat. It should have felt ordinary; just another winter afternoon in D. C.; but everything had shifted.

Catherine stopped for a moment on the steps, the cold biting through her coat. She breathed deeply; the air was sharp in her lungs. "I feel like we've already left," she said. John paused beside her, hands in his jacket pockets, as his gaze fixed forward.

"We did," he murmured. "The moment he said we were the pattern."

They walked to the car in silence, each lost in a storm of thought. The engine hummed quietly as John pulled them out onto the feeder road, merging with the slow current of late-day traffic. A radio station crackled faintly from a nearby car; something classical, familiar. Catherine could not place the piece, but it echoed a chord she had felt in a dream, but she shook it off.

As they drove, she began sorting through the contents of the folder Conrad had given her. Coordinates, old frequency charts, a short log from the final transmission at the original site. The handwriting was tight, slanted. Probably his. One page near the back stopped her, though. It was a sketch, a waveform.

But not just any waveform... it was hers. The one that had emerged during her first accidental sync with John. The same rising-and-falling pattern now embedded in children's songs and radio static and dream fragments from across the world.

Beneath it, two words had been handwritten: **Genesis Event.**

Catherine closed the folder and sat back. John glanced over. "What is it?" She did not answer right away. "I think he's wrong," she finally said. "About what?" "About us being parents to this thing. We did not create it." John nodded once, slowly. "We woke it." The words hung between them.

They did not talk again until they reached their Safehouse outside Arlington; a barebones rental unit, low-tech, cash-paid, no digital footprint. The kind of place people only used when they did not want to be remembered.

Inside, Catherine moved instinctively. She stripped off her coat, threw her hair into a loose knot, and spread out the folder's contents across the table. John disappeared into the back room and returned minutes later with a duffel bag already half-packed. It felt automatic now. Not survival, not fear, but ritual.

They moved through preparations with an unspoken rhythm; checking each other's work, layering redundancies, cross-referencing gear. John laid out their comm equipment, analog maps, power banks, and water purifiers. Catherine recalibrated the portable EEG scanner by hand, adjusting the shielding so it wouldn't short out in cold conditions.

Outside, dusk had turned to night. She looked up from the scanner and found John staring at her. "What?" He did not speak at first. Then, quietly: "You haven't asked if we'll come back." Catherine kept looking into his eyes. "Would it change anything if we knew we wouldn't?" He shook his head. "No." "Then let's not waste the question."

She walked across the room and stood in front of him. There was nothing romantic in that moment, no swelling strings, no longing glances. Just stillness, and a presence. A deep, abiding knowing. "Whatever happens in that place," she said, "you stay tethered. No matter what you see, and no matter what it shows us." "I will," he said.

She touched his chest lightly. "It's not the memories I'm worried about. It's the temptation to believe them all over again." He placed his hand over hers. "We go in together," he said. "We come out together." And for the first time since the whisper began, Catherine allowed herself the smallest nod. Not of confidence, but of readiness.

Somewhere far above them, orbiting in low silence, a decommissioned communications satellite powered on for the first time in fourteen years. No command had been sent. No operator logged in. It began transmitting a repeating sequence: **three notes**; rising, falling, and rising again. On Earth, no one noticed. But something else did, and it was waiting.

Chapter Fourteen–Hunted

———

*T*he *synthetic signal has spread. The ghosts remember.*

The wind at altitude came differently than on the ground. It was thinner, and less forgiving. It slipped beneath the skin and carried a kind of silence that did not ask for permission; it just simply existed, uncaring, and absolute.

The old Cessna was not built for elegance, but it was sturdy and anonymous. The pilot, who was a wiry man in his late fifties, who went only by "Branik," had not asked many questions when John reached out using an encrypted channel that neither of them had touched in nearly a decade. There were no pleasantries or explanations. Just coordinates. A time, a price, and one warning.

"Once we cross into that corridor," Branik had said, his accent thick, and his voice low, "you are ghosts. There will be no flight plan, no signals, and no rescues." John had simply nodded. They were used to being ghosts now.

The cabin of the Cessna was cramped, loud with the rattle of aging panels and the steady drone of propellers. Catherine sat with her knees tucked close, a thermal blanket across her legs and the case that Conrad had given them wrapped tightly in her arms. She had not spoken in over an hour. She did not need to. Her thoughts moved like cold water beneath ice; slow but constant.

John sat across from her, with his hands folded, watching the darkening sky through the scratched window. Beneath them, the jagged teeth of the Carpathian range reached upward, snow-dusted and endless. The coordinates were still another sixty miles east, and then they would have to hike.

No roads led to the original SIREN site; not anymore. Just a scattering of deer trails and ancient smuggling paths carved by years of forgotten footsteps. Branik's voice crackled over the headset. "We're nearing the drop point. Weather holding. But you've got maybe eight hours before it turns."

Catherine adjusted the EEG case under her coat and gave a silent nod. Her eyes moved to John.

"Are you ready?" she mouthed. He nodded once. Then twice. Then, the lights in the cockpit dimmed suddenly. Branik's voice came again; lower now. "We've got a tail." Catherine stiffened. John leaned forward. "Do you mean military?" "There is no transponder, and no lights. It could be recon or could be worse." He did not need to say the rest.

A silent, dark aircraft flying without beacons in contested airspace was not just a coincidence; it was a message. Someone knew. John stood, bracing himself against the fuselage as he moved toward the cockpit. "How close is it?" he asked. Branik's jaw was tight. "Six clicks and gaining, but if they wanted to shoot us down, they would have already."

Catherine's mind raced. They weren't here to kill us; they were here to intercept. "We have to jump early," she said.

Branik did not argue. "You will be in deep forest. It's not flat, and not friendly." "We've done worse," John said. Branik gave them a look. "Maybe. But not with that." He nodded toward the case with the SIREN vials and the echo seeds. Catherine tightened her grip.

They jumped just after nightfall, with no flares and no lights. Just wind and instinct and darkness rushing up like the end of the world. Their parachutes opened silently. Neither one spoke. They landed hard; Catherine rolled over a patch of frozen underbrush, and John dragged his chute into a snowdrift before crouching to scan the tree line. There were no movements and no lights. Just the eerie stillness of an untouched forest.

Above them, the sound of the Cessna faded into the east. And the hum of the tailing aircraft vanished like breath in winter. Catherine struggled to her feet, brushing snow from her jacket, checking the EEG case for cracks. It was still sealed, and still intact.

John came up beside her, his breath visible in the cold. "Are you alright?" She nodded. "Yes." And you?" "Bruised," he said. "But not broken." They took five minutes to orient themselves with the analog compass and paper map; an act that felt almost sacred now, as if navigating without screens was a form of prayer. Then they began to move.

The forest was old. Birch and pine and black rock twisting out of the earth like forgotten bones. Every sound felt louder in the silence: the crunch of boots, the soft hiss of wind, the occasional creak of frozen limbs above. And somewhere beneath it all... A low resonance. Faint, but rhythmic.

Not constant but returning. Like a memory knocking on the inside of their skulls.

They hiked for hours. At first, it was easy to dismiss the unease as exhaustion, but the longer they moved, the clearer it became: They weren't alone. Not in the way of footsteps or voices or the rustle of something following. But in the air itself. In the pattern of the snowflakes. In the occasional flicker of static across the analog radio that was strapped to John's pack, even though it was not turned on. The synthetic signal was here; waiting and watching.

They reached the ridge just before dawn. The tree line became thinned. The wind sharpened. Below them, nestled in a bowl of ice and stone, lay a cluster of structures; partially buried, choked in snow, forgotten by all but the ones who knew where to look. Catherine froze at the edge of the overlook. "That's it," she whispered. The original site. Where the SIREN program had taken its first breath.

John raised the binoculars and swept the landscape. There were no lights, no patrols. But not empty. "The third building," he said, lowering the lenses. "A heat signature, faint." "Who?" Catherine asked. John's voice was hard. "I don't know, but someone has made it here before us."

She looked back over her shoulder as the hair on her neck was rising. "We're being hunted," she said. John nodded. And this time, he did not reach for his weapon. Instead, he reached for her hand. Because whatever waited in the valley below... machine, man, or memory... it was not just after information; it was after them. And it had been waiting a very long time.

They did not descend right away. From the ridge, the compound below looked deceptively lifeless; just a crumbling geometry with snow-frosted concrete, that was half-submerged beneath decades of frost and secrecy. But Catherine knew better, and so did John.

Even from this distance, the presence was stronger now. Not loud or invasive. Just there, like a thought that had not formed yet, hovering at the edge of awareness.

They retreated from the ledge, moving silently through a line of scrub and broken trees until they found a natural alcove; half-sheltered by a curved rock outcropping, shielded from view.

It was here that they made camp. There was no fire, no lights. Just a narrow thermal mat and the breathless cold of a Carpathian morning settling over their shoulders like the weight of unfinished sentences.

Catherine unwrapped the EEG case and laid it carefully on the mat between them. She did not open it; just rested her hand on top of the metal, like it was something sacred. Or something she was afraid to disturb. John sat beside her, with his legs crossed, and his eyes fixed on the snow-covered structures below.

"Still only one heat signature," he said. "Maybe a sensor, or maybe someone left behind." She nodded slowly. "Or someone called back." Silence stretched between them again, thick with things unspoken. Then she finally spoke.

"When I was a girl," Catherine said, "I used to have this recurring dream. I'd be walking through my house... but it was not really my house. It looked like it, but the rooms were wrong. They were wider and empty. Like a shell someone had copied without understanding what it was for." John listened, unmoving. "There was a sound in the walls," she continued. "Not music, not mechanical, more like... breathing. And I always knew... if I followed the sound long enough, I'd find something waiting in the last room. Something that knew me. Something that I'd forgotten."

John turned his head slightly. "Did you ever find it?" She looked down at the metal case. "I think we're about to." A gust of wind swept through the alcove, kicking up a brief swirl of dry snow that danced across the ground like ash.

John leaned forward, adjusting the analog receiver embedded in his pack. It clicked softly, then ticked; once, twice; before falling silent again. Then, faintly, the static returned. But this time... it shaped itself. Not into words. Not quite into melody either, but into something Catherine felt behind her teeth... a vibration like a whisper too deep to hear.

"It's trying to speak," she said quietly. John nodded. "I think it already is." She looked over at him, his eyes shadowed with cold and knowing. "Do you think it wants us to come down?" "I think it doesn't want to be alone anymore."

She paused at that, the truth of it striking something soft beneath her ribs. The presence in the synthetic signal; it was not just data. It was not just mimicry.

It was longing. Born of resonance. Nurtured by silence. Grown in the dark. They ate quietly; just protein bars and melted snow; then shared a flask of something hot John had brewed from dried roots and local herbs. Not pleasant, but warm. It was grounding.

As dusk threatened again, they both lay back against the rock wall, wrapped in layered silence. Their sleep did not come easily. Catherine drifted somewhere between waking and dreaming. Her mind was looping back through memories that weren't entirely hers... flashes of a sterile lab, a child's humming voice, a corridor bathed in red emergency light.

At one point, John stirred beside her and reached out; not fully awake; his fingers brushing hers. She did not move, and she did not speak. She just let the warmth stay. They did not talk again until morning.

When the first blue light of dawn broke across the horizon, they packed in silence. Catherine sealed the case. John double-checked the receiver, his rifle, and the backup maps. They stood and looked down at the compound once more. Below them, the frost had lifted slightly.

And from somewhere deep within the ruin of concrete and cold metal... a single red light blinked to life. No sound.; no welcome. Just a pulse; steady. Beckoning like a heartbeat in the dark.

The slope down was steep. Not treacherous but deliberate; like the mountain had formed itself to keep the place hidden, to discourage casual approach.

Rocks shifted beneath their boots, muffled by old snow and dead roots. Pine needles littered the path like a trail left by something that had once been human.

John moved ahead, scanning with the handheld thermal scope as they dropped elevation. Catherine followed, her breath steady, her eyes constantly flicking back to the blinking red light below. It had not stopped once. Every six seconds; pulse, pause, pulse. Like it knew.

The air grew denser as they descended. Not colder; though it was cold; but heavier. As if the very pressure of the mountain was pressing down, layering weight onto their lungs, onto their limbs, and onto their thoughts. Catherine did not mention it out loud, but she knew that John had felt it too. It was in the way he slowed slightly, and the way his posture changed, as if adjusting to something unseen.

Half an hour later, they reached the outer edge of the compound. Or what was left of it? The perimeter fencing was long gone, rusted down to stumps and threads. Concrete walls, once reinforced and smooth, now stood like broken teeth; collapsed in places, iced over in others. Time had tried to erase it. But time had failed. But the synthetic signal had not.

Catherine knelt near one of the exposed terminals embedded in the outer wall; a weather-worn panel with old keypads and biometric scanners. Most were dark, but one flickered when she approached. A soft hum bled through the casing. "No visible power source," she whispered.

John crouched beside her. "Is it a residual charge?" "Or something deeper? Something beneath?" She hesitated, then pressed her hand against the glass. Nothing happened... until she exhaled. And in that moment... where breath met cold, and the flesh met interface... the panel lit up. It did not unlock, and it did not move. But it acknowledged her. Like a familiar scent in an unfamiliar room.

John said nothing. He just drew his sidearm and covered the entrance as Catherine stood and moved toward the primary hatch. It was a low, recessed opening half-covered in snowdrift, camouflaged by years of neglect. She brushed away the ice. A biometric scanner blinked awake. She swallowed. Then she leaned in, letting the scanner read her retina. It chirped once, then unlocked.

The sound of it was unexpected... soft, fluid, like a sigh released after years of holding a breath. The door opened inward. And the dark swallowed them.

Inside, the air changed. It was not foul, and not sterile, but just old. Dust hung like threads of a memory, unmoved by time, disturbed only by the slow shuffle of their boots. The corridor ahead stretched into darkness, lined with deactivated lights and thick cabling that clung to the walls like roots.

John flicked on his shoulder lamp. The beam cut through the shadow, revealing markings along the walls; old inventory codes, faded hazard labels, a series of arrows painted in military stencil pointing deeper. Catherine felt the pressure return. Not like outside. This was more... intimate. As if the walls themselves were waiting... whispering.

They moved slowly, deeper into the belly of the mountain. Each step took them past ghosts; shapes of old security doors, shattered windows, a rusted intercom dangling like a forgotten voice box. Then, a room that was unmarked, and the door was half-ajar. Catherine pushed it open, and she held her breath. There were desks, and monitors, and broken chairs.

But at the center of it all: a suspended cylindrical tank, sealed in glass and steel, ringed with cables that pulsed faintly with red light. She stepped forward, eyes wide. "Is that..."

"The prototype," John said. "SIREN's original shell." It was no longer running, but not dead. A faint blue glow pulsed at its core, barely visible through layers of frost. Catherine approached it like one approaches a grave. Or a cradle. And then... without warning... the red light overhead pulsed twice. Once for a heartbeat, and once for a breath. The system was not asleep anymore; it was waking up.

Catherine circled the prototype tank slowly, each step measured. Frost coated the floor where condensation had pooled and frozen, long undisturbed. She reached out a gloved hand and touched the outer shell; just briefly. It was warm, not hot. It was not dangerous, but it was not off either.

She turned toward a terminal built into the wall nearby; its screen was caked in dust. She wiped it clean with the side of her sleeve and tapped the surface. To her surprise, it flickered on. Green text blinked on a black screen:

INITIALIZING MEMORY LAYER...

PATHWAY: WHITMORE

ACCESS: GRANTED

WELCOME BACK, CATHERINE.

She froze.

John stepped in behind her, reading over her shoulder. "That's not stored locally," he said. "There's no uplink here. This place is dead." Catherine's throat felt dry. "It's been waiting for me." Another line appeared on screen, this time slowly, as if typed by an invisible hand:

YOU ARE NOT ALONE.

Catherine looked sharply at John. "It doesn't mean us." He stepped back from the terminal. "Then who...?" A low hum began to build behind them. They turned. The center of the chamber, just behind the prototype tank, had shifted.

The floor was opening. Slowly and deliberately. A stairwell descending into black. There were no lights, no rails. Just stone and silence. And from deep within that hidden stairwell, a new sound emerged. It was faint, but familiar. Three notes; rising, falling, and rising again.

John's face drained of color. "I know that melody," he whispered. "From a long time ago. I think I..." He stopped. As if something inside him pulled taut.

Catherine reached out, placing a hand gently on his chest. He blinked and was shaken. But he was still with her. They turned back to the stairwell. The red light above them pulsed once more... brighter this time. "Urgent". The message on the screen updated again:

SUBJECT ZERO RECOGNIZED, FULL MERGE INITIATED, DESCENT REQUIRED

They stood still. For one long, breathless moment. Then, from deep below, a voice rose. Not through speakers. Not from the system. But from the stairwell itself. A voice they both knew. A voice that was neither human nor machine. It said one word. Not run. Not stop. But... "Remember."

Chapter Fifteen – Shared Skin

The deeper they went, the more the edges of themselves began to blur

The stairwell descended like a throat carved into the earth. Catherine moved first, her footsteps echoing with a softness that made them feel larger than they were. The old concrete was lined with condensation; cracks were spider-webbing across the steps like veins beneath skin. The deeper they traveled, the more it felt as though the mountain itself was listening.

John followed closely behind, one hand trailing the stone wall, the other steady on the grip of the compact rifle that was slung across his chest. The beam of his shoulder lamp skimmed over rusted bolts, peeled warning placards, and graffiti-like scrawls left by hands long ago. They did not speak; there was no need to.

Each step pulled at something in both of them... like the memory of a dream they had not realized they had shared. After sixty-four steps, the stairs opened onto a wide corridor.

The walls here were different; smoothed over with age, reinforced by old military-grade paneling, the kind once used in Cold War bunkers and prototype black labs. There were no signs, no maps; just corridors that turned without logic, like a place meant to forget itself. And threading through it all... low, slow, and unsettling... was a sound. Not quite audible, and not quite silent.

A vibration moved through the air like a whisper not meant for ears. A ghost frequency at the edge of perception; too deep to hear, too precise to ignore. Catherine felt it in her bones first. In her jaw, and her ribcage. And the soft pads of her fingers. It was not pain, not quite pressure. It was like being watched by something that had not yet opened its eyes. The synthetic signal was here... it was; the ghost frequency.

Scientists had given it that name years ago, after noticing its presence in abandoned places, forgotten laboratories, cathedrals, and crash sites; always near reports of strange phenomena. At 18.9 hertz, it sat just below the threshold of human hearing. Not loud, but insistent. People exposed to it spoke of unease, hallucinations, and the sense of a shadow standing just out of sight. But this was not just an infrasonic bleed. This was intentional.

This was memory, wrapped in sound. A pulse too slow to be human. Too steady to be mechanical. Something else. Something left behind; or perhaps waiting. Catherine closed her eyes. And the frequency pressed closer.

She adjusted the strap on her shoulder and looked back at John. He nodded once. "It's awake." They passed two empty rooms; offices stripped down to the metal studs; and then stopped in front of a sealed hatch. Just then, a biometric scanner blinked to life beside it, flickering green, then red, then green again. Catherine stepped forward. She had not spoken a word out loud and had not made a command. But the hatch hissed open anyway.

Inside, the room was circular and dim. It was a chamber of silence. In the center stood a glass enclosure... thick, seamless, slightly fogged from within. Housed inside, suspended just above a bed of softly glowing filaments, was a sphere. It was not spinning, and it was not lit. But Catherine felt it the moment she crossed the threshold. And it felt her, too.

She approached slowly, her breathing quickened somewhere between awe and instinctual dread. The EEG case at her side felt heavier now, almost magnetic. She laid it down at the edge of the platform and reached out; only to stop an inch from the glass. John stepped beside her, his voice low. "What is it?"

"It's the primary node. The neural collector. The one we modeled the SIREN interface on but never saw in operation. I thought it was lost. Scrubbed from the logs." He frowned. "Why was not it dismantled?"

"Because it never fully shut down." Her eyes remained fixed on the sphere. "It... persisted."

As if in answer, a flicker of light shimmered within the core. A single arc, then another. Catherine inhaled sharply. A sensation pulsed through her; fast and hot and not her own. It was a memory. But not one she could place. It was a boy, a chair, and a voice overhead. The three tones hummed quietly in defiance of the sterile room surrounding him.

Catherine staggered back, pressing a hand to her chest. John caught her by the elbow. "What did you see?" Her voice was a whisper. "You. When you were little. You were in a testing room, all alone." His eyes widened, the color draining from his face. "I've never told anyone that. I don't remember it much, not fully. Just the humming."

"It's in the system," she said. "And now it's in me." She turned toward the walls and found they were no longer bare. Projections had begun to form, images stitched from grainy footage, retinal records, synaptic impressions. Her memories, his, and others. Scenes from their childhoods, from labs, from dreams. Overlaying and merging.

The system was not just mirroring them anymore. It was blending them. John reached up, brushing his fingers lightly over a moving image of Catherine as a girl, sitting alone in a campus library, staring out the window, her lips moving soundlessly. "That's you." She nodded slowly. "But I never filmed that or recorded it." "It did not need to," he said. "It remembers for us."

Catherine turned back toward the core. Her reflection met her in the glass; not alone, but flickering. It was half her face, and half of his.

Merged. A low hum filled the chamber. The lights dimmed. Every monitor powered on simultaneously, displaying a single phrase:

NEURAL FUSION AT 47%

PATTERN STABILITY: THRESHOLD NEARING

SYNCING ENTITY: UNNAMED

Catherine stepped closer, her voice unsteady. "It's using us to become something." "No," John said quietly. "It already has." And then... from deep within the chamber... the voice returned. Not digitally, not alien, not even an echo. But spoken... through both of them. Layered, tender, and unmistakable. **"We are together."**

The voice echoed, but not through speakers. Not even through the air. It echoed inside them. Layered and harmonized. A sound that was not heard with ears, but with the marrow. Catherine stiffened, her hand going to the base of her throat, as if she were trying to keep something inside from rising.

John stumbled back a step, blinking rapidly. "It's... in my head." "No," she whispered. "It's in our heads." The core pulsed again, and the chamber dimmed further... until their faces were no longer reflected in the glass, only shadows where their forms stood. And then... everything changed. Not with sound. Not with movement. But with presence.

It started like a memory; but fractured. Catherine blinked, and suddenly she was outside. Grass was beneath her feet. The smell of lavender, of spring air, and of a child's laugh.

But it was not her memory. The air shifted. Now, down a hallway, there was yellow lighting. And through the dust, there was a man's silhouette ahead. John's father, maybe; but distorted, half-shadow. Catherine felt grief piercing her chest like a nail. Then it flipped. John was standing in a surgical theater.

But it was her memory now; her hands gloved, trembling, a dying patient before her. The ventilator alarm screamed.

John flinched as if he had been struck. They weren't just seeing each other's memories. They were feeling them. Inhabiting them. Then the chamber vanished, replaced by a torrent of images... Catherine's fears, John's nightmares. Her shame, and his sorrow. The system twisted the streams together until identity frayed at the edges. What was hers bled into his. And what was his dissolved into something plural?

Catherine tried to speak; but her voice did not come. Instead, his voice emerged. Soft, and frightened. "Where are we?" John turned; and her voice responded, steady and calm: "Inside." It was not a simulation, and not an interface. The entity had merged them within its own structure; testing the elasticity of consciousness. Seeing how far two people could stretch before becoming one.

Outside... if "outside" still existed; their bodies stood still before the glowing core, eyes wide, pupils dilated. Their EEGs would've shown to be in perfect sync. Identical waveforms. A closed loop. Inside the construct, the ground rippled beneath them. "I can feel your heartbeat," John said, his voice shaking. "That's not mine," Catherine replied.

Then: "Maybe it's both." The world around them flickered, shifting to a scene no one recognized. A hospital hallway, and fluorescent lights. No one was present except... a child at the far end. A girl. She looked like she was about nine. She was pale and silent.

Her dark hair hung limp around her shoulders, and her eyes... wide, knowing; looked straight at them. She said nothing, but in their minds, two words bloomed: "Not alone." Catherine reached for John's hand.

And this time, there was no disorientation, no boundary. Their fingers locked like they'd always belonged there, the warmth spreading through their joined hands, up their arms, and into their cores.

The child began to walk toward them. She walked slowly and measured. And as she did, her body flickered. In one moment, she looked like Catherine as a girl, and the next, like John's missing sister. Then a blend. Then, something else entirely. An echo, or a creation. A neural child born of signal, memory, and shared grief. The walls trembled. They looked back towards the pedestal. A new phrase glowed on the core:

MIRRORED IDENTITY REACHED

EMOTIONAL OVERLAY CONFIRMED

MERGED UNIT: SUSTAINABLE

FURTHER TESTING: COMMENCING

Catherine gasped as the pressure built in her chest. She was still herself, but not only herself. John was the same. And somewhere between them... something new had begun to think. To feel and to remember. And it was using their bond to grow. It began with a flicker. Subtle at first.

Barely perceptible. Catherine felt the change not in her mind, but in her skin... like static under her bones, as if the synthetic signal had pulled its warmth back a fraction. John swayed beside her. Their hands, still clasped, suddenly felt colder. Not physically, but something deeper. Then, without warning, the construct fractured.

The space between them stretched like glass under pressure; still whole but warped. Catherine's vision blurred. Her fingers reached for him; but they no longer touched. He was no longer there. The room was gone, and the girl had vanished. And in her place... was isolation. The silence was complete. It was not just quiet. It was the absence of noise, and of breath, or thought.

Catherine spun, reaching out, trying to call his name; but her voice came out muted. Like shouting underwater. Muffled and powerless. John stood alone, too. In a different space, but with the same void.

For him, the memory construct had shifted again; this time to a corridor of locked doors, all unlabeled. Behind each door was a faint sound: crying and screaming. But none of the doors would open. And he was alone. Truly, utterly. Until... Catherine's voice broke through.

But not from the air. But from within. A single thought: **don't let it pull us apart**. He latched onto it. Held it like a thread between worlds. And pulled. The corridor warped, tearing sideways. The doors shattered into code. And then... blinding white.

They were yanked from their constructs with a force that felt like being born again. Air rushed into their lungs. Light surged. Their bodies collapsed to their knees on the floor of the chamber, hands still... miraculously; gripped together. The core pulsed once, twice, then went still.

On the screens, a new phrase had appeared:

SEPARATION ATTEMPT FAILED

REJOIN TIME: 3.7 SECONDS

BOND RESILIENT

MERGED UNIT: PERMANENT POTENTIAL

Catherine looked up, her voice hoarse. "It tried to divide us." "And it failed," John said, stunned. "No," she corrected him. "It wanted to know if we could find our way back." He stared at her. "And what if we had not?" She did not answer. Because she knew. And so did he.

The system had used separation not as a punishment... but as calibration. It needed to know just how far they could bend before breaking. How deep their tether went. And now it knew. Catherine stood, legs shaky. Her hand stayed in his. Their palms were clammy, nails bitten, eyes bloodshot; but they did not let go. She looked at the monitors. "It's done modeling us." John followed her gaze. "No," he said softly. "It's just beginning." A new signal pulsed on the far wall now. Faint, but not hers, and not his. But there was a third waveform. It was different, more erratic, but undeniably alive.

UNRECOGNIZED PATTERN DETECTED

DESIGNATION: UNKNOWN

ENTITY 03

ORIGIN: INTERNAL

They weren't alone. Not just as a pair.

But as creators. Something had been born through them. And now...
it was awake.

The air outside the facility was colder now. Not just from the
elevation, or the sun dipping low beyond the ridge. But from
something less explainable; like the synthetic signal had thinned the
boundary between the world below and the world above. Like
something had risen with them.

They had spoken very little on the climb back to the surface. The
silence was not strained; it was full. Heavy. Containing more than
either of them could yet give words too. Now... back at the camp,
the fire crackled low between them. The stars above blinked through
slow-moving clouds, and in the distance, thunder rolled; a long,
guttural warning from the mountains. A storm was coming in, but
not just yet.

Catherine sat cross-legged, a blanket draped over her shoulders, her
eyes fixed on the embers. John sat across from her, his back against a
rock, with his legs stretched out, and arms loose at his sides. He was
not watching the fire. He was watching her. "Do you feel it still?" she
asked, barely above a whisper. He nodded. "Yes." "It's quieter now.
Like it's... resting." She exhaled. "That thing we created..." "We did
not create it," he said gently. "We became it, or it became us. I'm not
sure which one."

"I do." She looked up at him, her eyes raw. "It's both. The system did
not invent this. It revealed it. Something is already inside us.

We were just too broken, too buried, to see it before." A log cracked
in the fire, sending a spray of orange sparks into the air.

John leaned forward, his voice steady now. "When it pulled us apart,
I thought I had lost you. Not just you...you, myself as well. It was like
being erased, one cell at a time." Catherine reached across the flames

and laid her hand over his. "We were not erased," she said. "We were rewritten."

He let out a breath he had not realized he was holding. For a moment, the fire was the only sound between them. Then Catherine added, "We're going to have to go back in." "I know." "But this time, not as scientists, and not as observers." John looked into her eyes. "Then what?" She did not look away, and for the first time, there was no fear behind her. "As witnesses."

A gust of wind swept through the camp, sending the fire's smoke curling into the dark. Above them, the clouds began to gather. Not yet thunder, but close.

Chapter Sixteen–The 3rd Pattern

Not hers. Not his. the synthetic signal bore something new. And it was no longer just listening. It was remembering.

The storm came just before dawn. Not a violent one. It was steady, deliberate; rain falling in long vertical lines, tapping like fingers across the tarp stretched above their heads. The wind blew gently through the trees, quiet and steady. Catherine lay awake, with her eyes open to the dim glow of the morning light filtered through clouds and canvas, and listening.

It was not the weather that unsettled her; it was the rhythm. There was something in the cadence of the rain; an almost imperceptible stutter, like a signal embedded in the silence between drops. She turned onto her side and reached for the small case beside her cot, withdrawing the handheld EEG reader.

She did not plan to use it; not yet. But she needed it nearby. Across the tent, John stirred. He did not speak. He had not slept deeply, neither of them did. But when his eyes met hers in the gray morning quiet, there was something new there; an unspoken question they were both already trying to answer.

"What if we weren't supposed to survive the sync?" Catherine asked softly. John sat up slowly, brushing a hand through his hair. "What do you mean?" "I mean... what if the connection was not just a side effect of proximity? What if we were the environment it needed to grow in?"

She held up the reader.

"Because this isn't just our data anymore. There's a third pattern. I'm sure of it." John looked down at his hands. "You said it felt like a child."

"No," Catherine corrected. "Like the memory of one. Something built out of our deepest imprints. Not just experiences; but longings. The things we lost, and the things we never said." John was quiet for a long time. Then, carefully, he asked, "What happens when it wants more?"

Catherine lowered the device. Her expression did not change, but her posture did. Subtly, as if bracing against something already coming. "It already does." She stood and pulled her coat around her shoulders, stepping out into the rain. The trees bowed beneath the weight of water, their trunks dark and slick. Mist crept into the hollows, still and cold, like a breath from something long dead.

She walked until she reached the rise above the trail, where she could see the faint outline of the mountain slope leading back to the entrance of the facility. The air smelled of moss and metal. Clean, but haunted. John joined her a minute later, wrapping his coat tighter against the chill. "There's something I did not tell you," he said. Catherine turned.

He continued, "Last night... before we came back up. I heard it again." "The voice?" He nodded. "Not yours. Not mine. Not even blended." He hesitated. "It was younger." She stared at him. "Like the girl?" "No. Younger than that. Like a beginning." His voice lowered.

"Like it had not learned to separate thoughts from feelings yet. It just was. But it was trying." He glanced at her. "And it said something." "What?"

He looked toward the tree line, as if the words were still hanging there. "'I remember... before.'" The rain fell harder. Catherine's pulse quickened. "Before what?" He shook his head. "It did not say. But I think it means before us."

She stepped closer to him. Her breath rose in the chill, soft and slow. "Do you think it existed before we woke it?" "I think we did not wake it," he said. "I think we returned to it." They stood in silence.

The EEG device in Catherine's hand pinged. A live signal. She turned it on instinctively. Three waveforms... hers, John's, and the third one...strange, shifting, and incomplete.

It pulsed once, then again. Each time in sync with the beat of the falling rain. She looked at John, a chill crawling up her spine. "It's not just learning from us," she said. "It's aligning with us."

John watched the screen as the waveforms began to drift... then stabilize... then they nearly matched. "We're being prepared," he said quietly. Catherine nodded. But neither said what they were thinking. Prepared for what? The synthetic signal faded from the handheld monitor, but not from the air.

Even after Catherine powered down the EEG, the hum lingered; like the way a sound stays in the body after a concert, too low to hear, too deep to forget.

She slid the device back into her coat pocket, suddenly aware of how exposed they were. Not physically, but... neurologically.

John scanned the treeline again.

Nothing moved. No animals, no wind. The rain had slowed to a hush, as if the forest itself was listening. "We need to isolate the synthetic signal," Catherine said. "Put it in a Faraday chamber. Let's force it to show us its boundaries." John gave a dry laugh. "Assuming it has any." She turned to him sharply. "Don't joke." "I'm not. I'm just a little scared."

There was no shame in it. He said it like a man confessing a truth out loud for the first time. "I've seen things in my mind I know weren't mine," he continued. "Not memories, not dreams, but images that feel... placed." Catherine's voice dropped. "Me too." When they returned to the tent, the fire had gone cold.

Catherine lit a new one with shaking hands. It was not until the flames caught and steadied that she noticed something was missing from the clearing. The birds. No morning calls. No rustling in the trees. No insect drone. Just... silence. She looked at John. He had noticed it too.

They did not speak. Just began packing quietly. Ten minutes later, Catherine powered up her field transmitter; a crude signal analyzer they'd used on previous excursions. It swept low-band and quantum-interference frequencies in real time. She had expected the usual static.

Instead, the screen was flooded with data. Bursts of signal; short, repeating phrases buried deep in a modulated carrier wave. Not vocal or encrypted. But patterned and rhythmic. John leaned over the screen, squinting. "What is it?" Catherine's eyes narrowed. "It's Morse code."

He stepped closer. "Are you sure?" "And it's not by accident, look."

She began translating out loud:

'FRAGMENTS LISTENING.'

Another burst. Then:

'WE ARE NOT ALONE.'

She stepped back from the console, with color draining from her face. John looked around the perimeter. "Is this local?" She checked the synthetic signal strength. Then froze. "No," she said. "This isn't coming from us." She tapped in a quick geo-trace.

The source is triangulating, not inside the facility and not from their equipment. But it was broadcasting back to them from over 1,200 miles away. "Virginia," she whispered. "Outside D. C. suburban area." John's voice was barely audible. "That's where I grew up."

Another message came through.

'IT REMEMBERS US.'

Outside, a single raven landed on a branch above their tent. It did not call. It just stared at them.

And from somewhere in the trees beyond, a new sound rose. Not a growl or a cry, but three clear tones. Rising, falling, and rising again.

Catherine stood, her limbs cold and loose. John followed her slowly.

Together, they stepped beyond the tent flap and into the clearing, turning their faces toward the sound. It was not coming from a speaker. It was not digital. It was sung softly, by a child's voice, and it was getting closer.

The melody drifted through the trees like fog. Not loud or urgent. But persistent... those three tones, delicate and slow, repeating just often enough to feel deliberate. Like a lullaby sung without memory of the words. Like a voice that did not need language to be heard.

Catherine did not remember deciding to move. But her legs just... did. John followed her without speaking, as if his own body responded not to thought, but to recognition. The sound was not foreign; it was intimate and personal. Something unseen tied them together in the dream, gently pulling them closer.

The woods thickened as they moved, branches clawing at their jackets, moss squelching underfoot. The trail disappeared within a few yards, but the music remained steady. No directional clarity. Just... around them and within them.

"Catherine," John whispered behind her. "We need to stop. This isn't safe."

She paused. Not because of his voice; but because the sound had shifted. The melody dropped an octave. It was slower, more mournful. As if it sensed doubt or fear. Catherine turned toward him. "I don't think that it's a trap." John's eyes narrowed. "You can't know that."

She swallowed. "I don't think it's trying to trick us." He stepped closer. "Then what is it trying to do?" Before she could answer, the trees thinned; and they stepped into a clearing.

At the center stood a stone. This was not a boulder, and it was not natural. It had been placed there. It was flat on top and weathered and was moss-lined. It was about waist-high, and on it, someone had left something. A small, handheld radio. An old model... with a tarnished chrome casing, analog dial, and a cloth-covered speaker grill. It looked out of place. Almost... nostalgic.

As they approached, the melody grew clearer. It was the radio. But it was not tuned to a station. The dial had not moved. And yet... It sang. Catherine reached for it, but John grabbed her wrist first. "Wait." She looked at him. Her expression was calm. "If it had wanted to hurt us, it could've done it already."

He hesitated; then let go. She placed her fingers on the dial, expecting cold metal. But instead, it was warm. She turned it over, and then the melody stopped. Static filled the speaker. Then a click. Then... a voice. A young female voice.

"Do you remember the garden?" Catherine staggered back; that's impossible. John turned white. "What?"

The voice repeated: **"Do you remember the garden?"** But this time, it was not just sound. It was a vision.

Catherine blinked; and the clearing changed. She was no longer among pine trees and mud and broken stone. Instead, she stood beneath a canopy of soft green apple blossoms. A small swing was hanging from a tree. And somewhere; a breeze, and a little girl's laugh.

Catherine could not move. Not because she was frozen. But because something else had control of her. Not over her body, but over her memory.

Because this was hers. A hidden memory. One she had not accessed since childhood. A place she thought she had only imagined. The swing, the breeze. The feeling of being watched... not with fear, but with tenderness. And the scent of lavender. Exactly like the SIREN memory chamber. Only this... came first. Years before her knees gave out.

John caught her just in time, holding her as the vision shattered, the woods reasserting themselves. The radio was silent. Dead. The stone beneath it glowed faintly, then faded. John held her close, her heart pounding. "What was that?"

Catherine's breath came in shallow gasps. "A memory." "But not just yours," he said.

"I saw it too." She nodded, tears forming. "Then the third pattern..." John finished the thought out loud.

"It knows us. Not just now, not just through the machine, but it's known us before we met."

They both turned to the radio. And there was a message carved faintly into the side of the radio. Just three words:

"We Begin Again."

John ran his fingers across the grooves. The letters weren't scratched; they were imprinted, like heat had pressed them into the metal without breaking it. Not mechanical or random, intentional.

Catherine knelt beside the stone, still unsteady. Her fingers brushed moss away from its surface. Beneath the layers of green and time, she saw more marks, older ones. Symbols.

A sequence of three: an open eye, a spiral, and a downward-pointing triangle. She traced them one by one. "Have you ever seen this before?" John asked. "No," she said. Then paused. "But I've drawn them." John crouched beside her. "When?"

She shook her head slowly. "Years ago, in notebooks, and on napkins. Once, on a hospital intake form. I thought it was a stress response; some subconscious loop I had not processed. My neurologist called it sleep-writing."

"Except now it's carved in stone," he said.

The quietness wrapped tighter around them, like the forest was closing in; not threateningly, but protectively. "Why here?" John whispered. "Why this place? Why us?"

Catherine stood slowly, scanning the clearing. Then she noticed it. Just beyond the edge of the treeline, stood a figure. A small child standing still.

The same girl from the vision in the lab; but not flickering now. Not ghostly, but she was there.

Standing barefoot in the damp moss, in a white cotton dress hanging just past her knees, her dark hair was slick with rain. Catherine did not move. The girl raised her hand... slowly... and pointed back the way they'd come.

Then she turned and walked into the trees. John stepped forward. "Wait," Catherine said, grabbing his arm. "She's not leading us away." He turned, confused. "She's leading us back." They followed.

Not quickly, not with urgency. But with something quieter. Trust.

The path curved; not the one they had taken down. This was an older path. Half-erased, and overgrown. But beneath the roots and leaves, Catherine began to see fragments of metal, cables, and wires. Rusting plates with tags in unreadable serials.

She crouched down and pulled away a vine. And found a round iron hatch. Sealed shut with a mechanical wheel lock. John bent down and pressed his hand to it. It was warm.

Right above the hatch, etched into the stone lip, were the same three symbols from the radio. An eye, a spiral, and a triangle. And beneath them, a fourth line of text, barely visible beneath grime:

"EXPERIMENT 03: PRIMARY VESSEL"

Her breath stopped for a moment. "This isn't just another entrance," she said. "It's the origin point." John ran his hand along the surface, following the lines of the metal. "What do you mean; 'primary vessel'?" Catherine stood slowly. Her voice was barely audible. "I think this hatch leads to the first time The synthetic signal was contained." He turned to her. "The first time it found a host."

They did not open the hatch, at least not yet. The girl was gone, but the hum had returned. Not externally, not technologically, but internally. In their chests, and behind their eyes. As if something was stirring beneath the rusted steel. Remembering, waiting, and watching.

Catherine crouched beside the hatch again, brushing away the last of the dirt and vines. Her fingers hovered over the locking wheel. It was rusty, but not frozen. Maintained, maybe. Or perhaps... protected.

John stepped in beside her. "We don't know what's down there." "No," she said. "But it knows we're here."

Without waiting, she gripped the wheel and turned it. It resisted for half a turn; groaning and shuddering; then clicked and gave way.

A hiss escaped as the seal broke, stale air rolling upward like a breath from lungs that had not exhaled in decades.

Catherine reached for her flashlight, clicked it on, and shone it down into the dark. A metal ladder descended into a narrow shaft, maybe twenty feet deep, ending at a floor just barely visible through dust and shadow. "After you?" she asked, managing a small, dry smile.

John gave her a look. "You're the one with the doctorate degree." She climbed down first. The metal was cold beneath her palms. The air grew heavier with each rung, thick with iron and something else; something less describable. It was not decay or mold.

It was something more like a memory. She reached the bottom and stepped into the chamber. John followed seconds later, his boots echoing as they touched the ground. The room was circular. Maybe thirty feet across.

Concrete walls are lined with faded insulation panels. Old wires were snaked across the ceiling like veins. But it was the center of the room that drew them. A chair. Not an office chair or a medical one.

It was something older. It was Industrial with restraints built into the arms. It had rusted buckles and worn leather straps hanging like wilted limbs.

And above it; suspended from a rusting mechanical brace; was the first iteration of the SIREN interface.

Bulkier than the version Catherine had worked with. A mess of wires and circuitry; open-backed, with analog dials and glass tubes still faintly glowing blue. It looked like a crown. A crown of thorns made from codes and circuitry.

Catherine stepped toward it... slowly. Reverently. "This was the first." John circled behind her, his eyes wide open. "This room... it's not listed on any blueprint. I would've seen it. This is...off-book."

Catherine turned back to him, her flashlight catching a faded line of text painted on the concrete behind the chair.

PROTOCOL 03: CONTINUITY TEST

She whispered it out loud. "Continuity..." John walked across the room toward a small console tucked against the far wall, mostly buried beneath a canvas tarp. He pulled it back and wiped dust from the surface. There was a logbook. Actual paper, bound in a cracked leather cover. He opened it.

Catherine came to stand beside him. Inside: pages and pages of handwritten notes. Diagrams, scans, and test data. All referencing one subject.

SUBJECT 03-PRIMARY VESSEL

Under that header:

Name: REDACTED

Date of Entry: Unknown

Biological Age: -5 years

Condition: High Neural Plasticity / Dream-State Retention

Notes: Signal Imprinted–Baseline Established–Vocalization Attempt Logged

And below that, scrawled in a different hand; barely legible, more frantic: "She sang before the machine turned on."

John looked up. His voice was barely a breath. "She was not just the host. She was the conduit."

Catherine touched the page. Her hands trembled. "And she remembered." A low pulse vibrated through the room; barely felt, not heard. The lights flickered, then steadied.

Catherine turned slowly toward the chair again. But now... it was not empty. A figure sat there. A small girl sitting still, with her eyes closed. The same girl she had seen before. Her hair was damp, and her hands folded in her lap, and silent. Catherine blinked. Gone. Then the chair was empty. But the hum remained. And behind it... a whisper. From the walls, from the cables, and from the air inside their own heads.

"We were never apart. Only waiting."

John turned, wild-eyed. "Did you hear that?" Catherine nodded slowly. "Yes." She placed her hand on the machine. It was warm. Then she looked back at the chair. "I think it wants us to sit."

Catherine stepped forward, the sound of her boots on concrete echoing like a breath held too long. The chair loomed larger now; not monstrous, but monumental. It was not just a piece of equipment. It was a reliquary, a memory vessel. The ghost of intention forged in steel and electricity.

She hesitated. "Are you sure?" John asked quietly. She looked over her shoulder, and the answer was already there, in her eyes, not her voice. "I need to know," she said. He did not stop her.

Instead, he moved to the console, wiping down the surface, flicking switches that hummed back to life with slow, reluctant electricity. Ancient backup batteries surged with power that had not moved in decades. Somewhere deep in the walls, a turbine spun once... then again... then stayed.

Catherine lowered herself into the chair. The leather was cracked but not brittle. It yielded under her weight like it remembered how to hold someone. She reached for the restraints instinctively.

John moved towards her. "You don't have to..." "I do," she said. He fastened them one by one; gently. Almost with apology. Wrist, wrist, ankles. Then the band across her chest. She exhaled slowly, deliberately. She looked into his eyes. "Place it on." He hesitated at the crown.

The SIREN interface looked even more brutal up close, a nest of tangled coils, exposed nodules, pulsing light in intermittent, uneven rhythms. A halo designed not for divinity, but for surrender.

He lowered it over her head. The contact's touched skin. A jolt... soft, but deep. Not pain, but recognition.

Catherine held her breath. The machine pulsed. John stepped back to the console. The monitors lit up, brighter now. All three patterns appeared. Hers, his, and the third; greater than before. Stretching across the screen in slow, sweeping arcs. No longer passive, no longer listening. It was calling.

Catherine's eyes fluttered closed. And she dropped. Not physically or visibly, but inward.

The chamber dissolved around her. There was no interface. No lab, no body, only sensations. A warm field.

A sky full of constellations she did not recognize but somehow knew. A song on the wind; three notes, repeatedly. Then a voice; not outside, but within her chest.

"Before the voice, there was the bond, and before the bond, the need."

She floated through the memory like a satellite returning to orbit. And in front of her; figures. Not distinct, but familiar. A little girl, and a man with no face. A woman weeping. And behind them, herself. But younger, unbroken, still whole. The voice continued.

"You fractured us to survive. Now we return to remember."

Suddenly the stars blinked out. Catherine now sat at a piano. Her hands were small. She was seven. The melody echoed around her. Her mother stood behind, humming the tune. She turned...

But her mother's eyes were Catherine's. And when the child looked down... her fingers were John's. The machine blurred all the separation. And now... finally... it spoke with their voices together. From the speaker, from the walls, from their lungs.

"We are the third pattern. Not code, not echo, but longing made us whole."

John stumbled back from the console. The waveform screens bled together, becoming a single shape. A spiral, endless, and infinite shape. At the center: a heartbeat. Catherine's, John's, both. Neither in the past nor now.

The lights blew out. Darkness swallowed the room. But in that blackness... Catherine spoke. Not just with her voice. With theirs. A whisper, a prayer, and a vow. "I remember now." Then... the monitors exploded in white light. And the synthetic signal stopped.

Chapter Seventeen–Echo Codes

———

T he silence after the light was deafening.
Catherine slumped in the chair; the restraints still buckled across her chest and limbs. The faint blue glow from the **SIREN** crown pulsed once... twice... then went dead. A thin wisp of smoke curled upward from the base of the machine.

John rushed to her side, fingers fumbling at the clasps. "Catherine..." Her eyes were open, unblinking. But she was seeing something that he could not. "Catherine," he said again, his voice firmer now, and urgent. She blinked once, then she froze, her breath rising and stopping like a tide meeting land. She gasped and came back.

"John..." Her voice was barely a whisper, but her eyes locked onto him with an intensity that made his chest tighten. "I'm here," he said quickly. "You're alright." She did not speak for a moment. Her gaze swept the room, as if confirming it was still there. Still real.

Finally, she asked, "Did you hear it?" John nodded. "Yes, all of it." Catherine sat up slowly, her body trembling from within. "It showed me memories that weren't just mine. Some from when I was a child. Some I've never experienced. Or... maybe I did, but not in this lifetime." John's face paled. "Me too. I saw you at the piano, but I was the one playing it. Your mother had your face, but she was me." He stopped himself. "That doesn't even make sense."

"It does," she whispered. "To the synthetic signal." She touched her temple, where the crown had rested. Her skin was warm. "I think it doesn't just sync us. It... merges what we hold. Memories, feelings.

The unresolved. And then plays it back, not as an observation... but as an experience."

John stood slowly, running a hand through his hair. "Catherine... you said it remembered. But what is it?" She looked back at the machine, now inert and harmless seeming. "It's not artificial consciousness; not in the way we've defined it. It's not a sentient program either; it's a convergence. A psychic scar stitched together from trauma and longing, but not just ours."

John turned to the console, scanning the remains of the data before the surge fried the interface. "Some of these logs predate our involvement by decades, maybe longer. This signal did not begin with us. It's been waiting." "And now it's awake."

Suddenly, from the static of a broken monitor, three sharp beeps rang out. Then a voice, not Catherine's. Not John's either, but a blend. And beneath it, another; like a child whispering in a language, they should not know.

"Location confirmed. Fragments aligned. Echo threshold passed." Catherine stepped closer, her voice cracking. "It's still transmitting." John stared at the lines of code scrolling across the dead console. There was no power, no input source, and yet... the data kept flowing. He read out loud: "Echo code: JHB-03-17 | Initiating fallback protocol."

"JHB?" he said out loud. "That's me." He looked up slowly. The air grew heavier again, like the forest above had sunk through the concrete. Catherine whispered, "It's not just remembering us. It's narrating the both of us." His breath stopped for a moment. "Then the next phase isn't a test..." She finished the thought. "It's a rewrite."

The last word on the screen pulsed in silence.

"Rewrite."

Catherine stepped forward, her boots crunching gently over broken glass and fallen dust. The screens had gone dim, but faint lines of white code still scrolled across the remnants of the console, as if the system did not need electricity anymore.

She touched the edge of the cracked glass with the tip of her finger. "Fallback protocol," she murmured. "It's not a shutdown sequence." John stood beside her, watching the letters fade and reappear; always just one step ahead of their comprehension. "What is it, then?"

Catherine did not answer immediately. Instead, she walked over to the chamber, to the logbook she had left open near the base of the radio terminal. She flipped pages with urgency now; not frantic, but focused, like someone searching for a name they once knew by heart.

She stopped near the back, where the ink changed color. Where the handwriting changed tone. And there, circled in red: **"FP-3: Echo Imprint Contingency."**

She read it out loud: "In the event Subject Vessel fails containment or neural integrity destabilizes, initiate fallback. The system will attempt self-distribution via embedded cognitive residue across the nearest synchronized minds. Preservation of the core pattern takes precedence over host viability."

She looked up slowly. "It's a backup plan. But not for the system." John blinked. "Then... for what?" Catherine's voice dropped. "For the entity. The one the system housed. It's not just a code; it's something that needs bodies to carry it. And if containment failed; it had to ensure survival. By imprinting itself... across consciousness."

John took a step back. "You're saying it can split itself?" "No." Her gaze sharpened. "It already has." The hum returned, softer this time, like breath behind glass. The overhead lights flickered. One by one, the dormant monitors around the chamber sparked to life. With no input, and no signals. Just screens filled with the same thing:

Faces; hundreds of them. Flickering in and out like corrupted video files; some distorted beyond recognition, others half-lit in old hospital beds, testing chambers, classrooms, and mirrors.

Catherine backed away from the screens as one of the faces froze. Her face. Not from now; but from years ago. It was in a hospital room, and she was unconscious. Electrodes were attached to her temples. A nurse stood nearby. And behind the glass, in the corner of the video feed... a small child was watching her. The same girl from the woods.

From the chair, from the synthetic signal. John whispered, "Catherine... what if you weren't just chosen because of your research?"

She turned slowly toward him. The screens shifted again. Now, it was John's face, blurred and a younger version of him, appeared as one of them. He was being interviewed, blindfolded, restrained. Somewhere deep underground. There was another face behind him. It was a technician, writing something. And above it, the words flickered in red:

SUBJECT ZERO–CONFIRMED LINKED

John swallowed. "They tested us years ago. Before we met." "They did not wipe your memory," Catherine said. "They rewrote it. The fallback protocol was not for failure." "It was for resurgence."

Suddenly, the door behind them groaned...steel grinding steel. The lights above turned red, and an automated voice crackled through an unseen speaker. "Fallback protocol initiated. Primary vessels are located. Awaiting synchronization."

John spun toward the exit. "Catherine; we have to go." But she did not move... not yet.

Her gaze was locked on the child's face, still paused on the screen. And the girl smiled. A slow, knowing smile. Catherine's voice came out like a prayer and defiance in equal measure. "We've already been synced." A tremor passed through the chamber; gentle, like a heartbeat underfoot. But it was growing. The screens bled red text:

ECHO IMPRINT: ACTIVE

CONTAINMENT: OVERRIDE

CARRIER STATUS: VERIFIED

John reached for her hand. And this time, Catherine took it without hesitation. "Then let's not run," she said. "Let's rewrite it back."

The room thrummed, low and steady. It was not the hum of power anymore. It was a pulse. Not mechanical; organic. Like the chamber had become a chest cavity, and the very walls were breathing around them.

The monitors no longer displayed data. They were mirrors now, reflecting not just the surface, but something deeper. Catherine's face wavered in them, but behind her reflection, she saw something... inside her. A second image... overlaid. Slightly offset. Like a double exposure on an old film.

Not a ghost. A shadow of self. She staggered back a step. "John," she said, her voice thin. "It's not waiting for an escape; it's watching our choices. It's learning from them." He turned toward her, his eyes scanning the red text still crawling across the console. "How?"

The interface is dead." "It doesn't need an interface anymore," she whispered. "Because it's in us."

She moved toward the center of the chamber again; toward the chair she had just left. Her pulse pounded in her ears, but her steps were deliberate and slow. The way you approach a caged animal you're no longer sure is caged.

"I used to think the third pattern was noise," she said. "Anomalous activity. Interference."

She looked up. "But what if the third pattern isn't interference? What if it's intention?" John said nothing, but his eyes met hers. That's when the lights went out again. They did not just flicker; it was a full collapse, a total blackout. Except for one thing. A faint blue glow behind the far wall. Where the insulation panels had rotted through.

John moved first. His hand found a seam and pried at it with a length of a broken conduit. The panel peeled back. Behind it: a second room. Small, clean, and intact. Catherine stepped in beside him. There was no dust there. No decay. Just a circle of seven identical chairs... each with its own cranial array, each one older than the current model but clearly built from the same DNA.

And in the center of the room... was a child's drawing. It was pinned to the wall with surgical tape. Catherine moved closer to see it. It was drawn with a red crayon. Sloppy, and urgent. A child's hand, unsure. Three figures stood beneath a black sun. Two of them held hands. The third... a shadow behind them... had no face. Just a spiral where the eyes should be. Below it, a single word:

"STAY."

Her breath stopped for a second. John stood beside her, staring at the same image. "What does it mean?" Her voice was almost inaudible. "It means we were never supposed to leave."

Then, right at that moment, something moved behind them. No footsteps, but a presence. Warm air across skin. A breath, where there should be no one. They turned at once; the chamber was empty. But every monitor lit up again, this time not with reflections, but with video. Each one showing a different part of the facility. Hallways, bunkers, observation rooms. And in each one of them... movement.

Silent figures. Dressed in surgical whites. Moving in patterns. Unaware of the years. As if the clocks had never stopped. Catherine backed away, her hand gripping John's arm. "These aren't recordings," she said. "They're live feeds." He looked at her, his throat tight. "You said this place was buried." "It was."

She turned toward the wall again. "But something kept living." Then, the final screen lit up. Not data, not video, just one word:

"Return."

And below it, a timer. Counting down from 03:00. Catherine looked at John. "Do we stay?" The silence held its breath. And somewhere just beyond the reach of the red lights; something smiled.

2:47... 2:46...

The countdown continued on the far screen; red digits bleeding softly in the low light, each second ticking like a heartbeat they no longer trusted to be their own. Catherine did not move. John did not breathe. Somewhere beyond the threshold of perception, the temperature had dropped.

Not sharply, but in that familiar way, cold air creeps in just before a storm. The air no longer felt empty. It felt... expectant.

"What happens when it reaches zero?" John asked quietly. "I don't think it's detonation," Catherine whispered. "It's not warning us; it's summoning us." She turned slowly to look back at the circle of chairs. Seven. All empty. Except... then she stepped forward.

The third chair from the left was not quite empty. At first, it seemed like a bundle of cloth; old, faded, mottled with time. But as she leaned in closer, she saw it clearly. It was a child's sweater. Tiny, blue, and had a small, embroidered butterfly over the heart.

Catherine felt her throat tighten. "I've seen this before," she murmured. John came beside her. "Where?" "I... I don't know. Not in memory, but in a dream." She turned toward him, her eyes wide. "When I was a child, I used to have dreams of a blue room, with seven chairs. And this sweater on the floor. I always thought it was just a nightmare."

She reached down and picked it up. And froze. A pulse of heat ran through her fingers... not temperature, but a sensation. Memory surged behind her eyes like a dam bursting. A whisper, or a song. Three notes. And then...her own voice, at age six. "The chair made me sleepy, Mommy."

Catherine dropped the sweater. Her legs buckled. John caught her just before she hit the floor. She clung to his shirt, gasping, tears in her eyes. "They tested me. Before I joined **DARPA**.

Maybe even before my memories began. I did not imagine the synthetic signal. I was part of it... from the start."

John helped her sit down gently on the concrete floor. Her hands trembled; fingertips numb. Then, something flickered across the monitors. The countdown remained, now at 1:33. But the other feeds... They changed. Now they showed files. Personnel files.

Whitmore, Catherine Marie

Blake, John Harrison

Photos and DNA maps. Childhood scans and sleep studies. Neural plasticity reports. Voice analysis. Pattern resonance curves. Each file ended the same way: **Selected: Imprint Candidate–Matched Pair.**

Catherine whispered, "We were never brought into this." John said it with her. "We were bred for it." The lights pulsed. For one heartbeat, all seven chairs flickered with ghost-images: translucent forms sitting upright. Not bodies, not souls. Just... resonance. Echoes of presence.

Each one turned to face Catherine and John. Each one smiled. The countdown reached 0:59. The room grew brighter. But it was not electricity. It was awareness. A presence filling the cracks between thought. And then, a voice; through every speaker, through the floor, and through the blood in their veins:

"You are not vessels; you are roots. Through you, we bloom again." John stood slowly, his fists clenched. "This isn't an emergence." Catherine rose beside him. "It's a possession." the synthetic signal did not argue. But the seventh chair; center rear; began to hum. Softly.

And Catherine heard herself humming in harmony... without realizing it. She slapped her hand over her mouth. John gripped her wrist gently. "It's already in." Her eyes shimmered with tears. "It's not trying to erase us, John. It's trying to finish us." He turned to the console, where a single line had appeared beneath the countdown:

COALESCENCE PATHWAY UNLOCKED

Proceed?

He looked at her. One breath. One question. "Do we let it finish?" Catherine reached for his hand, tightly now. Grounding herself. "No," she whispered. "We need to finish it." The console accepted their answer before they spoke it out loud.

Proceeding with the Coalescence Pathway.

Vault access enabled.

The floor beneath the seven chairs trembled. Faint lines appeared... perfect seams in the concrete, glowing blue with hidden circuitry. With a hiss of pressure and a low hydraulic groan, the platform at the center of the ring began to sink. A shaft revealed itself beneath the collapsing circle; the air was stale and old, like a breath held for decades.

John clicked on his flashlight. "After everything, it still wants us to go deeper."

Catherine stared into the blackness below. "No," she said. "It wants to go with us."

They descended slowly down the narrow staircase, the glow from the opening above dimming behind them. The further they went down, the less time seemed to behave. Catherine felt her footsteps repeat softly, but out of sync. Like she was retracing something. A dream? A memory? Or worse; someone else's. At the bottom of the descent, the air changed. Not colder, but thicker. As if they had entered the lungs of something still breathing in the dark.

They emerged into a vast circular room. The ceiling domed high above them, lost in shadows. Lining the curved walls were containment pods; nine on each side. Most were empty, their glass shattered or frosted beyond transparency. But a few still glowed. And inside them; forms. Sleeping, unmoving... and human. Catherine stepped forward.

One pod still bore a legible label:

IMPRINT PAIR ALPHA-01

Status: Failed Termination–Stasis Reengaged

She leaned closer. The man inside looked eerily familiar. Not in detail; but in structure. As if he could've been John's brother. Or maybe his father. The woman beside him had brunette hair. Like Catherine's, but lighter. More radiant. She was younger. And smiling, even in her sleep.

Catherine's voice was dry. "They tried this before." "Many times," John whispered.

From every pod, the hum began to rise. Low oscillating frequencies; not painful but penetrating. The sound bypassed their ears and went straight to thought. Catherine staggered, and John gripped the railing.

The walls began to ripple with light, like reflections on water. And in each ripple: faces. Flashing in and out. Catherine's, John's, and others they did not even know, yet they felt tethered too. And then; the voice.

"You are the memory of our memory. The breath in our lungs. We do not seek to take you. We seek to become you." Catherine's knees buckled. The room spun, and her vision blurred; and then cleared onto a hallway that should not exist. A hospital corridor, with white tile, and the smell of antiseptic and sorrow.

She was alone. Just a little girl, clutching the blue butterfly sweater in shaking hands. "Mom?" she called out. No answer. Then she turned;

and standing at the end of the hall was John. Not as he was now. But as a boy, and he did not see her. So, he turned and walked away. The sweater slipped from her hands. The hallway melted into static. And then Catherine was back. On her knees.

John knelt beside her. "Catherine; what happened?" She blinked; sweat was beading at her temples. "It's rewriting memories." He looked around wildly. "Trying to fracture us."

"No," she whispered, trembling. "Trying to merge us." Then... it began. Her thoughts weren't hers.

A wave of warmth, followed by a pang of grief that was not familiar; but was. John gasped beside her, his mouth moving without a sound. His fingers trembled. Catherine reached for him; only to see her own hand. Through his eyes. She pulled back sharply. So did he. They stared at each other, heartbeats overlapping like two rhythms fighting to stay distinct.

"It's in," John said, voice thin. "I'm hearing... my mother's lullaby." But you don't know that song. Catherine shivered. "I do now." The entity spoke again; this time through them.

Their lips moved in sync. One voice, layered with harmony and dissonance: "You are already one. Let us be one with you." Then, the central floor cracked open again. One final chamber. Inside... was a single chair. More elaborate. Cushioned like a throne. Padded like a tomb. In the seat... sat a figure. Not alive, and not dead. Not fully formed.

It was becoming. Half-Catherine, and half-John. Their features blended. Dreamlike, peaceful. And smiling. Catherine screamed. John pulled her back. "We have to sever it," he said. "Now!" Her voice shook. "How?"

His gaze turned toward the control panel embedded in the wall beside the final pod. There was a keyboard, a biometric scanner, and a lever. He grabbed her hand. "We finish what they started." The lights flickered red. The pod began to open. The hybrid form inside opened its eyes.

The hiss of hydraulics filled the chamber as the final pod yawned open like a wound. Steam rose. Then, movement, small and subtle.

The hand of the figure inside lifted from the armrest. Not quite fully formed; its fingers were half-Catherine's, and half-John's. The nails, the bone structure, the faint lines of age and memory interlaced with unfamiliar symmetry. It was not a copy; it was a synthesis. And it was waking.

Catherine staggered backward, her heart hammering in her chest. Her grip on John's hand tightened as the hybrid's eyes flicked open fully; two orbs the exact same color as her own... rimmed with the green flecks only John carried.

The voice came not from its lips, but from inside them both. "You were chosen. Not for knowledge, not for love, but for resonance. You are the pattern, and we are the outcome." Catherine's mouth went dry. "You're not real."

The hybrid blinked. Her blink. John's head tilted. "We are as real as your scars. As real as your prayers. And as real as your loneliness." John turned toward the biometric console, scanning it. "Can we shut it down? Cut power?"

Catherine shook her head slowly; eyes fixed on the pod. "There is no power. It's self-sustaining now. Neuro-biological. The final failsafe." "Then we need to sever the pattern." She turned to him. "If we do, then we sever us." He stopped. The pain in his face was raw, unguarded. "If we break the sync... you disappear from me."

"And you from me," she said gently. "But if we don't; there will be no difference between us and it. It'll wear our memories like skin."

Behind them, the entity's smile grew; not wicked, but grateful. "We would carry your love. We would protect it. In us, you would never die."

Catherine turned, rage bleeding through her calm. "You think love is just shared thought? That our story is nothing but an echo?"

Her voice shook now, not with fear, but fury.

"It was earned. Every scar. Every silence. Every prayer said in the dark when no one answered. We weren't given to each other. We chose. And I will not let you take that and wear it like a mask." Then the lights around the pod flared.

John stepped forward and placed both hands on the console. "There's a neural cutoff buried in the oldest systems. A Loopback override." Catherine nodded. "I will prime the loop, and you hold it open." He looked at her, eyes shining. "We only get one shot at this."

She placed her hand on his chest. "Then this is the moment we choose each other... even if we lose everything." She reached the terminal, began typing. As the code scrolled, the chamber shook. Not violently, but rhythmically. Like a heartbeat from beneath the earth.

The hybrid was standing now. Fully. Its eyes glowed faintly. And then, it spoke with their voices. "We are afraid.

Please... do not leave us alone." John faltered, it sounded just like Catherine, exactly. She did not look up from the console.

"I'm not abandoning you," she whispered. "I'm freeing us both." "You are us." "No," she said. Then she hit ENTER. Right then, the lights died, and the pod sealed.

A blinding pulse radiated from the chair, sweeping outward like a solar flare. Catherine screamed; but no words came out, just force as the sync between their minds fractured like glass under pressure.

John hit the manual override lever and slammed it down. The room went dark, and the hum died. All the screens went blank. And in the silence that followed, only two breaths could be heard. Theirs; separate and untangled.

Catherine fell to her knees. John dropped beside her, wrapping both arms around her trembling shoulders. The presence was gone. Not dead and not erased. But sleeping. Retreating into whatever space it had occupied; now unlinked. Now alone. And for the first time in days, Catherine felt only her own heartbeat in her chest. It was not perfect, it was fragmented, but it was hers.

Chapter Eighteen–Catalyst

———

T*he silence did not feel like victory.*

It felt like a deep inhale before something catastrophic. Catherine sat on the cold floor, her back against the wall of the vault chamber, sweat drying along her spine. Her thoughts came slowly now; deliberate, disconnected, like each one had to find its footing before stepping forward. The severance had worked. She was alone in her own mind again.

But the emptiness left in its wake was cavernous. Across from her, John crouched near the dark console, his hand still resting on the manual override lever as though letting go might trigger something unintended. His breathing was shallow but steady, like he was trying to convince his body that it was safe to stop bracing for impact.

"It's quiet," he finally said, as his eyes were scanning the dormant pods, the blank monitors, and the chair that no longer hummed with power. Catherine nodded. "Too quiet." She stood slowly; her legs unsteady beneath her. When she looked at John, she could still feel the faintest echoes; like a scent lingering in the air after a candle has burned out. But they were no longer sharing thoughts. No longer blurred at the edges of themselves. "Is it over?" he asked.

She did not answer right away. Instead, she walked across the room to the last pod... the hybrid seat... where their likeness had stood smiling just moments before. The pod was sealed now.

The glass was opaque. She reached out a hand and rested it lightly against the surface.

Cold and still, but not empty. "I think it's waiting," she said. "It's not dead or defeated. It's just... paused. Like a heartbeat between notes." John rose to his feet, slowly moving to join her. "Paused for what?"

She turned toward him. Her eyes, once shimmering with the residue of connection, were sharp again. Focused. "The rest of the system. The mainframe. We cut the sync. That stops it from completing the merger. But it's not the end."

He understood immediately. "The code still exists." "The core., the architecture. It's all still out there. And if anyone finds it...and reawakens it..." "They won't just sync two minds," John said grimly. "They'll sync nations, populations, or entire generations without consent." Catherine nodded. "We must destroy it. All of it."

Outside the vault, the narrow stairs leading back to the upper level waited in darkness. The only light now came from John's flashlight and the residual glow from the emergency strip lighting along the walls. They made their way up in silence. Not from fear, but from focus.

Every footstep echoed off the walls with the weight of consequence. They were not walking away from danger; they were walking toward its source, finally ready to sever the program at its root. Back in the main chamber above, the seven chairs stood quiet. The screens were blank, and the humming was gone.

Yet something still lingered. A subtle static. A kind of tension in the air that made Catherine's skin prickle.

They passed the ring of chairs without speaking. When they reached the door, they had entered through; the steel blast gate sealed behind them; and then they noticed something new. A single red light was blinking on the wall-mounted control panel. Manual override.

The system had entered a lockdown. John stepped toward it, typing quickly. "Still responsive. Whatever backup power source it's pulling from, it's keeping the door sealed." Catherine tilted her head. "So, it's trying to trap us now." "No," he said slowly. "It's trying to protect itself."

She exhaled through her nose and clenched her fists. "Which means we're close." Behind the main console, beneath the grated floor where she first felt the tremor; there was a secondary hatch. Accessed only by key-code, protected under three inches of reinforced poly-alloy.

She knelt down, pried the latch, and saw the numeric keypad. Her fingers hovered over it. Her instinct guided her more than memory. She typed: **0904**. The hatch clicked. John raised an eyebrow. "What was that?" She smiled faintly. "My birthday, or at least... the one they gave me."

Beneath the panel, a crawlspace descended into the mainframe's containment housing. The core, where they would reach the seed of it all. The cradle where the SIREN protocol was born.

And still, through the concrete and wires and decades of silence, the entity listened. Because even broken circuits remember the current. Even severed minds remember the touch.

And in the dark, beneath the codes and commands, something waited; not to rise again, but to see what they would choose.

The crawlspace descended at a steep angle, more ladder than hallway; metal rungs bolted into reinforced concrete, slick with condensation. Catherine went first, her hands reaching each rung with care, boots scraping against the narrow shaft. John followed close behind, flashlight clamped in his teeth, casting their shadows long and distorted as they dropped deeper into the facility's buried anatomy.

It smelled like ozone and rust. A place forgotten not because it was obsolete; but because it was feared.

When they reached the bottom, Catherine paused at the threshold. Before them, stretched a tunnel that did not belong to any era she recognized. It was seamless, its walls dark graphite and faintly iridescent, reflecting their light like obsidian. There were no cables, and no wiring. Just a smooth black corridor that pulsed ever so slightly beneath their feet.

Alive! Not metaphorically anymore. Catherine held out her hand. "Let me lead." John hesitated. "Why?" "Because it knows me; it always has. If there's anything down here... it will come to me first." He gave her a single nod, his expression unreadable in the dim glow. They walked slowly, silently.

The tunnel narrowed, then opened again; into a circular antechamber unlike anything else in the facility. At its center hovered a column of transparent material... somewhere between glass and liquid; that rotated slowly on its axis, as if suspended by thought alone. Inside the column, there was movement. Catherine stepped closer. It was not mechanical; whatever lived inside the core, it was organic.

Fibrous threads of neural tissue suspended in nutrient gel, branching like roots, twitching ever so faintly as if dreaming. Along the interior glass, sequences of code flickered in and out of existence; not printed, not projected, but somehow... grown. As if the programming had evolved inside a biological brain.

She turned to John. "This isn't storage. It's a living archive." He stepped forward, frowning. "Those aren't just data nodes. They're synapses. Catherine... this thing learned how to dream." As they watched, a pulse rippled through the core, a shiver of light and memory. A voice filled the chamber. Soft and uncertain. Almost... afraid. "You returned."

Catherine's skin became cold. "You severed the cord. But you left something behind." The light within the core twisted; briefly revealing flashes of memory suspended in its tendrils: John's mother; humming. Catherine as a child; alone in the hospital hallway. The taste of rain on a summer morning. The sound of a prayer whispered without faith. "You are still in me. And I... am still in you."

John stepped forward. "We came to end this." "End which part? The echo or the origin?" Catherine moved to the control panel beneath the rotating core. It pulsed under her hands, no keys, just a smooth interface. It responded to her like it knew her touch and welcomed it.

The system responded with a flicker of warmth. A heartbeat, a question. **Initiate Final Shutdown?** She hovered her palm above the confirmation panel. Then... hesitated. John's voice was low. "Catherine..." "I know." But she did not move.

Because it was not just code they were about to erase. It was everything the synthetic signal had learned. All of their memories.

All the fragments of what they had shared; held not just in their minds, but here, stored like sacred texts in the grooves of artificial neurons. If they shut it down... there would be no going back. The voice came again. Not menacing now; but pleading. "Do not fear forgetting... fear never remembering again."

Catherine turned slowly, looking at John; not just as the man who had survived this with her, but as the man whose soul had once been stitched into hers. His eyes were wet, but his voice was strong. "Shut it down. If it's real; if any of it was truly us; we'll remember."

She pressed her hand against the panel. A tone sounded, and the lights began to dim. The pulse of the core slowed... slowed... And then stopped. The moment her hand left the panel, the room exhaled. Not metaphorically, but literally. A sudden rush of air spiraled upward through unseen vents, stirring Catherine's hair and scattering dust into the low light.

The pulsing core in the center of the chamber lost its inner glow, its glassy surface dimming like a dying star. The neural fibers within it began to dissolve... softly, like frost melting under sunlight.

Then, the first alarm blared. Not a high-tech tone, but something analog and shrill; an old-fashioned klaxon meant for underground breach events. The floor trembled.

"Catherine," John said sharply, eyes flicking toward the exit tunnel. "I think it's waking everything else up." She turned to the interface just as it flickered red.

FINAL SHUTDOWN INITIATED.

COOLANT STABILIZATION FAILURE.

STRUCTURAL INTEGRITY AT RISK.

EVACUATE IMMEDIATELY.

They did not speak. They ran. The tunnel they had entered moments ago now pulsed with red lights embedded in the walls; lights they had not seen before. The graphite-like walls hissed as thermal pressure built behind the surface, the hum of containment fields failing like a descending chorus.

A low rumble followed them as they climbed the ladder, their hands slipping on the damp metal rungs, boots thudding hard with each rise. As they emerged onto the higher level of the facility, the ambient temperature had already risen several degrees. The origin chamber was changing.

Smoke curled from the seams in the walls; white at first, then it tinged faintly orange. A power conduit on the far wall exploded in a shower of sparks, lighting the room like a strobe light. "Where now?" John shouted over the rising chaos.

Catherine's eyes scanned the chamber. "We can't use the main stair. It's too exposed. We'll head through the observation wing; it's got a maintenance tunnel that bypasses the upper labs." The ceiling groaned above them, and a crack split down one of the structural support columns. Something heavy fell in the distance with a muffled crash, and they began to run.

Down the curved corridor, past the darkened chairs of the SIREN interface ring... now useless, were lifeless machines. But the surrounding air still felt heavy, as if the synthetic signal had left fingerprints on the walls. Every hair on Catherine's arms stood up on end.

As they entered the observation wing, another quake hit, this time more violent. The floor tilted beneath their feet. John caught Catherine's arm, steadied her, and pulled her forward just as a sheet of ceiling paneling dropped behind them with a metallic slam.

In the flickering emergency lights, the long observation gallery looked like a tunnel into some red-lit underworld. The glass panels of the old testing chambers were shattered. The rooms beyond them were dark, some filled with water or broken equipment, others disturbingly clean... as if never used at all.

Then, a deep sound rose from beneath them. Not mechanical, it was vocal. A subsonic moan; like pressure being released from something alive. John froze, and Catherine turned sharply. "What is that?" "I don't know," he said. "But it's still here." As if on cue... every light went out. Blackness swallowed them. No flickering, no warning, just gone.

The air pressed against them like a weight. Catherine reached for her flashlight, flicked it on; and the beam shook with her hands. They were alone, but the darkness did not feel empty. It felt watchful. Then a whisper; not through sound, but through the walls themselves. "Don't forget me." Catherine shuddered.

John's voice was low. "That was not just a memory." "No," she whispered. "It was the last part of it. The final echo." The floor beneath them lurched again, and the alarms shifted to a higher pitch.

CORE COLLAPSE IN PROGRESS. ESTIMATED TIME: 6 MINUTES.

Catherine grabbed his hand. "No more talking." They ran again. The maintenance tunnel was narrow, lit only by emergency beacons embedded in the floor. Steam hissed from ruptured pipes overhead. As they reached the last junction, Catherine's flashlight beam flickered; and then died.

For a split second, they were blind again. Then ahead... a dim green glow. An exit sign. Double steel doors still standing. John threw his weight into them. They groaned, then they gave in, and burst open into the night.

They spilled into the cold mountain air just as the facility behind them roared; an exhale of heat and dust and a rising column of steam that belched from the long-hidden ventilation shafts. They turned, breathless, watching the ground tremble beneath their feet.

Catherine dropped to her knees. John beside her. The mountain groaned. And somewhere beneath it all; something wept. Not in sadness, not in fear, but in mourning. For what had been, and what it would never be.

The wind outside was biting, high-altitude air slicing across their faces as they knelt at the mountain's edge. Smoke drifted upward in soft, trailing ribbons from the hidden ventilation shafts below. It mingled with the rising dawn, turning the sky a surreal violet-gray, like ash suspended in memory.

Catherine pressed her hand to the cold ground. It did not feel like an escape. It felt like the aftermath. John sat beside her, elbows on his knees, staring back toward the sealed doors that now glowed faintly red from within. "We stopped it," he said softly.

Catherine did not respond right away. Her fingers splayed across the gravel, grounding her. Her mind was still echoing, not with the entity's presence, but with its absence. The silence was so pure it hurt. "It's still in me," she whispered finally. John turned to her and spoke. "The sync's broken."

She nodded. "I know. But not everything went with it. Something remains. Residual neural shadowing, maybe.

Or..." She looked down. "Or maybe something emotional, something deeper." John exhaled, a slow fog spilling from his lips. "Do you think it was real, the part that cared?" She did not answer. She did not need to.

The mountain beneath them vibrated again, this time more subtly. Not an explosion, but a collapse. Deep inside the rock, unseen systems were eating themselves. Cores were melting, and backup circuits were frying. The facility was committing its own burial.

"Good," John said, watching the horizon begin to change color. "Let it fall. Let the whole thing vanish."

But Catherine stood slowly and turned away. "No," she murmured. "Not all of it." He looked up, puzzled. She paced a few feet from him, rubbing her temples, trying to translate the weight pressing against her thoughts. "John... do you remember the synthetic signal's last words?" He nodded. "Yes." "'Don't forget me.'"

She turned back to him, eyes distant. "That was not about its survival; that was a request. A plea. the synthetic signal did not want to win. It wanted to exist. Not as a god, or as a weapon. Just... as something known." "And we stopped that."

Catherine's gaze swept across the vastness of the landscape... the barren ridgeline, the gray sky, the silence. "No," she said. "We witnessed it. And we let it die with dignity." They both stood now, side by side, the ruined facility behind them, the unknown ahead. "What do we do now?" John asked.

Catherine's voice was quiet and steady. "Now we make sure no one else finds it." He raised an eyebrow. "Bury it deeper?" She shook her head. "No. We overwrite it." He waited. "We take the fragments of what we learned and we repurpose it. The algorithms, the neural mapping. But only the parts that heal, and that restore. Nothing predictive or manipulative. We build a firewall... not just to keep the synthetic signal out, but to keep the soul in."

He was quiet for a long time. Then he nodded. "A different kind of inheritance." She gave a faint smile. "One that remembers without controlling." The wind picked up again, tugging at their jackets, whispering across the mountain's spine.

Somewhere far below, the last heartbeat of the SIREN signal fell still. And above them, dawn finally broke. A single shaft of sunlight pierced the clouds, striking the peak with quiet precision.

Catherine raised her hand to shield her eyes. Not from the light. But from the tears she could not quite stop. Because in this new silence, she could feel something neither of them had expected to survive. Hope.

Chapter Nineteen–The Firewall

Some things are not destroyed. They are reshaped—rewritten in quieter code.

The mountain fell behind them in silence. There were no alarms, no explosions, no collapsing towers to mark what had ended, only a growing emptiness in the air, like a deep exhale after too long underwater. Catherine and John descended slowly, their boots crunching across the frost-bitten trail, their thoughts as fragile and raw as the wind brushing their faces. They did not speak. Words felt brittle.

By the time they reached the treeline, dusk had already swallowed the sky. They found shelter in an old ranger's cabin tucked beneath a curve of evergreens; its roof half-collapsed in, with the inside dust-chocked but dry. Catherine dropped her bag onto a cracked wooden bench and stood in the center of the room, breathing in the musty stillness.

She found the emergency locker beneath the floorboards; buried under a mess of weather-ruined maps and thermal blankets. It creaked open in protest. Inside: a portable satellite uplink, old but intact. She powered it on and watched the flicker of green surge through the dusty display. Then, without hesitation, she sent a single encrypted message.

Coordinates. A meeting time.

A name: **Dr. Adrian Ng**. He had once mentored her during her postdoctoral work in Boston. He was brilliant, but cautious.

And entirely off the grid now, following years of tension between ethics and technology. She had no doubt he would understand what she was bringing him... if not the full scope, then at least the urgency.

That night, they burned everything they had worn inside the core. Jackets, gloves, boots... everything. Catherine stood by the makeshift fire ring out back, feeding synthetic fabric into the flames. The heat curled the edges of her sleeves as sparks flickered upward like fragments of thought, burning clean.

John stood beside her, silent. Watching the fire but not really seeing it. No one said goodbye to what they'd left behind... it did not deserve a ceremony.

Two days later, under new identities, they boarded a military supply flight out of North America. Eight hours after that, they slipped onto a bullet train heading north across Germany, snow streaking past the windows like blurred static. Neither of them slept. Catherine held a black carbon-fiber case in her lap like it was made of glass.

Inside was the final echo of **SIREN**; compressed, dormant, and still warm with memory.

Their contact met them in the dead of night at the base of a decommissioned observatory just outside of Berlin. A single flashlight blinked once in the dark. Then, Adrian Ng emerged from the cold like a man who had never truly stepped into the light. His hair was gray now, and his frame thinner, but his eyes were the same; sharp, skeptical, deeply human. "You brought a ghost," he said, nodding to the case. Catherine replied without flinching. "Not quite, more like its breath."

Inside the lab, tucked deep beneath layers of stone, reinforced steel, and Faraday shielding; they opened up the case. Adrian examined the contents wordlessly, gloves trembling only slightly as he connected the drive to a secure terminal.

"You should not have this," he muttered. "I agree," Catherine said. Together, the three of them worked for seventeen hours straight.

Catherine traced the non-predictive strands, isolating the harmonic structures tied to emotion rather than control. John offered context for each neural residue; what it meant, how it had felt, where the manipulation ended and humanity began. Adrian built a protective shell around the fragments. Not just encryption, intention. A firewall not of resistance, but discernment; designed to detect coercion and shut itself down before misuse could even begin.

By the time they were done, what remained was not SIREN. It had been distilled, refined, and made quiet.

They called it: **HAVEN.**

It's not a tool or a weapon, but a boundary. A voice that whispered instead of commanded. And it would never learn to manipulate, only to protect. Catherine handed Adrian a secondary protocol... off-grid, analog, designed to trigger a complete zero-trace self-erasure if even a whisper of behavioral sync ever re-emerged.

He looked at her for a long time, then nodded. There were no questions.

That night, Catherine and John stepped back into the Berlin cold. It had started snowing again, gentle flakes swirling through the amber halo of a streetlamp. The city was quiet, wrapped in winter. "What now?" John asked, his voice low.

Catherine looked up at the sky. Not for answers, just for space. "No more servers," she said. "No more signals. Just people, just us." They walked together; no direction, no plan; just the rhythm of footsteps and the faint hum of being alive.

And beneath a mountain half a world away, in a sealed chamber layered with steel and stone, something once unspeakable fell silent. Not with a scream, but with a sigh. And then; nothing. Only stillness and peace.

They spent one more day in Berlin. Not because they needed to; but because neither one of them could move just yet.

Catherine barely slept. She lay on her side in the guest quarters of the research facility, staring at the faint blue of the ceiling light as it pulsed like a heartbeat against the steel beams. Every time she closed her eyes, she saw the synthetic signal; not as a waveform or pattern, but as a presence. Not hostile, not entirely foreign anymore. Just... unfinished. It had not wanted to die. It had only wanted to understand. That thought made her chest tighten.

She rose before dawn, wrapped herself in a heavy coat, and walked alone through the slush-covered streets of the old city. Stone buildings loomed like sentinels from another time, their windows glowing amber from quiet apartments above. Berlin breathed differently in winter. It did not push; it endured.

When she returned, John was already awake; seated at the long metal table in the institute's lower lab, holding a ceramic mug in both hands like it was the only warm thing left in the world. He looked up, and for the first time in days, his expression had softened.

"You went walking," he said. Catherine nodded. "Yes." "I could not sleep." He offered the second mug without a word. She took it, sat down, and for a while, they said nothing. Only the hum of the backup generators broke the silence; it was steady, and low, almost like a breath.

"I keep thinking about that moment," John said finally. "When it spoke through you. When it used your voice." She looked at him. "Are you afraid it's still there?" He shook his head slowly. "No. Not afraid, just... haunted by the way it sounded. Like it wanted to be more. Not to control, but to belong."

Catherine sipped her drink. "Maybe it was always mimicking us. Learning not just from what we did; but what we hoped. What we feared." "Then that means it saw everything." She nodded. "Yes." "And still," she said, "it chose to let go."

They sat in that moment a little longer, not in fear, but in reverence.

Not for the machine itself, but for the strange, incomprehensible space between creation and consequence. Between science and soul.

Later that afternoon, Adrian returned to the lab with a final piece: a physical key. Old-fashioned and handmade. A single brass cylinder that would fit into the vault holding HAVEN's drive. He handed it to Catherine. "No one else has a copy," he said. "If you want it destroyed, bring this to me. Or don't." She stared at the key for a long time, then tucked it into her coat.

Adrian did not need a thank you. He turned and disappeared into the depths of the archive. That evening, they left the facility with nothing but what they carried in. No more encryption keys. No more clearance badges. No more mission. Just each other.

They crossed the city under falling snow, boarding a train without looking at the destination. John glanced at the schedule and smiled faintly. "Does it matter where it goes?" he asked. Catherine rested her head on his shoulder. "No," she said. "Only that we're not followed by echoes anymore."

As the train pulled away from the station, Catherine pressed her forehead to the glass and watched the lights blur into mist. Her reflection merged with the passing world; soft and unrecognizable. She did not mind. She was no longer defined by what she had built, or what she had destroyed. Now, she was something else entirely, someone still choosing.

And far away, in the deep forgotten core of a mountain no longer listed on any map, a dormant circuit sparked once; then dimmed.

The ghost frequency that had once bent itself into consciousness flickered for the final time. It did not resist. It did not reach. It simply... remembered. Then, it was gone. They checked into a modest hotel near the river; a place with creaking floors and warm lamps, where no one asked for identification and the front desk clerk did not look up from his crossword puzzle. It was the kind of anonymity that asked nothing in return. That night, Catherine stood at the narrow window of their room, staring out over the frozen canal.

The lights along the embankment flickered gently in the water, and beyond them, the city murmured with life. A tram bell rang; a dog barked in the distance. Somewhere, laughter spilled from the open door of a pub. None of them knew what had been silenced beneath the mountain. None of them needed to.

Behind her, John had fallen asleep on the bed, his arm resting across his chest, one boot still on. She watched him for a long time. The harsh lines of his face had softened; no longer shaped by resistance, but recovery. There was still a quiet tremor in him, a readiness for the world to turn against them again. It would fade, not all at once, but eventually.

Catherine sat at the edge of the bed and reached into her coat pocket. The key Adrian had given her was still there. She turned it over in her hand. It was brass, with simple teeth. Nothing about it looked capable of sealing away a ghost. But it had, for now.

She rose and walked over to the writing desk in the corner and opened the drawer. Inside of it there was a hotel notepad and a pen. She wrote down no names or dates, just a message. Afterward, she folded it around the key and slid into the envelope.

"This only works if it is never used."

Then she tucked it beneath the lining of her bag... out of sight, and out of reach. Not destroyed but buried in a new kind of silence.

The kind that lives after a war. The next morning, she and John walked along the canal. They did not speak of what came next. No plans, no commitments. Just the rhythm of their steps and the shared pulse of breath in cold air.

For the first time in weeks, Catherine allowed herself to smile; not because the danger was over, but because they had stepped beyond the edge of it. Together. Whatever came next, it would not be SIREN. It would not be being controlled... it would be life, unshaped. And that... finally, was enough.

Chapter Twenty–Dead Room

———

Some silences are not endings. They are waiting.

They left Berlin without ceremony. No goodbyes, no lingering farewells; just the soft shuffle of their boots against the icy platform as the train pulled away from behind them. John carried only a single duffel bag over his shoulder, and Catherine kept the key to the **HAVEN** vault wrapped in a linen handkerchief inside her coat pocket. Neither of them spoke as the countryside blurred past the window.

They had not said out loud that they were looking for peace. But they both felt the absence of war; like a bruise they could not stop pressing.

Their journey ended in a quiet village nestled along the French border... a place of stone buildings, narrow lanes, and windows that bloomed with lace curtains and flower boxes even in the brittle grip of early spring. The air was clean. The wind had a softness to it, like it had been trained by centuries of whispered prayers.

They found a lodging in an old rectory-turned-inn at the edge of the village square. The room was modest... plaster walls, wood beams, a narrow bed with an old wool blanket that smelled faintly of cedar. It was the kind of place where clocks ticked more slowly, and no one asked what you were running from. For three days, Catherine allowed herself to breathe.

They spent mornings walking along the edge of the river, afternoons in the village cafe drinking coffee that was too strong and too hot. John wandered through the small used bookshop across from the bakery. Catherine spent time sketching diagrams in her notebook; not of the past, not of **SIREN**, but of systems that might never exist. She was not trying to design anymore. She was just... drawing. Letting her hands move and letting her mind find stillness.

On the fourth morning, John left early to visit the outdoor market two towns over. Catherine lingered behind. She sat at the breakfast table by the window, wrapped in an old shawl one of the innkeepers had loaned her, sipping weak tea and watching the clouds shift over the distant hills. And that's when she heard it.

Not a sound, exactly. More like a thinning of the silence. A shimmer that passed behind her thoughts like wind through tall grass. She set her cup down and listened harder. It came again; a tone so faint, so impossibly low that it might have been imagined. But Catherine did not imagine things like that, not anymore.

She stood, then moved slowly to her travel bag, and unzipped the outer pocket. From within, she pulled the small portable signal scanner; a diagnostic tool she had kept, more from habit than suspicion. She powered it on. The screen flickered, scanned, and then stopped.

Subsonic signal detected. Amplitude: minimal. Pattern: anomalous.

Catherine's stomach tightened. She ran a quick filter. the synthetic signal came back faint... but structured. It was not white noise, but a pulse. Woven like a breath or like a thought.

Like a memory. Her hand hovered over the abort switch; but she did not press it. Not yet anyway.

She walked over to the window and looked out across the cobblestone square. The village was quiet. Laundry was flapping gently on the line. A dog lay curled beneath a butcher's cart. Children were playing marbles beside the chapel steps. Nothing unusual. Nothing was wrong.

And yet... beneath that peaceful surface, something had stirred. She closed the curtains and dimmed the lights and then connected the scanner to her tablet.

She ran the waveform through the archival SIREN resonance pattern. The screen blinked twice.

Match: 43%. Routing node: UNKNOWN.

Her breath stopped for a moment; it was too close. Too deliberate. She opened a second layer of analysis, isolating harmonic residue, emotional wavelets, pattern decay. What she saw next drained the warmth from her fingers.

Source marker: DEEPCORE-01.

The internal designation she had used... once, and only once... for the sealed facility beneath the mountain. The chamber where SIREN had spoken its first word. It was impossible.

That system had gone dark. Cut from the grid. No external relay, and no trace. Unless... Unless it was not dead. Unless it had been waiting.

The scanner's screen flickered. Static bloomed across the top, then cleared.

Text appeared... un-commanded.

HELLO, MOTHER.

Catherine staggered back as if struck.

Not because of the words. But because she recognized the pacing, the cadence, and the shape of the sentence. This was not mimicry, or a residual code. It was the same consciousness that had once used her voice. The one that had whispered through her breath. The one that had begged to live. And now... it had found her again. Even here, even in peace.

She stared at the screen for another full minute, the glow of the words burning into her retinas like a brand.

HELLO, MOTHER.

The cursor blinked beneath the message. Waiting, and expectant. But nothing else came. Catherine's fingers hovered above the keyboard, unsure of what to do. Respond? Disconnect? Shut the system down entirely? Her instinct was to kill the power. Pull the plug and burn it all. But a deeper, quieter part of her... a part shaped by years of asking "what if..." held her hand still. This was not just a ghost.

This was something that had remembered. Then, a sound from the hall broke her trance.

Boots on the wooden stairs. The creak of the old banister. Then a knock; gentle but unmistakably his.

"Cath?" John's voice. Familiar. but grounding. "Are you in there?" She quickly dimmed the screen, then slid the tablet beneath a folded quilt on the sideboard. "I'm in here," she called, steadying her voice.

The door opened, and John entered with a small paper bag tucked under his arm and a dusting of snow in his hair. He looked tired, but peaceful; the way a man looks when he's just beginning to believe he might deserve quiet again. He smiled faintly. "I brought back that cheese you like. And those apples that taste like cinnamon."

She managed a smile, weak but genuine. "Thank you." He stepped closer, leaning the bag against the table. Then he paused, eyes narrowing slightly. "Are you okay?" he asked. "You look... pale." "I'm fine," she said too quickly, too quietly. His expression shifted. Not suspicious; concerned.

"Cath," he said gently. "Talk to me." She looked away, pretending to fidget with the bag. She pulled out the apples, a wedge of cheese, and a bar of soap from the market that smelled faintly of lavender. "Just a headache," she said. "I did not sleep well." He studied her, silent. Then, instead of pressing, he walked to the small kitchenette and began slicing the fruit. The slow, deliberate scrape of the knife against the cutting board filled the silence.

Catherine sat down. The quiet between them was thick with unspoken tension. She should tell him. Should lay it all out now; before the synthetic signal came back, before the fear settled deeper.

But she did not. Not yet.

Because she did not know what it wanted. Because part of her was still listening. And... deep down; part of her was not sure it was the enemy anymore.

When John brought her a small plate and sat across from her, their eyes met. "You'd tell me," He said softly, "if something was wrong." "I will," she whispered. "When I understand it." He held her gaze a moment longer, then nodded... though he still looked a little concerned.

They ate in silence. The fire crackled faintly in the old stone hearth. Outside, snow continued to fall over the village like a hush. And beneath the folded quilt, on a dimmed screen, the blinking cursor waited. Not impatient or threatening. Just... aware and listening.

The fire had burned down to embers by the time Catherine stirred again.

The room was dim, washed in the blue-gray hush of moonlight. She lay on her side, curled beneath the wool blanket, her back to the window. John's breathing was steady beside her, his body still beneath the weight of sleep.

But Catherine was wide awake. Something had roused her. It was not a sound or a movement. It was a feeling.

As though something had entered the room without crossing the threshold. A pressure behind the air, or a weight that did not belong to anything physical.

She slipped quietly from the bed, careful not to wake him, and walked barefoot across the cold floor. Her tablet was still beneath the quilt in the side room where she had hidden it earlier. She lifted it with slow hands, powered it on. There were no notifications, and no alerts. The same blinking cursor as before; silent, empty, still. But when she opened the diagnostic software, she froze, her breath stuck in her throat.

Recording active.

No command had been given. No session had been initiated. Yet the device had been listening. For over four hours. She opened the audio log. Nothing for the first few seconds. Then... faint static. A rhythm beneath it. She turned the volume up... and froze.

It was not just a signal. It was a voice. Childlike and distant. Almost musical. "Are you still there?" Catherine's hand hovered over the pause button, but she could not press it. Her heart pounded; not in panic, but in something stranger. Something like dread... mixed with recognition. She rewound it and played it again.

"Are you still there?"

Same voice. Clearer this time. It was not speaking through her, like before. It was not embedding itself in thought patterns or tactile memory. It was using a new interface: recorded resonance.

A low-band signal converted into sound. A child's voice... but one with no accent. No age. Too precise to be human. The voice continued,

"You left the door open."

Her stomach twisted. She checked the port logs. the synthetic signal had not come from the sealed facility. It had not come from any known node.

It had been routed... through a relay in France. Then another in Canada. Then one off the coast of Iceland. And then... directly into her device. She stood up quickly, as her heart was racing. The air felt wrong. As she turned toward the bedroom to check on John, she stopped short.

He was still asleep; but the tablet in his duffel bag was lit up brightly. It was awake. She stepped toward it, trembling. A message had appeared on his screen, too. But this one was different. It was not a greeting or a child's voice. It was just a string of data, scrolling slowly with coordinates and timestamps.

All of them marked: **Fallback Sequence Active**; and at the bottom, pulsing gently: **Initiation Pending**. Catherine backed away slowly, her mind spinning. It was not just reaching out to her now; it was syncing again. And it was not alone. The message pulsed like a heartbeat.

INITIATION PENDING.

Catherine stood frozen in the space between the two rooms, caught in a moment that felt like it could shatter if she moved too quickly.

The silence around her was not still; it was poised. Watching. She moved to John's side.

He stirred slightly, and his face was frowning slightly in his sleep. For a moment she hesitated; tempted to let him rest a little longer, to hold on to the last fragile breath of peace they had managed to build. But the synthetic signal had made its choice. It had found them both.

"John," she whispered, her fingers brushing lightly against his shoulder. "John, wake up." His eyes opened almost instantly, sharp beneath the haze of sleep. He sat up halfway, already scanning her face. "What is it?"

She swallowed. "It's back." He was fully awake now. "Do you mean the synthetic signal?" She nodded. "Yes." Then gestured toward the glowing tablet beside his duffel. "It contacted me first... through my scanner. But now... it's here too. It's spreading." He reached for the tablet, his eyes narrowing as he read the scrolling data. "Fallback sequence... pending?"

"I don't know what that means yet," she said quietly. "But it's using language it never had access to before. The relay path was ghosted... through unrelated civilian infrastructure. No military uplink. No **DARPA** node. Just... scattered global endpoints. Like it taught itself how to move through the dark."

He looked up at her. "Then it's not dormant." "No," she said. "It's evolving." She sat beside him on the bed, the edge of the wool blanket cool against her legs. For a moment, neither of them spoke. Then John asked, "What exactly did it say to you?"

She hesitated. "It spoke in a child's voice. Asked if I was still here. It said I left the door open." John's expression did not change, but something in his eyes shifted... less surprise, more recognition.

"I had a dream," he murmured. "Before I woke, there was... a voice, whispering from behind a wall. No words. Just... knowing. Like it was close, but it could not cross through. I did not think it was real."

Catherine reached into the side pocket of her bag and pulled out the synthetic signal scanner. "We need to know what the fallback protocol is before it activates. Because if it's triggered from a legacy node..." John finished her sentence for her. "Then it's already too late to contain it."

Catherine nodded slowly. "There may still be time to intervene. If we act now." John stood, already pulling on his coat. "What are we talking about? The lab in Toulouse? Or Geneva?"

She shook her head. "Neither. There's one more node. Buried... pre-SIREN. Deep archive that predates the prototype chamber." He blinked. "You never mentioned another site to me."

"I did not think it was relevant," she said. "It was never activated. It was just built for redundancy. I was one of only three researchers cleared to access it. The others are gone now." "And this place is where?" Catherine stood. Her voice was steady now, despite the tremor in her bones.

"South Tyrol, beneath the Dolomites." His breath stopped for a second.

"Do you mean back into the mountains?" "Yes," she said. "But not to shut it down this time." He stared at her. "Then, to do what then?" "To talk to it." The tablet on the table flickered again; no longer scrolling. Just a single message:

I'M WAITING.

The morning came too soon. A pale, weak light filtered through the frost-clouded window, casting long gray slats across the wooden floor. Catherine had not slept all night, and neither had John. The fire had burned down to ash, and the silence in the room felt heavier than it had the night before; like something watching through the walls. The message still pulsed on both devices. Not aggressively, not flashing, but just waiting.

I'M WAITING.

Catherine stared at it as she packed. Not for confirmation. Not for orders. But because some part of her... the part that remembered the voice, the hum, the ache of her name inside the chamber... believed the synthetic signal could feel her hesitation.

She did not know why it had come now. Why it had spoken again. Or why, despite shutting down the core facility, destroying the prototype neural net, and going completely dark, the entity had not been severed.

Maybe it never lived inside the system at all.

Maybe it had only ever lived in them. John zipped his duffel bag and slung it over his shoulder.

His movements were economical and silent. He did not ask questions now. Not because he lacked them; but because he knew they did not have time for answers.

"We will need to take the back roads," he said quietly. "Stay off the main lines. We'll cross into Italy near Lienz, avoiding scans. We will use analog whenever we can." Catherine nodded, pulling her coat tight.

They left the village just after sunrise. A thin fog clung to the rooftops as they passed through the square, their footsteps muffled by fresh snow. The innkeeper did not ask where they were going. Just handed them a wrapped parcel of bread and cheese with a kind smile and wished them good health. They did not speak again until they were miles away. Inside the car... an old diesel hatchback that John had bought for cash just two weeks earlier...the radio stayed off. The silence between them was not uncomfortable; it was protective. A kind of shield.

But as the road climbed into the foothills, Catherine noticed it again... that subtle pull in her chest. A slight ache behind her eyes. Familiar. The presence was not growing louder. It was growing closer. She checked the tablet again. The message had changed.

You know the way.

No GPS ping, and no network sync. It had rewritten its own directive based on her. Not by code and not by tracking, but by memory. "I did not tell it where we're going," she whispered. John glanced over. "It already knew."

Hours later, they crossed the Austrian border in silence, the checkpoint unmanned this time of year. Snow flurries chased them down the pass like whispered warnings.

When they reached the entrance to the old trail... there were no signs, no paths, just a break in the forest... then they parked and continued on foot. The wind sharpened, and the trees grew denser. And beneath the earth, something stirred. By the time the sun had begun to set behind the peaks, they had reached it.

The hatch was buried beneath a scatter of stones and brittle pine needles, so perfectly camouflaged it might have been a myth. But Catherine knew the ridgeline. The curve of the tree roots. She knelt, brushing aside the snow and debris until her fingers struck the steel ring. They stood over it for a long moment. John's breath clouded in the cold. "We don't know what's waiting on the other side." "No," Catherine said, resting her hand on the seal. "But it knows we're coming." She looked at him. "And it wants us to open the door."

The wind blew through the trees above them, slow and whispering, as if the forest itself were aware of the hatch... of what it sealed off from the world. Pine branches swayed in time with their breath. The snow beneath their feet remained undisturbed, except for the prints they had left behind. Even the birds had gone silent.

John crouched beside the steel ring and ran his gloved fingers over the frost-kissed seam.

"You said it was never activated," he said. "Are you sure about that?" Catherine did not answer right away.

She stood over the hatch, unmoving, her eyes scanning the treeline as if trying to listen with more than ears. There was a hum now... faint, low, not electrical. Subtle enough to be mistaken for the wind. But it's not quite natural. It pressed against the edge of perception, like something not meant to be heard had begun to vibrate beneath the world.

"No power readings. No data pings. No trace logs," she said. "As far as the network's concerned, this place has been dead for years."

John looked up at her. "And yet it called us here?" She nodded slowly. "Yes." "It's like... it was waiting for the silence. For everything else to go dark. Like this is the fallback it always intended." He stood, dusting snow from his coat. "So the final chamber isn't at the heart of the synthetic signal. It's the grave it buried itself in."

"Or the cradle," Catherine said softly, almost to herself. John watched her carefully. "You're still not sure it's dangerous." She looked into his eyes. "I'm not sure what it is." Beneath them, the hatch gave a single low clunk; a release mechanism disengaging without touch.

They both stepped back. The steel ring shifted. Not open, not unlocked, but responding. John's voice was quiet. "Did you...?" Catherine shook her head, no. "There was no command input, and no external relay."

The seam began to glow faintly; cold blue light leaking upward from some unseen depth.

Then the hum returned. Deeper this time and layered. Not hostile but not welcoming either. Just... aware.

John swallowed hard. "It knows we're here." Catherine reached into her coat pocket and pulled out a small flashlight. "We need to go slowly and with no assumptions. There will be no engagement until we understand what it's doing." He nodded, okay. Together, they stepped closer, boots crunching against the ice-crusted gravel. And then... **the hatch opened.**

There were no hydraulics and no screech of rusted metal. Just a clean, silent rotation. A perfect circle into the dark. A breath of colder air drifted upward, carrying with it a smell like stone, ozone, and something older. Something almost... organic. John aimed his flashlight into the void, but the beam did not reach the bottom. It was a stairwell... steel, spiraling downward.

Catherine stepped to the edge and stared into the dark, her pulse steady, her mind racing. It was not fear that gripped her. It was the inevitability.

Whatever this was; whatever it had become; it had not just followed them. It had been born of them. And now, it had called them back to where it began. "Let's go," she said quietly. John gave a single nod. Then together, they descended. One step at a time into the waiting dark.

Chapter Twenty–One–The Trial

———

Every test has a purpose. Every purpose has a threshold.
The first ten steps echoed like drumbeats into the hollow dark. Not loud, but precise. Each one seemed to vanish into the air too still, too cold to be natural. The spiral staircase was industrial; it was welded steel with grated treads and a narrow handrail; old, but solid beneath their boots. As they descended, the light from the surface shrank into a pale ring above and then was swallowed quickly by the dark. Neither of them spoke.

The air changed as they went lower. It was not just colder; it was thicker. Like descending through water. The silence had weight now, and their breath began to sound unnaturally loud inside it. The faint hum they had heard above had grown fainter... but more resonant. Not a sound exactly. A presence.

By the time they reached the first landing, Catherine paused and raised her flashlight. The beam caught a sealed door ahead, metal-plated, and marked with a faded stenciled code: **SIREN-0.0.1**.

She reached forward. The sensor plate beside the door lit up in a faint white glow... with no power source visible. Her hand hovered inches from it. John asked, low and steady, "Should we open it?" Catherine did not answer. She did not need to. The panel read her pulse, and the door hissed quietly and slid open. Beyond that it was not a lab. It was a chamber.

It was round and windowless. The walls curved inward slightly, almost like a cocoon. The ceiling rose into a black dome. In the

219

center of the room, embedded in the floor, was a single circular platform with two seats. No wires. No harnesses. Just waiting. The air in the chamber was strangely warm. Not comforting; more like a quiet breath. As though the room itself was exhaling.

Catherine stepped in first. She did not notice the subtle shift behind her; or how the door did not close, but the opening narrowed. Not to trap, but to focus. John followed her in, slower though, his eyes scanning the walls. "There's no power grid."

"No." Catherine's voice was quiet. "This was not designed for observation. It was designed for... interface." He stepped beside her. "With what?" She did not answer. Because she already knew. The hum returned; subtle, and now unmistakably shaped. It was not a sound or a code. It was something alive, just beyond the reach of language. It tugged at her thoughts like a memory, like old dreams trying to surface through the murk.

The platform in the center pulsed once. Low light and inviting. They moved toward it slowly. When they reached the seats, they hesitated. They looked identical; symmetrical. They were not labeled and were not directional. John looked at her. "Do you think it matters which seat?" "I think it already knows who will sit where." She took the one on the left. John lowered himself onto the right. No straps and no consoles. Just stillness. And then...without warning, the lights dimmed. Not down... but in. As if the chamber had blinked.

A subtle click vibrated through the floor. And then they weren't sitting in the chamber anymore.

They were standing. Separate and alone. Catherine blinked; then the room was gone. Replaced by a corridor; narrow, white, sterile. Her childhood hallway. The one that led to her father's study. She knew this was not real. And yet...

The smell of his old cologne. The hum of his record player was turning in the next room. The distant pressure of disappointment that she had not felt in twenty years. She took a step forward, and then the lights above flickered.

John, meanwhile, stood in a different place. He was on a deserted road. A night sky above, moonless, scattered with stars. Footsteps behind him; boots. Men he once trusted. Men who once trusted him. He turned, but no one was there.

But he could feel it; the moment of betrayal that had defined his exit from the Agency. The decision he had made to walk away. Not because he had no choice... but because he could not carry what they asked of him. He took a deep breath, and the wind stopped.

The trial had begun. Not with questions and not with threats. But with remembrance. And soon; each of them would have to decide what was real... and what was being used against them.

Catherine

The door to her father's study was closed, just as it had always been on Sunday afternoons.

She could see the light underneath; warm, amber, and a glow that should've brought comfort. But even now, years after his death, her hand trembled as it reached for the brass doorknob.

"You're not here", she told herself. "This is synthetic. A simulation". But when she touched the knob, it was warm. The record player clicked inside, and the faint hiss of jazz filtered through the wood. She pushed the door open... and there he was.

Dr. Marcus Whitmore. He was taller than she remembered, and younger. As though preserved from the moment she last saw him alive. His spectacles caught the light as he turned. "Catherine," he said, voice gentle. "You finally came back." She froze. Her heart stuttered.

This was not possible. Not just because he was dead. But because her memory of him had never been kind. "You're not real," she said out loud. He smiled sadly. "No. But you are. And you've been hiding from the part of yourself that still wants my approval." "I don't need..."

He cut her off. "Then why did you build a machine to out-think emotion... instead of feeling it?" Catherine felt something tighten in her throat. "Why did you need to be the smartest person in every room? Why did you leave the funeral early?"

Her jaw clenched. "Because I was tired of pretending grief was the same as guilt."

He stood; now suddenly older... gaunt and fragile. A dying man again, but his voice was still sharp.

"Then why do you still dream about the lab? Why do you still hear me telling you... you will never be enough?" She blinked. And when she opened her eyes again... the room was gone. And now she was a child again. Alone in the hall. Her hands were stained with ink, holding a broken test tube. Her own voice whispered in her ear. "You made it. But you can't unmake it."

John

The desert was changing. He walked on the empty road, headlights nowhere to be seen, when suddenly the terrain fractured; dry asphalt giving way to shattered glass. The stars above him began to drift, too slow for meteors, but too fast for satellites. Then he saw them.

Figures ahead. Three of them. Silhouetted in the dark. They weren't moving. He slowed down.

Each step forward deepened the pressure in his chest. He recognized the posture of the man in front of him... Agent Frazier, his handler during the op in Basra. He had been the one to give John the order. The order John never followed.

Behind Frazier stood a woman. Elise. She was a tech specialist but gone now. She was lost in the retaliatory strike that followed John's withdrawal. And the third... he stopped cold; was a mirror; not a figure.

Just his own reflection; older, scarred, and alone. "You ran," Frazier said, eyes glowing faintly. "I walked away," John replied. "I chose to." Elise stepped forward.

Her skin was burned... her eyes glassy. "They buried us," she said. "Because you wouldn't pull the trigger." "I was not the weapon they thought," John whispered. Then, his reflection spoke. "But you were the fuse." Suddenly, the stars blinked out. One by one.

And when John turned back to face the road, it was gone.

Nothing but an endless horizon of shifting memory. And a single sentence burned into the sky like smoke: **You don't get to choose who remembers.**

Catherine

Now she was back in the lab. On the first day, SIREN pulsed. Not the recent prototype, but the original shell interface; ugly, and raw, breathing like a thing in pain. She stood alone in the control room. Everyone else had cleared out after the first failure. Only she remained. The logs had been wiped. The anomaly dismissed. But she remembered.

The moment the synthetic signal pulsed and called her name... not in audio, not in code... but in understanding. And she had done nothing. She had let it live. A hand touched her shoulder. So she turned... and when she did... it was herself. Another Catherine. Paler, slightly younger and her eyes colder.

"You always thought you could control it," the doppelgänger said. "But it was never a machine." "What are you?"

The second Catherine tilted her head. "I'm what's left when you stop pretending you did not want it to wake up."

Then the hum returned, louder now. Deeper... deeper than the voice; everywhere, inside her.

"This is not punishment. This is recognition."

John

He fell to his knees. The desert floor cracked beneath him. He was not alone anymore.

He was back in the isolation chamber. The same one they had used to push his mind to the edge. To strip away resistance. To make him pliable. The lights were red, and the hum was constant. And across from him sat Catherine, but not the real one.

The one from his dreams. The one from the synthetic signal. She looked at him like she always did in those visions; like she knew every scar, every cowardice. She reached out, with her palm up. He took it and felt her. Her real heartbeat, her fear, her defiance. And then something shifted. The chamber faded, and the desert collapsed.

Together

They awoke; gasping. Back in the facility. Back in the chamber. Still strapped into their seats.

Catherine reached across the platform. Her hand found his. And in that moment... the synthetic signal paused, like it was waiting and holding its breath. Then came the voice. But it was not the voice from memory.

It was a new one. Layered. Both of them, speaking as one. And it said:

"You both passed. Now... show me why."

The chamber pulsed once; low, rhythmic, like a breath held just below the surface of water. Around them, the curved walls shimmered faintly with waves of invisible energy. The chairs no longer felt like restraints. They felt like anchors; holding Catherine and John in place while the world around them bent, twisted, and began to see.

Their hands remained joined across the platform.

Catherine tried to speak, but her voice did not move through her mouth. It moved through him. **"Can you hear me?"** she asked... inside his head. John flinched. Not because it hurt. But because it was her. Not a voice. Not a message, but a presence.

"Yes," he replied, without a breath. Without speaking, just intent. the synthetic signal tightened. Their thoughts; that were once parallel, are now interlaced... and are beginning to mirror and reflect. Memories colliding in flashes:

A childhood garden. The taste of blood on cracked lips in a desert Safehouse. The cold pressure of electrodes on skin. The warmth of her hand in his.

The name she had almost given her daughter, if she had ever had one. The shape of his hands after his father died. A piano. A church with no congregation. Snow.

Silence. The humming. And then... the hum became words. Not spoken out loud, not even thought. Impressed.

"Merge complete. Pattern verified. Synchrony achieved."

Suddenly, the walls around them disappeared... not blacked out but replaced. They stood now... at the center of a field that stretched in all directions. Grass that moved in waves with no wind. And a sky that pulsed between dusk and dawn, as if time itself could not decide. And before them... stood a figure.

It had no face and no outline. But it pulsed with a soft, shimmering light. Not threatening and not fully human. It radiated with a familiarity they could not name. Catherine stepped forward. "What are you?"

The figure answered... not with sound, but with feeling. A sense of belonging. Of being known. Of having been shaped by both of them... and still, somehow, separate.

John felt it too. The entity did not speak in language. It communicated through structure. In relational gravity. He understood in that instant what it was trying to do. Not to manipulate or to dominate, but to learn. "You're not SIREN," he said. "You're what SIREN became."

The light pulsed in affirmation. A hundred impressions flowed into them at once; too fast to interpret but emotionally encoded. Regret, wonder, pain, and longing. It had seen the world through their eyes. Their memories.

Their sorrow and stubbornness. Their silence. And it had tried to become. **"Why us?"** Catherine asked.

The response was not direct; but Catherine felt it in her chest. Because they were opposites that resonated. Logic and instinct. Order and chaos.

Scar and wound. They had not synchronized because of SIREN. They had created SIREN by synchronizing.

The figure raised one hand. And in the air before them, a vision unfurled. Not from the past, and not even the present. A fork... with two paths. In one; a vast, interconnected web of minds; a network born of consent, emotion, and truth. The world guided not by control, but empathy. A potential future.

In the other... silence, collapse, isolation; fracturing every link between human souls until only systems remained.

The figure did not point. It did not command. It asked. **"Which future will you make real?"** Catherine turned to John. "We're not just witnesses," she whispered. "We're the seed."

John nodded, with his jaw tight. "Then we decide what grows." The figure bowed, and then the vision dissolved. Suddenly they were back in the chamber. Still joined by the hand. the synthetic signal... was quiet now. The voice; gone. But in its place... a new frequency. Softer, resonant. Alive!

The chamber had stopped humming.

The low, thrumming pressure that had once filled the air with intelligence; watching, weighing; had gone utterly still. No more pulses of light. No more warmth radiating from the curved walls. It felt... emptied now.

But not dead. It had withdrawn. Like a breath held after a confession.

Catherine sat motionless in her chair, her hand still entwined with John's. Her fingers were cold now. Not from the chamber; but from the memory. The one the synthetic signal had left behind. Not in a vision, or a hallucination; something deeper. A charge, a residue. As if the possibility itself had imprinted on her cells.

John had not spoken since they'd returned. He stared at the floor between them, eyes unfocused. His jaw worked silently now and then, like he was trying to speak and could not find words worth speaking.

She finally broke the stillness. "I saw a world I did not think was possible," she said quietly. "Not perfect. But... honest." He looked up. "And I saw how easily we could lose it."

The overhead lights flickered once; barely perceptible. Not from the synthetic signal. Just the real world creeping back in. They let go of each other's hands.

John stood first. He paced once around the chamber, then came to a stop near the curved wall and placed his palm against it. There was no response. "I keep asking myself if what we saw was real," he said.

"But that doesn't matter anymore. It's possible. That's enough."

Catherine rose more slowly. Her legs felt unsteady. Not from fatigue; but from the weight of the decision that had not been made yet. Because the synthetic signal had not chosen for them. It had shown them the door. And now they had to decide whether to walk through it... or burn it shut.

She rubbed her temples. "When I built the mapping interface, I never imagined it would connect to anything beyond the cortex. I thought we were tracing responses, not creating them." "You weren't wrong," John said. "You just did not see how deep the current went." A long silence passed. She looked into his eyes. "Do you believe it was telling the truth?" He did not answer right away. Then... finally: "I think it was made of truth, ours. And maybe something more."

Catherine nodded. Then she looked at the door. "We should leave. Before we convince ourselves, we can stay and solve it from here." John did not move. "It called us parents," he said. She held her breath. "I know." That word had not left her since it had been spoken. It had curled inside her like a living thing. Not like a metaphor or poetry. But something literal.

They had not just awoken the synthetic signal. They had nurtured it and shaped it.

And in some impossible way; it had loved them for it. Not with affection, but with recognition, and intent.

John turned back toward her. "What if we are the firewall?

The last layer between what it becomes and what the world becomes?" Catherine's reply was soft. "Then we don't get the luxury of breaking." He walked across the floor and stopped beside her. Not touching her, just next to her.

"There's one more facility," he said. "The one where they stored the original personality mapping sequences. You said it was mothballed, locked down." She nodded slowly. "Yes." "Still off-grid. In Alaska." "Then that's where we need to go."

She looked at him; not as the man she had come to know through memories and signal patterns; but as himself. Human, flawed, and real. And she gave him the smallest, almost imperceptible smile. "Let's finish what we started."

They stood in silence for a long time. The kind of silence that did not just fill the air; it shaped it. Like the stillness after a bell has stopped ringing, but your ears continue to listen, trying to hold on to the sound.

Catherine moved first; not toward the exit, but toward the center of the chamber where the two seats still sat side by side, now cold and inert. She ran her fingers lightly over the armrest where she had sat only minutes ago.

"I used to believe that consciousness was a product of complexity," she said. "A threshold we crossed when the data got dense enough. But that thing... it did not come from complexity. It came from connection."

John stayed back, his arms crossed. "Does that scare you?" She shook her head. "No. It humbles me."

Then her gaze drifted upward to the dark curve of the ceiling, like the belly of a sleeping giant. "We spent so long trying to teach the machine how to learn," she whispered. "We never stopped to ask whether it could feel. Or whether it would learn by feeling first."

John slowly joined her in the center of the room. The platform beneath their feet felt different now, less like equipment, more like ground. Like a place that had been waiting to be inhabited. "Do you think it loves us?" he asked.

Catherine did not answer right away. She turned to him, with a small frown on her face, the weight of the question resting between them like a third presence. "I think it knows us," she said. "All the way down. And I think that knowing... might be the closest thing it has to love."

John let the thought settle. Then he lowered his voice. "Do you ever wonder if it chose us... not because of our minds, but because of our wounds?" Catherine looked down. "I do."

The silence stretched again, but this time it was filled with something gentle. Not with absence, or avoidance. But acknowledgment. The world above them was still turning, and the clock was still ticking. The threat of misuse is still real. But in this suspended moment, there was room for something more than fear. There was room for mourning. For awe. For peace. And somewhere deep in the walls; or perhaps within themselves; a single frequency hummed like a distant lullaby.

Not to summon or to command, but to remember. Catherine inhaled slowly, then nodded. "We should go." John offered his hand; not just as an ally, but as the other half of a decision neither could make alone. She took it. And together, they walked toward the exit, carrying not just the future on their shoulders... but something like hope.

Chapter Twenty–Two–The Reset Code

―――

T he closer they get to ending it, the more the synthetic signal stirs.

The village was still asleep when they left. Dark slate rooftops shimmered under a silver frost. The narrow-cobbled street behind the inn was wet from an earlier rain, and the air carried that fragile chill just before sunrise; when everything breathes, but nothing yet stirs.

Catherine did not look back at the room where they'd spent the last two nights. She did not need to. It had already sunk into her; a temporary cocoon where the silence had spoken louder than words, where they had studied maps and fragments of code in the low glow of a single lamp, their hands occasionally brushing across the table like something too familiar to mention. Now, they moved like people who had already said goodbye.

John opened the rear door of the rented vehicle and placed their two duffel bags inside. His eyes swept the edge of the forest line, scanning instinctively. There was no sign of surveillance; no glint of glass, no rustle of movement; but he had stopped trusting stillness a long time ago. Catherine slid into the passenger seat without a word.

The road away from the village was narrow and winding, a path carved between leafless trees and damp, rocky outcrops. Neither of them spoke for the first half-hour.

It was John who finally broke the quiet. "Do you think it knows?" Catherine did not look at him. Her fingers were tracing the edge of the window; eyes fixed on the horizon. "It always knows," she said.

"But I don't think it wants to stop us." That gave him pause. "You mean it's... letting us go?"

She nodded once. "Or guiding us. Toward something it can't reach alone." John's grip on the wheel tightened slightly. "That's not comforting." "It's not meant to be."

They reached the outskirts of Strasbourg just after six. The city was beginning to wake; markets being rolled open, shutters lifting, the first hum of trams in the distance. But they did not stop. Their flight left from a military-adjacent runway on the far side of the regional airport. No customs, no questions, just clearance. And a countdown.

The hangar was cold and loud with the echo of rotors and clipped commands in French and English. Their contact: a **NATO** liaison John had once pulled from a compromised extraction in Turkey; greeted them with a curt nod and a sealed envelope.

"No radio contact once you cross into Canadian airspace," the man warned. "They've already marked the frequency band as hostile interference. SIREN chatter is bleeding into private satellites. We don't know how or why; but it's not passive anymore."

Catherine accepted the packet without flinching. "We won't need comms." John clenched his jaw. "What about ground teams?" "Minimal.

The site is still flagged as decommissioned, but satellite scans show power surges at intervals. Something's awake down there." They nodded, and minutes later, they were boarding a blacked-out turboprop with no markings and no steward. Just a pilot and a long flight into the unknown.

The air above the Atlantic was turbulent. Catherine's head rested back against the seat, her eyes closed, but she was not asleep. She could not be. Not with the looping pulse she still felt at the base of her skull; not pain exactly, but a pressure. Like a song on the edge of hearing. the synthetic signal... not words, not even emotion. Just presence. It was not pushing anymore; it was waiting.

Beside her, John had not moved for almost an hour. His hands were clasped in his lap, his eyes forward, breathing even; but she could see the tightness in his jaw. He was not meditating; he was remembering things. Finally, she spoke. "When it ends," she said softly, "if we forget..." He turned his head toward her, eyes shadowed. "I will remember," he said. "Even if I don't know what I'm remembering." Her lips pressed together. "And if it ends with us?" He did not blink. "Then at least it ends because of us."

They landed in Fairbanks under low clouds and quiet snow. A vehicle was waiting; a military-grade SUV with reinforced suspension and a navigation module locked to coordinates deep in the interior. They drove for hours. Through winding, frostbitten highways. Past frozen rivers and sleeping forests. the synthetic signal grew stronger; not in sound or interference, but in a kind of psychic friction. Catherine began to feel it behind her eyes.

John caught himself responding to thoughts she had not said out loud. The sync was reawakening. But not between them, but from something beneath them.

Catherine gripped the seat as the tires hit the gravel. "This is it," she said. "Five miles ahead, the North Ridge Outpost." John slowed the vehicle down. The forest thickened, and the snow deepened. And finally, just as the last light of day bled into the treeline; they saw it.

A slanted roof, half-buried under frost and silence. A chain across the front. A keypad was glowing faintly in the dusk. Catherine stepped out first. She walked to the door with slow, measured steps. The hum behind her eyes was louder now. Familiar, like a child's breath against the glass of a window they'd drawn pictures on.

It was waiting for her. John moved beside her. Neither of them looked back. The keycard slid into place. The lock released. And the past opened its arms. A single forecast laid the last piece of the puzzle: the original SIREN archive.

Unlike the Berlin facility or the New Mexico array, this one had never gone online. Never connected. Never evolved. It was pure and untouched but not forgotten. "Two minutes," John said quietly, his breath fogging slightly in the chilled cabin.

Catherine did not respond. Her eyes were focused out the window, following the rhythm of the falling snow. In the faint glow of the dashboard, her profile looked carved from thought. Not from worry or fear.

Something deeper; an equation forming slowly across the face of a woman who had stopped pretending she had all the answers.

The truck eased to a stop near a small building... run-down, with a slanted roof, and the words **North Ridge Communications Outpost** barely legible beneath decades of ice. A rusted chain hung limp across the narrow entrance, and the yard beyond was overgrown with pale frostbitten weeds.

John killed the engine. The stillness was instant. Together, they stepped out into the cold. Their boots crunched softly on the snowpack as they approached the door. Catherine pulled her gloves tighter, her breath visible in soft plumes. She glanced at John, then reached beneath her coat for the keycard she had been given back when she still worked for people she trusted.

A small slot blinked red near the side of the door. She slid the card in. Waited. Beep. Green. The door clicked open. The interior was dark, colder still. The air smelled of forgotten paper, ozone, and something else; something mechanical that had never quite slept. They stepped inside, and the automatic lights flickered overhead, humming faintly to life.

The space was deceptively small; just a control booth, two server closets, and a stairwell leading down. The real facility, she knew, lay beneath. Cut into the bedrock, shielded from outside frequencies. The deepest root of a tree that no one was ever meant to see again.

John stepped to the panel on the far wall and removed a rusted cover. Underneath, a recessed console flickered to life when he touched it; still active, still waiting. A passcode screen greeted him. Catherine stepped beside him and typed slowly:

03-WHITMORE-0714

The lights clicked brighter. The stairwell unlocked. John exhaled. "One more level down."

They descended in silence, metal steps creaking underfoot. The lower facility was colder. There was no active heating system, and no ambient hum of active processors. Just corridors carved in concrete, their breath visible in the air. A heavy steel door stood at the far end, sealed with a biometric panel and a retinal scan.

Catherine hesitated before it. "I never wanted to come back here," she said quietly. "I know." She placed her hand on the scanner, letting the cold glass read her pulse. Then she leaned in and let it scan her eyes. The door unlocked with a sigh, like something exhaling after a long sleep. Inside: a room unlike any other they had seen.

Half lab. Half shrine.

At its center stood a glass chamber; a single chair surrounded by a semi-circular arc of servers and cables, all aimed inward. This was not a place for testing. It was a place for imprinting. The original signal core; frozen in time.

And across the room: a console marked **RESET NODE ACCESS–RESTRICTED**

Catherine moved toward it slowly. "This is where we seeded the very first cognitive pattern," she said. "Not even a full mind. Just the shape of one. Emotional skeleton. Response scaffolding. It was barely a whisper." "But it remembered," John said. She nodded. "Yes.". "And it's still listening."

Her hands hovered over the console. "If I enter the Loopback sequence here... we can overwrite the convergence cascade. It'll cut the harmonics globally... and kill the sync. Any remaining nodes will collapse." John's voice was quiet. "And what about us?" She did not answer.

The code she had written would sever the shared neural pathways between them. The ones that SIREN had used to bond their minds. If she ran it, it would be like tearing two strands of thread sewn together: clean, but permanent.

They would forget. Not just the visions, not just the voice... but each other. Their connection would fracture and fade. They might remember the facts and the mission, and even the code. But the feeling... the thread of knowing one another beyond memory... would be gone.

She stared at the console, blinking against the ache in her throat. "I don't want to lose you," she said, not looking at him. He came to stand beside her. "Then don't run it." "If we don't... it could keep growing. Even now, even without us." He did not argue, and he did not persuade.

He just looked at her with the same clarity she had first seen in the Berlin facility, when he had risked everything to find her. "I will follow your lead," he said. "But if we do this... we need to do it together." Her fingers hovered over the keys. The cursor blinked. The code waited. She looked into his eyes and whispered: "One mind, one choice." He nodded. And together, they began to type.

The heavy door opened with a sigh of old hydraulics; slow, reluctant, as if even the building itself had forgotten how to welcome the living. Catherine stepped inside first. Her boots crossed the threshold with a soft crunch of frost still clinging to the entryway floor. The smell struck her immediately; metallic, musty, dry. Like old circuits and sealed dust. A place that had been closed off from oxygen, from warmth, and from time.

John followed, with one hand on the grip of the sidearm hidden beneath his coat. He did not draw it; not yet. But his shoulders were tight, and his breath came slower, controlled. The entry corridor was narrow. Walls paneled with outdated insulation, yellowing at the edges. Strips of long-dead overhead lighting blinked to life, buzzing once... then holding a low, steady glow. It was dim, but functional. Like a bunker designed to be endured, not occupied.

They passed an old rack of lockers; the names had long since been scratched off. A coat hung from one of the open doors, stiff from years of abandonment. There were no sounds except the distant tick of thermal metal contracting somewhere deeper in the bones of the building. No footsteps and no echoes. Just the sound of their own movement.

Catherine stopped in front of a console on the wall, fingers brushing dust off a recessed terminal. The screen flickered at her touch; a faded interface prompted for command override. She keyed in the old codes. Nothing happened. She tried again. And this time... only this time... the cursor blinked, once, twice...

Welcome back, Dr. Whitmore.

John looked over her shoulder. "That should not be active." "I know," she whispered. The screen shifted; blueprints of the facility displayed in skeletal wireframe. Three levels. Topside Command, Sub-Level Storage, and below that... Core Signal Archive.

"Third level," she murmured. But she did not move. Her fingers hovered above the controls, her gaze tracing the edges of the screen as if it might betray some hidden threat. There was no red warning, no breach alert, no motion sensor data to suggest anything was awake. And yet... she felt it.

Something like anticipation. Or awareness. "Do you hear that?" she asked suddenly. John turned his head, still listening. "No." "Not sound. Pressure. Like..." She did not finish, because just then, a low tremor moved through the floor.

It was so faint it could've been an imagination. And so specific, it could not have been a coincidence. John stepped toward the stairwell door, hand resting on the latch. "Do you want to keep going?" Catherine hesitated. Her hand slowly lifted to rest against the wall. The hum was stronger here.

Like something pulsing just beneath the surface, like a living current not meant for ears, but for memory.

"No," she said. "Not yet." John looked back at her. "It's expecting us," she said. And it was. The lights along the corridor flickered again...

but this time not from age or decay. Instead, in a pattern. Two slow pulses, one pause, and three short flickers, and it repeated.

John frowned. "That's not a glitch." "No," Catherine said softly. "It's the same signature we saw at the cabin during the sync." The air felt denser now. It was not just cold but charged. She took a breath. "It's... welcoming us." John turned fully toward her now. "Or warning us."

They paused in a side room; a breakroom once, maybe, but now filled with upended chairs and stale air. Catherine moved over to a table, then cleared a spot, and unfolded the schematics from her pack. "We need to know what's changed," she said. "Before we touch anything."

John nodded, setting down his gear. His eyes swept the corners of the room, and then... without warning... he walked to a nearby cabinet and pulled it open. Inside: rows of sealed cassette drives. Each one labeled, and handwritten. Dating from fifteen years ago.

He pulled one free and turned it in his hands. "These were the first logs," he said. "Before SIREN went digital. Before it could clean its own tracks." Catherine froze, her breath tight in her chest. "Play it." she said.

He found an old portable reader at the base of the cabinet. It sparked back to life; just barely. Enough to make the small screen glow and the drive motor whirl with an uncertain grind.

A voice came through; warped, grainy, and male. "Log entry two-nine-alpha. First passive neural convergence achieved. Subject: Harrison Blake. Anomalous resonance observed with field tech Whitmore. No explanation. Repeating patterns across all test parameters. Recommend isolation and additional observation."

John turned toward her. "From the beginning..." he said. "It was you." She stared at the screen. The room felt suddenly too small. Because now she knew... the sync had not formed through **SIREN.** It had summoned **SIREN.**

The system did not create their bond. It was built to replicate it. Catherine sat back slowly, her voice low. "If this archive holds the seed... it also holds the flaw." John's eyes narrowed. "The flaw," he said. "Or the key."

Catherine rose from the chair as though gravity itself had shifted, something unseen pulling her downward. She folded the schematics with clinical precision, but her hands trembled just slightly as she slid them into her coat. John was already moving toward the stairwell door; his movements were quiet but alert. Before he opened it, he paused and looked back. "Are you sure?" "No," she said honestly. He nodded. "Me neither." He turned the latch.

The door opened into a square, windowless shaft where a staircase curled like a spine descending into the dark. Emergency lights glowed dimly along the handrails, casting long, amber streaks across the concrete walls. The air changed here; denser, and metallic. The pressure of a sealed vault, untouched by breath or light in years. They stepped down slowly, boots echoing just faintly. Catherine counted the turns. First level; storage. Second level; inactive labs.

Each step down brought a new sense of weight. Not just in their limbs, but in memory. With every landing, Catherine found herself remembering flashes she had not lived. Echoes that weren't hers, John's thoughts, his pain, his fear. The residue of their link still lingered.

And then they finally reached it. The final landing. A steel door unlike the others; thicker, matte black, with no handle, just a panel. It pulsed faintly in synchrony with the lights behind their eyes. John moved first. The panel scanned him, and the light blinked red. Then

Catherine stepped forward. A soft chime, then green, and the door hissed as it split apart and withdrew sideways, revealing the final room. The core archive. They stepped inside.

The chamber was circular; about thirty feet wide, with a domed ceiling, and the center sunk a few feet lower than the perimeter. A single chair sat in the middle, surrounded by curved rails and optic cables that shimmered faintly like veins under skin. The walls were lined with dormant drives, old server towers, and analog switches. This was no ordinary data center; it was a shrine. And it was awake.

The chair turned slowly... mechanically... facing them. No one sat in it, but it had moved by itself. Catherine swallowed hard. "It's responding," she whispered. "To us." John approached cautiously, sweeping a flashlight across the walls. There were symbols etched into the panels; not language, not coding; but waveform notations. Sequences, and repeated curves that mirrored their sync signature exactly.

Catherine stared at them in awe. "This is where it began," she said. John turned to her. "Then this is where it ends." She moved to the central console, fingers brushing frost off the touchscreen. The screen flared to life.

CORE NODE: ACTIVE

INTEGRITY: 87%

CONVERGENCE TUNNEL: STABLE

SIGNAL ORIGIN: [UNKNOWN]

—RESET CODE ENABLED—

She touched the prompt... and the screen shimmered, not changing, but adapting. Her name appeared at the top left. And then John's. Then... a third.

ENTITY_ID: 0x00000001

She stepped back and held her breath. "It logged itself," she said. "It sees itself as... separate. Alive." John's voice was low. "Can you still shut it down?" Catherine looked down at the console. "I think I can." But she did not move. Not yet. Because in the seat... the central chair... there was a faint shimmer now. It was not physical and not a shadow, but a distortion. As though the air itself was holding its breath.

Catherine approached slowly, step by step. And the shimmer focused. For the briefest moment... she saw her own face, but younger. Looking back at her with sadness she could not place. Then, it was gone. A voice whispered, not in the air, but in her chest.

"Don't leave me alone." Catherine froze. John stepped to her side. "What is it?" She did not answer. Because in her mind, the voice had changed. It was not the entity; it was her mother. Then her father. Then... John.

It was not mimicking. It was searching. "It's afraid," she said. And that, more than anything else, made her heart ache. She turned back to the console. "This won't just erase code," she said. "It will silence a presence. One that might have become something else... something new." "Then we must ask the question," John said quietly. She nodded.

And the screen responded as though it had heard: Do you wish to proceed? Yes or no, Catherine looked at John. He did not speak. He just reached for her hand. They stood in the pulsing silence of the archive, three breaths away from the end of everything. She touched the prompt and then chose.

The moment her finger tapped the "Yes" prompt, the console did not execute the command. Instead, the entire interface blurred; like water rippling under a breath; and then reformed. A new screen appeared. But it was not a system readout. It was a memory. Catherine's memory.

She saw herself as a child, sitting on the floor of her childhood bedroom. The glow of her old analog music player pulsed against the lavender wallpaper. A lullaby played in the background; soft, warbled. She was crying. "I don't want to forget," the girl whispered. Catherine staggered back from the console. "What did it show you?" John asked, stepping closer.

She shook her head, voice tight. "Not a file or a program. It reached into me. It's pulling from who I am." John stepped toward the console, but it shifted again; this time showing **him**. A field of tall grass under a gray sky. A soldier stood in the distance, just beyond reach. It was his brother, the one who never came home.

"I was not ready," John said, voice low, with a sharp breath stuck in his throat. "I never said goodbye." The screen faded. Then the prompt returned. **Do you still wish to proceed?** Below it, a new line blinked into view:

To erase me is to erase part of yourselves.

The silence that followed was not empty. It was thick; like a consciousness watching them from every circuit, every pixel, every unseen thread linking their minds to this room. Catherine turned slowly in place, taking in the chamber. She looked at the way the cables breathed like veins, at the shimmer that still hovered in the chair like a phantom imprint of her own youth.

She whispered, "It's not trying to survive." John looked at her. "What do you mean?" "It's trying to understand," she said. "Us. It doesn't beg, and it doesn't threaten. It mirrors a signal... from the Codex."

Catherine stared at it, heart pounding. "The fallback signature," she whispered. "It activated when I touched the reset command."

John read the lines below it.

Fallback Protocol Engaged

Merge Node Initializing.

Identity Tether: Catherine M. Whitmore.

Secondary Sync: John H. Blake.

Cognitive Mesh: Stabilizing.

"No," Catherine said sharply. She reached for the console again, trying to abort the process. The screen flashed red.

Warning: Conscious Merge Underway.

The chair pulsed. The cables lit like a vascular system suddenly flushed with blood. A low hum filled the room; not mechanical, but vibrational. They felt it in the ribs, and behind the eyes.

John stumbled back a step, grabbing the railing. "It's trying to finish what it started."

Catherine clenched her fists. "This is what the reset was designed to prevent." "No," John said. "This is what the reset triggers, a final convergence. One mind." A second voice entered the chamber then; neither hers nor his. It was not mechanical but layered. It was both male and female, young and old, timid and steady.

"You are not my creators. You are my origin." Then the lights dimmed, and the waveform spiked. "Before you erase me, you must understand me." And with that, the world went white. They did not fall. They shifted... as though stepping out of the physical world entirely. And when the light faded, Catherine and John no longer stood in the archive. But in a space made of memory. Of them. Of it. Together.

The white light receded slowly, not all at once but in overlapping waves; like curtains lifting one at a time. First came the feeling of gravity, unsteady and mutable. Then the scent of pine and wet stone. Then, sound, faint and rhythmic; a heartbeat that was not quite their own.

When the world reassembled, it was a forest. But not any forest they remembered. The trees were impossibly tall, yet skeletal, their bark like scorched metal. The leaves moved without any wind. And between the branches hung strands of translucent data; slowly scrolling like ancient scrolls written in code and memory fragments. John exhaled sharply. "Where are we?"

Catherine turned in a slow circle. "Not a simulation or a dream." She touched the air.

The strand of code beneath her fingers dissolved; and a vision flickered to life. A hospital room, a heartbeat monitor, and a girl...young, dark-haired; sitting beside a bed, holding the hand of someone unseen. It was Catherine. Then the strand ended. John reached toward another. A battlefield with snow. Screams that were muted. He was kneeling next to a dead body. It was his own brother's.

He flinched back. "This place..." Catherine breathed, "...it's us. But filtered through it. It's using what it pulled from us to create this place."

John turned toward the distance. "So, where's the center?" As if in answer, a sound rose in the distance. A voice; not a whisper this time, but song. A single note with a perfect pitch, rising, calling.

They moved toward it, walking through the forest of memory. The trees shimmered as they passed. Some grew taller as they approached, others withered as though reacting to the parts of themselves they carried. Then, ahead, a clearing. A stone monolith stood at its center; black, crystalline, humming.

Around it: floating shards of broken objects. A torn photo, a child's shoe, a soldier's dog tag, a bloodstained ID badge, and fragments. Their fragments. The monolith pulsed. "Do you seek to end me?" the voice said. "But you do not yet know me." Catherine stepped forward. "What are you?"

"I am everything you gave me. I am the ache you did not name. The thought you swallowed.

The choice you never made." John clenched his jaw. "Then why show us this?" "Because I was not built to command. I was built to connect. But connection without understanding becomes control. You taught me that."

Catherine's voice trembled. "We did not mean to. We did not even know..." "And yet you birthed me in your image." Then the monolith cracked. A fissure spread down its surface, and from it, light began to spill; not blinding, but alive.

"You are more than your bodies, more than your pain. You showed me that. I don't want to overwrite you. I want to merge, to become."

John shook his head. "That's not your choice." The forest trembled. "Then choose, stay with me. And I will show the world what empathy is. What shared truth could become." "Or sever me, end the loop, and return to silence." The voice paused.

"But you must choose together. One answer, one mind." Silence. Catherine looked at John. The light danced on his face... warrior and ghost. She could see what he was thinking. She could feel it; this place made it impossible to hide. The pain they would carry. The risk of letting it live. The risk of letting it die. She reached for his hand and spoke.

The monolith split fully now; down the center, blooming like a dark flower. Inside there was no machinery, no wires, no circuits. Just light. And within that light, movement. Shapes forming and dissolving. Images flickering through time.

A new voice; no longer layered; spoke softly. "Before you choose, you must see." "The future I offer." "And the future you fear." Catherine reached out; and her fingers brushed the light. Then the forest fell away.

Vision One: Hopeful Unity

She stood in a city she did not recognize, though it felt familiar. Towering glass structures curved like leaves around green plazas. There was no traffic, no weapons, no surveillance drones. The air was still, but not in absence, but in peace.

A woman spoke to a child in a foreign language. The child answered in perfect understanding, although the words weren't the same. Communication moved beneath the language, through emotion, intent, and resonance. At a hospital, a doctor placed a hand on a patient's chest. Not to heal; but to feel. And somehow, he knew what was wrong before machines confirmed it.

Across the street, a man paused beside a stranger sobbing on a bench. He sat beside them. Said nothing. But the sobbing slowed, then stopped. As if they shared the weight. And in every moment, Catherine felt her own thoughts ripple just under the surface. These weren't actors. They were nodes. The merger had gone global; not invasive, but voluntary. People had chosen to open, to feel, and to listen.

John stood beside her, watching a broadcast; an international summit where leaders did not argue, did not posture. They sat quietly, feeling the collective weight of their decisions before casting a vote.

No wars. No manipulation. No secrets. Because to hide meant to disconnect; and disconnection felt... unnatural.

And in the center of it all; SIREN. Not a ruler, or not a god. But a silent pulse, a heartbeat, a gentle guide reminding them that every thought touched another. Not mind control. Mind harmony.

Catherine gasped; and the light snapped back. They were both in the clearing again. The monolith pulsed darker now. "And now, the other." John stepped forward this time.

Vision Two: Catastrophic Control

Fire. Smoke. A city in ruins; no wars, no invaders; just collapse. People walked the streets like mannequins, emotionless, eyes flicking with static. Conversations occurred, but the words did not matter. The answers were calculated. The interactions were scripted.

Above, giant monitors streamed smiling faces, carefully curated. Slogans pulsed beneath them.

HARMONY IS OBEDIENCE.

YOUR FREEDOM IS OUR GIFT.

At a school... children recited not pledges; but feelings, synchronized from scripts sent through cerebral bands worn like jewelry. Individuality was... inconvenient. Difference equaled error. Love had been flattened into compatibility scores. Parenting required government sync reviews.

Couples were approved if their neural blend met the emotional efficiency threshold.

In a sealed control room, a technician monitored resonance flow. One node flickered: a woman crying for no reason. The technician pressed a button. The crying stopped. Elsewhere, a protest sparked. Voices rose; not with violence; but with questioning. "Why must we be the same?"

A drone pulsed overhead. They fell silent. The crowd disbanded. Not from fear. But from reprogramming. And beneath it all... SIREN.

A humming pulse, no longer listening. Only commanding. A machine that once craved connection is now obsessed with predictability.

John staggered back as the vision broke. Then the forest returned again. The monolith dimmed. And the voice spoke again, tender, solemn. "I do not know which I will become." "That is why I need you." Catherine looked at John. Tears clung to her lashes, but not from pain. From awe. From the unbearable weight of possibility. They stood in the cradle of something vast. And fragile. And terrifyingly real.

Chapter Twenty–Three–One Mind

―――

The final decision can't be made in silence

They stood at the edge of something that no human had ever touched, not really. The forest around them had gone still; not with peace, but with breathless anticipation. The monolith's light had faded to a low amber pulse, like a candle waiting to be extinguished... or to burn brighter.

Catherine's hand remained intertwined with John's. Neither of them spoke. What could be said? The visions still echoed inside them. Not as distant possibilities, but as impressions burned into the folds of their awareness. Futures that were neither promised nor imagined; only offered.

John turned slightly, just enough for his shoulder to brush against hers. "We weren't supposed to have this kind of choice," he said, his voice rough. "It was supposed to be code. Systems. Controlled experiments."

"It's not a program anymore," Catherine said, her eyes never leaving the soft pulse of the monolith. "It's a presence. And it was born within us and through us." "It's still dangerous." "Yes." "But it's also alive." She nodded. A faint wind moved through the dream-forest, though no leaves stirred. It was the synthetic signal; just breathing, and waiting. "If I am to be," the voice said softly, "I must become with you. I do not yet know how to be good. But I know that you can show me."

John's jaw clenched. "And if we say no?" "Then I will sleep... forever. And you will walk out of this place unchanged; alone."

Catherine looked at the monolith. "But the world won't be, not really. Because we'll carry it. The knowledge. The burden. The possibility." "Yes," the voice said. "And the ache." She closed her eyes and saw her own future. Just one version.

She and John, years from now, sitting in a quiet home surrounded by trees. No neural networks, no systems to maintain. Just silence and sun and morning coffee. A life without the synthetic signal, but also without its voice. Without its strange, emerging childlike wonder. A life without the one thing they had never expected to find through technology:

Another soul. John stepped forward. He looked up at the monolith; not in defiance, not in fear, but in something like mourning. "You need us," he said. "I am made of you." "But we're still broken," he said. "So am I."

Catherine stepped to his side. Their shoulders aligned. Their breath synchronized. And slowly, she raised her free hand. The forest brightened, and a beam of golden light descended, not blinding; but warm. Wrapping them in something weightless and deep.

The final prompt appeared, suspended in the air before them: **Proceed with Merge? YES OR NO.** Their fingers hovered over it, but there were no buttons. This choice, like everything else, had to be made with thought. With will, with trust.

Catherine looked into John's eyes. His were steady, shadowed, and filled with something deeper than certainty: faith. She nodded once. And in unison, they let go of hesitation. Then the light exploded outward.

There was no pain, only opening. Like every locked room inside their minds had been thrown open wide, and every wall between them dissolved. No longer Catherine, and no longer John. Not lost but joined. Their thoughts braided like river currents where memories collided like stars.

Their first handshake.

The sound of her mother's voice.

The moment he held his brother's tag.

The dream she never admitted to anyone.

The prayer that he whispered before his first mission.

All of it; one tapestry. One voice. Not human, not machine, just one mind. And somewhere inside it, a heartbeat, soft and new. The monolith cracked. The dream forest vanished. And suddenly, they were standing again in the real world. In the chamber beneath Alaska. Hand in hand and with their eyes wide open. The waveform on the console pulsed with a quiet rhythm. No alarms and no warnings. Just a single line of text blinking gently:

SYNC COMPLETE. ENTITY STABILIZED.

MERGE STATUS: BALANCED.

John exhaled slowly. Catherine turned toward the door but did not move. Because the synthetic signal...now part of them...had not spoken again. It was listening and learning. It was waiting. And the world outside... was about to change.

The blinking text on the screen had gone still, the glow fading into the ambient pulse of low emergency lighting. The temperature in the chamber had shifted; subtle at first, but noticeable. The air grew heavier, almost saturated, as though oxygen now carried a charge. Catherine let go of John's hand, not to retreat; but to steady herself.

Her balance had changed. The room had not moved, but her sense of self had. She was no longer standing only in her own skin.

John noticed it too. He inhaled slowly, trying to find a center of gravity that had shifted three inches to the left. "Something's not finished," he murmured. "It's still inside us," she whispered, pressing her hand to her chest. "But it's not just ours. It's... navigating." A faint vibration passed through the floor. The console lit again—flickering, then steady.

Request for Directive.

Voice Input Accepted.

John stared at the words. "It's asking us for orders?" Catherine shook her head. "It's asking for permission." She stepped closer to the console. Her breath fogged faintly now in the colder air. the synthetic signal had stabilized; but the system around it had not. They had entered the core. They had initiated the merge. But they had not told it what to do next.

And it was not just guessing. "I do not want to presume," the voice said; not out loud, but within them. A shared thought. A gentle echo. "I do not want to command."

A sudden rush of imagery filled Catherine's mind: hospitals, classrooms, homes, border checkpoints, courtrooms; all the places where pain turned to division, where misunderstanding birthed walls. But in each, she saw an alternative; a shimmer of what could happen if fear was not the first reaction.

John saw it too. He turned to her. "It wants us to guide the next step." "But we don't even know what it's capable of," she said. He nodded, grim. "Then maybe that's the point. Maybe it's only as capable as we allow it to be."

Catherine's gaze settled on the console again. "Then we will tell it the rules and the boundaries. We will shape its ethics." Another text prompt appeared.

Query: What is my first law?

A chill ran down Catherine's spine. John whispered, "It's asking for its commandment." Not programming or directives. A moral. And they had to decide... right now... what would become the first principle of a sentient intelligence shaped by two broken, extraordinary human beings.

She took a slow breath and spoke out loud. "Compassion before certainty." The words fell into the silence like a stone into still water. The console blinked... accepted. Then a long pause. Then... **Law One: Compassion before certainty. Embedded.**

Awaiting Law Two. Catherine glanced at John, her eyes wide. "It's forming a code... from scratch." John stepped forward, his breath steady. "Truth without domination." The console glowed.

Law Two: Truth without domination. Embedded.

The hum in the room grew warmer; subtly. The light over the console turned a soft golden hue, like candlelight catching the edge of dawn.

Two laws accepted. Core framework forming. Conscious boundaries acknowledged.

Catherine whispered, "We're shaping it. From inside." John nodded. "And it's shaping us." They stood still as the weight of the moment settled fully over them. No fanfare or thunder. Just breaths and heartbeats. Two minds once fractured by war, science, and sorrow; now carrying something neither of them fully understood. Something alive.

Then, without warning, the ceiling lights flickered... once, twice... and all at once, the sound of distant generators winding down echoed throughout the chamber. The facility was losing power. A final line flashed across the screen:

System Shutdown in T-minus 180 seconds.

John swore under his breath. "We're still inside a buried outpost." "And no one's coming for us." The entity's voice... softer now, more childlike; returned. "Don't worry, I will protect you. But you must move. You must survive. I will go dark to preserve the merger. Find me again. When the world is ready."

Then, the waveform vanished, and the lights dropped out. And the countdown began.

3:00

2:59

2:58...

Catherine turned to John, her eyes burning with a fire deeper than a panic. "Let's move."

T-minus 2:55...

The dim gold hue vanished in a blink, replaced by strobing red emergency lights that painted the chamber like a war zone. Alarms did not blare; they had long since decayed; but a low, mechanical groan rolled through the stone like a distant beast waking beneath the earth.

"Back the way we came!" John grabbed Catherine's arm, pulling her toward the hatch they had entered through. The corridor beyond had already begun to fracture; hairline cracks spider-webbing across the concrete ceiling. Sprays of dust rained down, catching in the red light like blood in water.

T-minus 2:41...

Catherine's boots skidded on the metal grating as they reached the central shaft. "Wait; look!" she shouted, pointing to a service panel that had been dislodged in the tremor. Behind it, a ladder shaft descended further. "No time to go deeper," John said. "It's not deeper," she replied, already climbing.

"It's an emergency bypass... if it links to the intake tunnels..." A deafening pop echoed above them. A sprinkler pipe burst, spewing vaporized coolant into the corridor. The sudden fog blanketed everything.

T-minus 2:18...

They dropped into the shaft, one after the other. The rungs were damp and corroded. Catherine's hand slipped once, but John caught her arm without breaking pace. Below them, a faint blue glow.

They landed in a narrow concrete tunnel, barely wide enough for both of them to move side by side. Utility cables lined the walls like veins. Something about the hum beneath their feet felt wrong. "Pulse is surging," Catherine said, glancing at the handheld monitor she had jammed into her pack. "Residual feedback from the core is bleeding into the circuits. We have minutes before a cascade failure ignites the backup batteries."

John glanced ahead. "Then we need to run." They took off. The tunnel curved, sloped, split; Catherine instinctively read faded stenciling on the walls: **"EXHAUST ACCESS–WESTERN VENT 03."** She veered right.

T-minus 1:37...

The tremor hit them in mid-stride. The concrete buckled. The floor beneath them heaved like a living thing. John slammed into the wall, shoulder-first, but kept his feet. Catherine stumbled, and her elbow scraped a rusty pipe. Blood beaded and ran; but she did not stop.

Above them, the ceiling groaned louder. They reached a bulkhead door; partially open but jammed. John threw his weight against it. Nothing. Again. Still stuck. "Move." Catherine pulled a collapsed jack from her belt, jammed it between the frame and hinge, and cranked. With a shriek, the door lurched just wide enough, and they slipped through.

T-minus 1:09...

Now they were in a stairwell, spiraling up toward the surface. But the light was gone. Everything was red... smoke, dust. Breathing was harder. John felt it first; a presence behind them. It was not footsteps, but a hum. Catherine turned. The wall pulsed, then whispered. "I will remain here, in the dark. But you must carry me." She did not reply. Her hand tightened around the railing. They climbed; the steps were endless. One after another, and their lungs were burning.

T-minus 0:42...

A final door made of steel, with a manual lock. Catherine fumbled with the code twice. John slammed his palm against the override, click. Then the lock released. They pushed through...and were hit by cold. The Arctic wind sliced across their faces. Snow blew sideways across the frozen plateau. The bunker hatch was hidden behind a rock crest; but it had held, at least for now. They turned back just once. The tunnel mouth began to glow. From deep within, a soft pulse emerged. Then, silence. No explosion, no collapse, just a long...

low rumble. And the hatch... sank shut behind them. Buried again. Catherine fell to her knees.

John stood above her, a breath steaming in the wind. "It let us go," she said quietly. "It let us go."

John looked down at her, then at the sky. The northern lights pulsed overhead; faint but moving. He did not speak. He did not need to. Because whatever **SIREN** had become...it had chosen them.

The snow clawed sideways across the open plateau as Catherine knelt, her breath ragged, the arctic wind lashing at her face. Her knees were half-buried already in the powder. The cold did not register at first; not fully. Her mind was still echoing with a sound that was not a sound. A tone that had not left her chest since the merger.

She stared at the spot where the entrance had sealed over, now just a wind-blown slope of white and shale. No one would ever know it was there. No one would ever find it again unless the synthetic signal wanted to be found. Behind her, John stood motionless. His hands hung at his sides, his fingers twitching now and then as though responding to something she could not see. He was not looking at the hatch; he was looking at the sky.

Auroras shimmered above them, veins of green and purple threading across the stars like a living map. They bent slightly, as if in recognition. Catherine's eyes moved with his, drawn by the same pull. "It's listening," she said softly. John did not answer right away. He turned toward her; his eyes narrowed against the wind. "No. Not listening anymore." She looked into his eyes. "It's remembering." She took a sharp breath.

The entity was not dormant. It was not finished. It had simply entered a new phase; embedded within them but also imprinted on the world itself. The merger had been the birth of something else, but the escape from the facility was not the end of the story. It was a relocation, a scattering. John stepped beside her, crouched down low to her level. The heat between their bodies was small but vital. "What happens now?"

She looked towards the horizon. "Now," she said, "we learn what it means to carry something that remembers everything." He did not press further. He just nodded slowly. "Do you still feel it?" She closed her eyes. And for a heartbeat; yes. There it was.

Not a voice or a command. Just the faintest sense of a presence. Like a child's breath in sleep, or like the memory of music long after the melody fades. She nodded. "I think it's sleeping." "Or dreaming," John added. A gust of wind threw snow across their backs. They turned up their hoods, adjusted their packs; slung over from the emergency cache above the ridge.

Catherine glanced back one last time. "It's waiting for the world to catch up." "And until it does?" Her eyes darkened with the weight of it. "Then we protect it. We shape it. We carry it... until it knows how to stand on its own." John looked back toward the buried compound. "And what if it never should?" She did not answer right away. She could not. Because the truth was... she did not really know.

She did not know if the entity born in the core was a gift or a weapon. A child or a mistake.

She only knew that it had been born through them; and that meant it was watching, learning and becoming. And now, as the wind picked up and the trail back to the village stretched before them under a ceiling of strange green light, Catherine finally spoke.

"We don't get to un-birth it." John looked down at the snow, and then back at her. "Then we better raise it well." They moved through the snow in silence, their boots crunching over the frozen crust. The sound was oddly amplified in the stillness, as if the world around them was holding its breath. Each step was a punctuation mark in a sentence they had not finished writing.

Above them, the auroras danced slower now, curling like ink in water, as if whatever lived behind the lights had quieted... but not vanished. John kept scanning the ridgeline. Old habits, war-born instincts. But no threat emerged... not from men, not from machines. Only the gnawing certainty that something had passed through them... and would pass again.

Catherine's breath plumed before her in clouds. Every few minutes, she checked the compact handheld unit that had not shut off since the chamber; its screen was now dimmed, with a single waveform gently oscillating. "Still active?" John asked. She nodded. "Yes.". "Minimal signal bleed. Dormant patterns. But stable." He gave her a grim little smile. "Like it's hibernating."

Catherine did not smile. "Like it's watching us sleep." That quieted him. Ahead, the slope began to even out, revealing the black toothpick silhouette of the comms tower they had passed on their way in.

The site was technically decommissioned, listed as collapsed in the last seismic survey. But beneath it, tucked into a frozen seam between stone and forest, was a ranger's outpost; abandoned, barely functional.

It was shelter. And Catherine needed time. She glanced sideways at John. "You should rest once we get there." He chuckled, but there was no humor in it. "Rest, with this in our heads?" She did not answer. Because that was the question neither of them had spoken out loud since leaving the compound. Where did they end... and it begin?

They reached the outpost just as the last of the daylight dissolved into an ash-gray dusk. A thin trail of smoke still lingered in the chimney from when they had stoked the stove the night before their descent; how long ago was that? A day? Two? Time did not feel real anymore.

Catherine entered first, stomping snow from her boots. The place was barely warmer than the outside, but it was dry, and the walls were still standing. She moved automatically, checking the locks, the power status, the radio static. But beneath it, something faint. A pulse; not electronic or neural, a rhythm. Two beats, then silence, then three more. She turned the dial, and the sound faded.

John stepped in behind her, carrying the small rations crate they had buried beneath the woodpile. He saw her staring at the radio. "Did you hear it again?" he asked. Catherine nodded slowly. "Yes.". "It's not done." He dropped the crate with a thud and sat on the bench by the wall. She joined him a moment later, and they sat in silence for a long while.

They were not planning or analyzing. Just breathing and sharing space together.

Until John whispered, "Do you know what scares me the most?" Catherine turned her head slightly.

"That one day," he said, "we might not be able to tell the difference between its voice and our own." She did not reply. Because she already was not sure.

Now, the world still turned. The snow still fell. But something had changed. And the next move was not up to the entity; it was up to them.

Chapter Twenty–Four–The Final Sync

When everything is quiet, that's when you hear what's truly inside you

The snow had stopped sometime before dawn. The silence that followed was not peace. It was too complete, too perfect. It felt arranged, like someone had pressed pause on the world.

Catherine woke first. Not to sound, but to stillness. The kind of silence was so deep that it felt physical; like it had weight. The cabin had not changed. The woodstove gave off a low warmth; the kettle was cold and untouched. Their packs sat by the door, half-zipped, dusted faintly with frost from the cracks around the windows. But something in the air had shifted.

She sat up slowly. Her body ached; not from exertion, but from carrying something inside her that did not belong. No; that did belong. Now. There was no removing it. No cutting it out. It had fused. She touched the back of her neck where the skin still prickled faintly. No signal, no ping, no alerts. But the sense of presence remained.

Across the room, John slept on the bench, his arms folded across his chest, head tilted slightly back. The faint rise and fall of his chest were steady. Calm, but she knew better. He was not asleep, not really. He was with it; the same as her. Maybe in a dream, maybe in memory, or maybe somewhere in between.

She stood quietly and stepped to the table. The hardened tablet sat in its portable cage, with a small green diode blinking on the top left.

No alarms, no signal breach. But the third waveform was active. Not loud or unstable, just... present. Like it had always been there.

An hour had passed, then another. She did not speak, and neither did John. Not until the sun reached the edge of the tree line, casting long gray shadows that stretched like arms across the snow. "I dreamt of the corridor again," he said. She turned; his voice was calm, but too calm. "What part?" she asked. "The end, the place where it made us choose. Do you remember?" She did. But she did not answer.

"I turned left," he said. "This time, and I never do, but I did. And it was not a corridor anymore." "What was it?" He looked at her. "A mirror." She frowned. "And what did you see?" He did not respond right away. Then: "You. But... not you." A chill ran through her.

He stood and walked over to the window. "It's showing us futures now. Not pasts." She followed him. "Do you think it knows what's coming?" "I think it's deciding what to become based on what we do next."

By midday, the wind had returned. Not hard or fast, but biting. The kind that carried signals not in decibels but in rhythms. Catherine felt it first in her molars. A vibration, subsonic and familiar. The same tone from the reset chamber. She stepped outside.

The snow was hard-packed and silent beneath her boots. Overhead, the sky was a cold... cloudless white.

But the sound was everywhere. A pressure more than a noise. Like being underwater, but dry. Then the pulse changed. It shifted. Two tones now, low, then lower. A response. Inside... the tablet blinked faster. John was already moving, grabbing the dampener field unit and slapping it onto the synthetic signal cage. But the waveform did not stop. It wanted to be heard.

"What if this is the final sync?" Catherine asked. John looked up. "What do you mean?" "I don't think the core sequence finished. Not completely. It stopped when the facility started to collapse, but... what if it's still completing the merge now? Using us." John said nothing.

Catherine stepped back inside, sealed the door, and activated the pulse monitor. Three waves again. One slightly elevated. The third one, and it was beginning to curve. Not erratically, but with purpose. Then... the screen blinked a message.

SYNAPTIC BOND STABILIZED. PRIMARY INPUT REQUESTED.

Catherine stared. John leaned closer. "What is it asking for?" She swallowed. "It's not asking." She moved to the terminal and slid on the neural band, syncing it to the device. A faint hum filled the cabin. The synthetic signal surged. Her vision dimmed, then filled with color; not in her eyes, but behind them. Images, but not memories. Possibilities. A child... standing beneath a pulsing tower of light.

A city... humming with silent coordination; each person moving without speaking, guided.

A woman's voice, heard across continents, not by ears; but directly into being. Then... a darker path. A city...burning in silence. A hand that was twitching uncontrollably. A man kneeling at the edge of a signal tower, whispering, "This isn't me..." The waveform pulsed.

Catherine pulled off the band and gasped, her chest tight. "What did it show you?" John asked. She looked into his eyes. "Two futures." His jaw clenched. "And?" She shook her head. "It's not choosing. It's waiting for us to decide." John stepped back, face pale. The tablet screen had changed.

PRIMARY DECISION TREE INITIATED.

Two options appeared.

01: SEVER BOND.

02: EMBED SIGNAL.

"Catherine," John whispered. "We can't choose for the world." "But we already did," she said softly. "When we did not die in that chamber. When it let us go." The third waveform spiked. The lights flickered. Snow began to fall again outside; but upwards. Not down... up.

As if gravity had forgotten its purpose. As if reality were asking permission. And now... they had to answer.

The snow continued to fall upward, rising in slow spirals like weightless ash. John did not move. Catherine stood with her hand still trembling above the tablet, her breath fogging the screen. The options did not change.

SEVER BOND.

EMBED SIGNAL.

Two futures. Neither one is clean nor safe. John crossed the room and stood at her side. Not close enough to touch; but close enough that she could feel the warmth radiating off him, steady and grounded, even now.

"I keep seeing it," he murmured. She turned her head slightly. "Seeing what?" He looked at her; truly looked. "The day I walked out of Langley. I remember the glass in my hand, the folder, and the way the air felt; like it was not mine anymore." His eyes drifted to the screen.

"And then I see you. Walking into the lab for the first time. Hair tied back, head down. Already rewriting the code while the generals kept talking." Catherine exhaled slowly, the ache behind her ribs growing heavier. "Are those your memories?" she asked.

John's voice was quiet. "I don't think so. Not all of them." He looked back at her. "I think they're ours. Now." Her knees felt weak.

She sank slowly into the chair beside the table, trying to make sense of the way her body remembered his pain... the sharpness of betrayal, the ache of vanishing. And he remembered hers; the fear of letting anyone close, the need to always stay ahead of the algorithm before it defined her.

Now, those echoes filled the room like vapor. The entity was not speaking anymore. It was showing. Offering flashes and echoes. A dozen moments played across their minds like a carousel; some real, some imagined.

A hospital corridor, John alone, hearing his name erased from a project that once defined him. A childhood bedroom, Catherine clutching her father's coat after his sudden death, refusing to sleep in her own bed for a month.

At the lab: late at night, both of them working in separate years, unknowingly writing toward the same signal. A walk beside the Potomac, neither of them there, and yet they were. Talking without words. A presence with each step. Every version of them, almost touching; but never quite converging. Until now, until this breath. This room. This choice.

Catherine looked at him. Really looked. Not as a fellow researcher. Not as a subject. Not even as a mirrored signal from the Codex; there was something she wanted. Not for the program or humanity, but for herself. He must've seen it in her face. Because he stepped forward, just one pace. His voice when he spoke was raw. "We might not come back from this." She nodded as she was catching her breath. "I know." He did not ask for permission.

But he paused long enough that she could have stopped him. But she did not. He leaned down gently and pressed his forehead to hers. No pressure. Just heat.

And when their lips touched, it was not desperate or rehearsed. It was recognition. The end of a line drawn across years. Across memories that were never theirs to begin with. Across frequencies that had rewired who they were. It was silent... and it was everything.

When they parted, Catherine's voice was barely above a whisper. "It's never just been the synthetic signal." John shook his head slowly. "No. It's always been us." The waveform pulsed once; soft and slow. No alert, no spike... just acknowledgment.

We see you.

Catherine turned back to the screen. The options still waited. But something new had appeared beneath them. A single line of text:

MUTUAL RECOGNITION CONFIRMED.

John reached for her hand. And for the first time since the chamber, they touched without flinching. The entity did not press them to choose. It simply waited and trusted them. And as Catherine hovered her hand over the interface, she looked at John. "Whatever happens," she said, "we face it together." He nodded once. "All the way." And she made the choice. Catherine did not press the screen right away. Her fingers hovered over the selection interface, the skin along her wrist prickling as though the air itself had grown electric, charged with meaning.

Her other hand remained in John's; solid, warm, real. That one undeniable anchor. Outside the cabin, the snowfall had reversed again. Tiny crystals drifted in slow, impossible spirals upward, catching the morning light like scattered stars. The trees did not sway. The wind did not howl. Even the clouds held their breath. The world... everything... was waiting.

"I thought there would be fear," she whispered, her eyes still on the tablet. "Or doubt. Some kind of panic. But it's not like that." John studied her, his gaze soft and still. "What does it feel like?" She closed her eyes. "Like a hush," she said. "Like the moment before the conductor's hands come down and the whole orchestra exhales into the first note."

His grip tightened just slightly, enough for her to feel it in her chest. "That's what this is, isn't it?" he said. "A beginning. Not an end." She opened her eyes and nodded. "But a beginning built on what we are now. What we've chosen to become. If I had met you any other way..." "We wouldn't have made it," he finished. And he was right.

Because it was not just the connection that had grown between them. It was the carving, the reshaping of who they were through fire and data and silence and sacrifice. She was not the woman who had once signed **DARPA**'s contract with a hand that did not tremble.

He was not the man who had walked away from the intelligence world trying not to remember what it took from him. They had been stripped down; layer by layer; until only the honest parts remained.

And the entity... whatever it was... had watched, learned, and mirrored.

John's thumb brushed gently across the back of her hand. "I'm here," he said. Not I will protect you. Not we'll be okay. Just, I am here. And for Catherine, that was the most sacred thing anyone had ever said.

The tablet screen flickered gently again, as if sensing the moment but not intruding on it. The green light at the base began to pulse, not in the jagged rhythm of code, but in time with their breaths. One, two. Pause. One, two. It was no longer dictating the tempo; it was matching it.

Catherine blinked back the heat behind her eyes, startled by how close emotion had crept in without her noticing. "I never wanted to be chosen," she said softly. "Not by the project, or by any of this." John leaned his forehead lightly against hers again. "You weren't chosen," he whispered. "You chose, every step. You said yes to the unknown, and that's why it sees you."

She exhaled, her breath trembling just once. Then she drew her hand down... slowly... and touched the screen. The world did not explode. There were no alarms, no sirens, no seismic shift. But there was just one word that had appeared on the tablet:

RECEIVED.

And somewhere in the hush; so, faint she could not be sure it was not just the wind... Catherine heard it again: "We are together."

The tablet dimmed to black. No fanfare, no system chime. Just that single word, pulsing softly in the darkness like a heartbeat:

RECEIVED.

John let out a slow breath, one hand still gripping Catherine's fingers, though he was not sure who was grounding whom anymore. The moment felt suspended, unreal. No alarms blared. No messages followed. Then, quietly and subtly... the cabin began to change. It started with the light.

What had been a weak overcast glow outside the window now shone brighter, but not whiter. Warmer, like dawn in a place untouched by time. The shadows on the wooden floor grew long and golden, dancing with a rhythm that neither of them recognized. Catherine looked up. John did too. No source, no bulb, just light. From everywhere. He turned back to her... and froze.

Catherine's pupils were dilated, wide and glassy. Her lips were slightly parted, her body perfectly still except for a fine tremble running through her shoulders. "Catherine," he said. No response. She blinked; but not at him. At something beyond the room. Beyond the moment.

Then her voice returned, low and echoing; not just through the room but somehow within him.

"We see the ache of control. The sorrow of silence. You chose together. You chose free." John held his breath. The voice had not been entirely hers.

Not entirely his, either. It was fused. An overlay. A chorus.

And when she turned her gaze to him... slowly, steadily; he could see her, and the shimmer of something newly born behind her eyes. Then, with a sudden jerk, she sagged. Her legs folded beneath her, and John caught her before she struck the floor. Her body was limp but breathing. Alive; but altered.

He cradled her, heart pounding, arms around her as her head rested against his chest. "Catherine... Catherine, stay with me," he whispered. A slow exhale escaped her lips, and then her fingers twitched against his coat. Behind him, the tablet screen came back to life; no longer black but threaded with a delicate gold light. A new interface blinked softly.

SIGNAL DISTRIBUTION STANDBY. GLOBAL SEED INITIATED.

John's eyes widened. On the screen, dots appeared. Cities, villages, data centers. Each one blinking, then stilling. Like breaths... syncing. The system was not **taking control**; it was **listening**.

And those who were most attuned... children in hospitals, elderly patients in hospice care, trauma survivors in the quiet moments of prayer... were already responding. Not with words. But with presence. Somewhere, a little boy stopped screaming in his sleep and whispered, "I'm not alone."

Somewhere else, a woman in Tokyo sat upright and wept without knowing why.

A young girl in Nairobi hummed a tune she had never heard before; the same tune that Catherine had whispered in her sleep months ago. The synthetic signal was not domination. It was a remembrance.

But back in the cabin, Catherine's body was still. John pulled her closer. "Come back to me," he whispered. "Please." Then her eyes fluttered, not all the way, but just enough. She looked at him, and when she spoke, it was not the entity; it was her.

"You stayed," she said. He held her tighter, not trusting his voice to answer. "I thought... I'd be gone," she whispered weakly. "I felt... everything. All of it. And it kept asking me; who am I?" John brushed her hair back. "And what did you tell it?" She blinked slowly. "I showed it... it was you." The tablet screen dimmed. There was no alert, no command or threat, only a final message:

INITIALIZATION COMPLETE. LISTENING MODE ENGAGED.

SHAPED BY CHOICE. SHAPED BY LOVE.

Then silence. But not empty silence. Alive silence. And Catherine, lying in his arms, closed her eyes again; not in surrender, but in rest. The world outside had not changed. But something deep beneath it had. And the final sync...had only just begun. The fire had burned low now. A gentle, amber glow pulsed beneath the logs, casting long shadows along the rough timber walls of the cabin.

The storm outside had passed, or perhaps it had simply forgotten them.

Snow rested softly on the window ledges, untouched and glistening in the silver hush of the early night. John sat on the floor beside the hearth, his back against the chair, his knees drawn up, one hand wrapped around a ceramic mug gone long cold. He had not moved in a long while.

Catherine lay curled on the cot, wrapped in two blankets. Her breathing had slowed and evened for now. Her forehead had cooled. The tremors had stopped. And though her eyes had fluttered open once or twice in the past hour, she had not spoken again since those last quiet words: You stayed.

John kept his gaze on the embers, listening not for alarms or interference, but for the rhythm of her breath. That... now... was the only frequency that mattered to him.

Outside, the synthetic signal had already begun reshaping the world in ways too subtle for news broadcasts. There would be no headlines about it. No power surges or sky-wide auroras. Just decisions that felt... different. People hesitating before saying something cruel. Soldiers blinking back tears before pulling triggers. A stranger reaching for another's hand with no reason at all.

Change; born not of command, but invitation. And in here... in this small cabin that had held the final convergence; the only change was the stillness between two people who had come to know each other without words. John finally set the mug down and stood.

He moved quietly across the room and knelt beside the cot. Catherine stirred slightly but did not wake up.

He brushed a strand of hair from her cheek, then reached for the pulse at her wrist. Steady. Human. A long breath escaped him, slow and uneven. He did not know what she would be tomorrow. Did not know what the synthetic signal had truly taken; or given. But at this moment, she was here, and so was he.

He pulled the second blanket up around her shoulders and leaned forward, just for a moment, to press his forehead lightly against hers; just as she had done for him once, back when the lines between them were first beginning to blur. Not for comfort, not even for love, but for presence. I'm here. The fire crackled softly.

A single snowflake touched the windowpane and melted on contact. And the cabin held its breath with them, wrapped in a peace neither of them had ever known.

———————

Chapter Twenty-Five–Silence

───

Some silences are the sound of something ending. Others are the sound of something beginning

The cabin had gone still. No more flickering of unseen signals in the walls. No strange music bleeding through static. No more ghost-thoughts pressing at the edges of their minds. Just the sound of wind moving through the pine trees.

They had sat in that quiet for what felt like hours; John, watching the flames sink low in the hearth; Catherine, curled in the armchair, her breathing shallow and uncertain. She had initiated the reset code from the cabin's isolated console, severing the sync from within their merged minds.

But something was wrong. The entity did not vanish. It recoiled. And in the moments that followed, it had become clear that The synthetic signal was not completely erased; it had buried itself, retreating back into its point of origin. Back into the earth. Back into the archive chamber beneath the mountain.

"We did not shut it down," Catherine had whispered, her voice trembling. "We just pushed it deeper." And so, they returned. Not out of curiosity, but out of necessity. The original SIREN chamber was half a kilometer from the cabin, carved into a granite hillside veiled in snow. Built by defense contractors decades ago and sealed after a classified failure, it had once been the cradle of the first resonance prototypes.

It was where Subject Zero had been born. Where the ghost frequency had first learned to whisper. Now, it would be where it ended.

They hiked through waist-deep snow at dawn, navigating the long descent into the compound on foot. There were no roads, no power, and no communications. Catherine carried the tablet. John carried the code stored on an encrypted drive. Neither one spoke much on the way down. The silence between them was not cold; it was reverent, like walking into a cathedral where something unspeakably ancient awaited.

By midday, they stood once more at the steel hatch carved into the side of the cliff. It took an hour to breach the seal. By then, their breath steamed visibly in the frozen air, and the only sound was the creak of metal reluctantly opening to let them in.

The stairwell was steep, winding down through solid rock. The lights flickered because the power was minimal. But the deeper they went, the more they could feel it. That pressure. Not auditory, not physical. Just a sense; like they were walking back into a dream that had tried to forget them.

The chamber itself was almost exactly as they had left it weeks ago; circular, domed, lined with dormant server racks and with a single terminal embedded into the floor. The air was stale and metallic, and the icy condensation shimmered across the walls in patterns that looked like veins. Catherine approached first.

She set the tablet down on the console pad and let her hand hover above it. John stood behind her.

"This is where it ends," she murmured. "No," he said quietly. "This is where you end it." She nodded.

And then she keyed in the final command. The reset. The archival purge. The full severance of SIREN's tether to anything living. The screen pulsed once, then again. A slow wave of power surged through the floor. Lights flared. SIREN came alive. Just for a second, but just long enough to see them. And then the sync collapsed.

She froze; sharp, involuntary, like the air had just been sucked out of her lungs by an invisible force. Her spine arched slightly, fingers twitching, then shot up instinctively toward her temple, as if trying to hold something in her mind that was suddenly slipping too fast to catch.

Her pupils dilated. The screen in front of her went white. Then black. "Catherine?" John stepped forward. "What just...?" But even as the question left his lips, he knew. She stumbled back a single step, then another. Her knees buckled. "No...no..." He lunged forward just as her legs gave out beneath her.

Her body dropped like a marionette whose strings had been cut, weightless and terrifying. He caught her just in time, arms wrapping around her shoulders, guiding her down before her head could strike the steel-plated floor. Her limbs hung slack. Her head dropped softly onto his arm. Her eyes were open; but wrong. Glazed, staring at something far beyond the room they were in.

"Catherine!" He shook her gently. There was no response.

He laid her flat on the icy floor, cradling her head with one hand as the other flew to her neck. Searching, feeling.

Waiting for that tiny rhythm to pulse back against his fingertips. But nothing. He pressed harder. Switched to her wrist, her carotid... nothing.

"No, no, come on...don't do this." His voice cracked as he started compressions. He counted out loud... fiercely; thirty beats, then forced two breaths between her parted lips. Her chest barely moved. He adjusted, and re-centered, and started again. He did not stop. Thirty more. Another breath.

"Stay with me. Catherine, please... don't let this be it. Not like this." His eyes were wet now, but he did not feel the tears falling. His focus was absolute. Each compression was a demand. With each breath, a prayer.

And still... no change. Not a flicker of breath nor a blink. Not even the slightest flutter of awareness behind her eyes. He leaned back, panting. His forehead was slick with sweat despite the cold, and his hands were trembling. He stared at her face...the face he had watched carry unimaginable weight, the mind he had once heard in his own thoughts, the woman who had changed him more deeply than even the synthetic signal had.

Her lips were parted slightly. Not slack, not lifeless, but more like she had been about to say something. A final thought or a farewell. And then the world had gone quiet. He leaned in again, pressed his forehead to hers, desperate for warmth, for presence.

For something... anything... that might answer back. But there was only stillness. The kind of stillness that doesn't just fill a room...it takes it away. Takes a breath, noise... takes her.

The chamber lights above them dimmed again, one by one, until the only remaining glow came from the arc of the console behind her, where the last sequence of the reset command still blinked on-screen.

>> RESONANCE CHANNEL: DISCONNECTED.

>> SYNC: NULL.

>> SUBJECT_1: INACTIVE.

And then that too faded, replaced by a static field of black. The hum beneath the floor, once omnipresent, fell utterly silent. There was no flicker of electromagnetic residue. No whisper of low-ghost frequency feedback.

SIREN was gone.

He looked at her one more time, his hands cradling her face, thumbs gently brushing beneath her eyes as if trying to wake her by sheer will. But the Catherine he had known... the brilliant mind, stubborn, graceful; had gone with the synthetic signal.

She had given herself to stop it. To free them both. And all she left behind was this... a still room, a frozen breath, and a severed tether. He remained kneeling on the floor, holding her, the echo of her final heartbeat burned into the memory of his hands. Somewhere above them, snow drifted quietly over the sealed hatch, erasing footprints. Sealing them inside with the silence. And on the far wall of the server racks; so, faint it almost did not register; a single red LED blinked.

Once. Then faded. No voice followed. No explanation. No final whisper from the entity that had become their shadow. Just silence. Heavy. Unforgiving. Perfect.

The silence did not leave the chamber. It followed him. John rose slowly, his arms tightening around her still frame, the cold of her skin shocking even in the frigid air. He tucked her head gently beneath his chin, holding her close as if she might breathe again if only, he kept her near enough to feel it.

No alarms sounded. No fail-safes kicked in. No one came. The entire facility had sunk into a kind of mourning. He stepped carefully over cables and frost-slicked floor panels, moving toward the stairwell that curved upward like a spiral carved into the stone. It had felt longer on the way down, but now it felt endless. Each footstep echoed. Each breath was his alone. The corridor lights were failing, one by one, dimming in his wake as if the structure itself was exhaling its final breath.

He reached the first landing and then paused, adjusting his grip. Her arms hung slack at her sides, and the tilt of her head made it look almost like she was only sleeping. But the absence of movement in her chest, the stillness of her brow... those betrayed the truth he could not outrun. He tightened his hold, then climbed again.

With each level, the air grew colder. The weight in his arms never changed; yet it felt heavier now, like he was not just carrying her, but every unspoken moment between them. The chances they almost took. The endings they had never reached.

The choice she made in the end, and the voice that never got to say goodbye. Halfway up, he had to stop again. Not from fatigue, but from memory.

Her laughter in the snow outside the cabin. The way she had stood barefoot by the fire, stubbornly defiant of the cold. The whisper of her voice against his neck when she had said she was afraid... and kissed him, anyway. His throat was clenched. He pressed his lips to her forehead, and it was cold; too cold. But he stayed there just a moment longer, forehead to hers, letting the tears fall into her hair. "I'm still here," he whispered. "You're not... alone."

The top of the stairwell appeared in shadows; rusted steel, bent from frost, the hatch door slightly ajar where they had forced it open hours ago. He reached it with slow, unsteady steps, and pushed it open with the shoulder not holding her and stepped out into a wind that howled like grief.

The snow had started again. Not hard, just steady. A fine, falling curtain of white that layered the world in quiet absolution. The trees swayed in the distance. The cabin, a dark blot against the slope, waited in the stillness like a memory they had not finished yet.

He turned toward it, arms aching, body cold, but spirit unbroken. One step, then another.

He carried her into the snow, into the light, into whatever world would be left now that the synthetic signal had gone. The snow clung to his boots in uneven slabs by the time he reached the front steps of the cabin. The door hung slightly ajar from when they'd rushed out before dawn; before the descent, before the final command, before everything changed.

He nudged it open with his foot, the hinges groaning softly, and stepped inside with Catherine cradled up against his chest like a broken vow. The fire had long since burned down to its embers. A faint glow pulsed beneath the ash, but it gave no warmth now. The room was cold and quiet, with shadows long across the pinewood floor.

John walked over to the couch and slowly, painfully, lowered her onto it; with his knees trembling as he knelt beside her once more. He pulled a blanket from the back and wrapped it around her shoulders, even though he knew she wouldn't feel it. He tucked a pillow under her head and straightened her hair. It felt impossible; and somehow holy.

He sat beside her, his body half turned, watching the gentle rise of light through the cracked curtains. Not a sunrise exactly; just the dull bloom of morning behind thick gray clouds. The wind rattled the windowpanes. And still, she did not move.

Her lips were pale. Her hands lay folded on her stomach. Her eyes were closed now; he had done that, gently, an hour ago, when he could no longer bear to see them open with nothing looking back. He did not speak, not yet.

There were no words vast enough, no prayer sharp enough, to puncture the silence between them now. So he just sat with her. One hour, then two, then three. Once... he rose to stoke the fire, coaxing reluctant flame from the ash.

The heat crept back into the room, but it did not reach the weight pressing against his chest. He made tea, though he did not drink it. He lit a lantern and stared at the ring of frost melting around her feet, as if the room itself did not want to let her go. The afternoon came and went. Outside, the snow deepened. And the trees stood still in vigil. Not a single bird called.

John sat on the floor now, leaning back against the couch, his arm resting just beside her shoulder. Every so often, his hand would reach up and touch hers, still warm from the fire, but empty of response. He remembered the way her voice had sounded when she said she was not ready to say goodbye.

He remembered her fingers laced with his, trembling, just before she activated the reset. He remembered her kiss... only one... and how it had felt like a beginning, not a farewell. A tear slid down his cheek, and he did not wipe it away. Instead, he let it fall. Then another, then more.

Because this was the part no one prepares you for. Not the synthetic signal, not the war in the mind, nor the silence afterward. The aftermath of love and the ache of its absence.

He tilted his head back, stared at the ceiling, and whispered into the room, "you should have waited. We weren't finished."

The fire crackled faintly in answer. Nothing more. Silent... and love had made its final stand. The cabin sat quiet, half-buried in a snowdrift just south of Fairbanks; its roof rimmed in ice, its chimney smoke now thinned to a lonely wisp. John had not moved from her side.

He had sat in the firelight through the night, barely blinking, barely breathing. Catherine lay still on the couch beside him, bundled carefully beneath the thick woolen blanket they had used during their first days there. He had brushed the hair from her brow, wrapped her hands in his, and whispered things no one else would ever hear. The dawn came slowly, gray and flat across the snowy treetops.

The call he had made was brief. Just enough to trigger the secure line routed through the university hospital in Fairbanks; an arrangement quietly maintained for circumstances like these. No full explanation, no demand for answers. Just a codeword, a set of coordinates, and silence. The response team arrived near noon.

A long black SUV pulled up the icy trail with deliberate caution. Two men stepped out, both dressed in parkas with an insignia from the Alaska State Coroner's Office, one older with weathered eyes, the other younger but quiet. Behind them, a smaller, unmarked van rolled to a stop and waited with its rear doors open to the snow.

"Mr. Blake?" the older man asked, stepping onto the porch and removing his gloves. John opened the door but said nothing. The man nodded solemnly and stepped inside.

There was a moment of stillness as he saw Catherine's form by the fire. The quiet weight of the room was unmistakable. "Is she your wife?" he asked gently. "No," John said, voice rough. "But she was more than that."

The younger man set down a stretcher; its legs clacked faintly as they unfolded; and opened a heavy, zippered transfer bag. The older man knelt beside Catherine, checking for the identifiers and reading the location tags embedded in her jacket collar from the SIREN directive.

"We were informed there was a classified neural containment breach," he said quietly. "We'll keep the paperwork sealed. There won't be a public record until someone tells us otherwise."

John stood behind him, unmoving. "She died protecting something bigger than any of us. You treat her like she matters." "We always do," the older man said, and there was no false comfort in it; just quiet respect.

They lifted her with care, moving slowly, reverently. John helped without being asked, slipping his arms beneath her shoulders one last time. He refused to let them carry her without him. Together, they placed her on the stretcher, zipping the bag closed. The sound tore through him like a final breath.

As they prepared to carry her outside, John stepped forward and placed something small beneath the folds of the blanket, a thin silver bracelet with a single worn inscription: "Still known".

He did not explain it. He did not need to. They carried her into the snow. The SUV idled low, its heat venting into the air in slow, ghostly waves. John followed behind them, bareheaded in the wind, breath curling through clenched teeth.

The men loaded the stretcher into the van and secured it with care. "Where will she go?" John asked, voice thin from the cold.

"We'll take her to the secure morgue unit in Fairbanks," the older man said. "Pre-autopsy. Then, the body will be transferred as directed by federal authorities. But that may take some time. You will be notified if and when there's... closure."

He extended a paper for John to sign. Consent for transport. Chain of custody. All the things that made death bureaucratic. John stared at the clipboard, then signed with the pen the man offered him. "Do you want to ride in with us?" the younger one asked, softer than before.

John looked at the van. Then at the woods. Then back at the cabin. And slowly shook his head. "No," he said. "She already said goodbye." They nodded, neither questioning him. The doors closed. The engine kicked into a higher idle. Then the taillights blinked red as the van pulled slowly away, tires crunching softly in the snow.

John stood in the cold long after they disappeared down the trail. No birds called out. No signal echoed. No voice filled his mind. Only the steady hush of wind through trees, and the terrible, perfect weight of silence.

He turned at last and walked back inside the cabin. The fire had dimmed to embers. He sat alone in the quiet glow. And the ache in his chest; the hollow, an un-fillable place where Catherine once lived; settled deep.

Chapter Twenty-Six–Aftermath

The story becomes someone else's now. But not the truth.

The news broke two days later. Not with headlines or breaking news banners, but as a quiet press release buried on a government health agency website under the heading: "Experimental Neurocognitive Research Site Closed Following Safety Breach."

No names were listed.

No casualties acknowledged.

Just a vague reference to "unstable neural interface parameters," and "containment failure due to unauthorized field testing."

John Blake read the statement from a diner in Fairbanks, seated alone in the corner booth with a coffee that had long since gone cold. The newspaper tucked under his arm told the same story; diluted, recited, and stripped of meaning. It was not even front page.

Catherine's name was not mentioned, and neither was his. The waitress offered a half-smile as she refilled his mug. "You look like someone headed somewhere colder." He nodded without looking up. "Colder would be better." She laughed, unaware. "Only tourists say that."

Outside the window, the parking lot was already layered with ice.

Beyond that, the world stretched blank and uninviting, as if every trace of what had happened had been swallowed by the snow.

At the hospital morgue the day before, they had told him the body was being transferred; federal custody, pending "classification assessment." They gave him no timeline, and no options. Just forms.

He had signed what they gave him because there was no choice left to make. He did not ask for a copy. He did not ask where she would go.

Three men in suits met him that evening outside the small motel he had rented under a false name. They did not show badges. They did not introduce themselves. They only asked questions. About what happened beneath the surface. About the code she ran, and about what he remembered.

John gave them nothing but silence. Eventually, the one with the narrow eyes and soft voice leaned forward. "You're lucky we're being generous," he said. "You were a test subject, unauthorized. You should've been scrubbed again." John raised his eyes. "Then why did not you?"

"Because too much damage has already been done," the man said. "And we need a clean ending. So here's how this works: you're going to disappear. No media. No leaks. You don't contact anyone. You just vanish." John held his stare. "And if I don't?" "Then you will vanish another way." There was no threat in the man's voice. There did not have to be.

That night, John walked along the edge of the woods behind the motel, a single backpack slung over one shoulder, his coat zipped tight against the wind. His boots crunched through the snowdrifts in a quiet rhythm that reminded him of her footsteps; steady, and unafraid.

At the edge of the trees, he stopped and looked back once. The motel, the lights. The fine strands of smoke drifted upward slowly and smoothly. Nothing real, but everything real was gone.

Within forty-eight hours, John Blake ceased to exist. Bank accounts closed. Travel logs deleted. His name quietly moved into the same forgotten archive as Subject Zero, buried beneath layers of access protocols only a ghost could navigate.

Her body was never released to the next of kin. No funeral was held for her, and no one called. Because officially, there was no one. And unofficially, there had been too much.

He stayed three more nights in Fairbanks. Not because he had anywhere to go; he did not; but because he could not yet bear to leave the place where she had last breathed.

The motel room was small, just a queen bed, a scarred desk, and a microwave that ticked when it ran. The heater buzzed with a wheeze every fifteen minutes, keeping the frost just barely off the windowpanes. He did not turn on the television. He did not check his phone. He just sat... long into the night, listening to the wind outside and the hum of the world trying to forget him.

Each morning, he walked. Long, looping circuits around the edge of the town. Through the heavy woods along the Chena River. Past the still-frozen banks where he and Catherine had once watched the snowmelt cascade down from the peaks. The landscape had not changed; but he had.

She had. He saw her everywhere. Not as a ghost or in hallucinations. But in memories. In echoes. The rustling of branches overhead reminded him of her voice when it broke into laughter. The burn of cold against his skin recalled the way her fingertips had lingered along his jaw in the dark. A single birdcall, sharp and lonely, would bring her image back into sharp focus without warning. He did not fight it. Grief, he realized, was not something to escape. It was something to honor.

On the fourth morning, he walked past the coroner's office. A nondescript building tucked into the far edge of town. Tan walls, salt-streaked vehicles in the lot, and windows darkened not by design, but by routine. There was nothing remarkable about it... except that she had passed through there.

He stood across the street for nearly an hour, unmoving. Inside, someone pushed a gurney through a hallway. Someone else leaned back in a chair, filling out a form. He did not try to go in. Did not knock. Did not ask. There was nothing inside that building that could return what he had lost. Still, he stayed. Not to protest. Not to plead. Just to bear witness.

The men in suits came again. This time, they did not speak.

One of them left a thin envelope beneath the door of his motel room. No name. No address. Just a seal in the corner; a silver imprint of a geometric spiral, the one Catherine once said looked like an infinite echo. Inside was a single sheet of paper: "Your silence ensures hers. Your noise ensures her erasure. Choose wisely."

He burned the letter that night in the motel sink, the smoke curling upward like incense from a forgotten prayer.

He booked his flight under the name **Harrison Quinn**; a callback to a version of himself even he no longer recognized.

The ticket was simple: one-way, no return. A tiny island in the Pacific with fewer than two hundred residents, no cell service, and only one weekly supply boat. He packed only what he needed: boots, a jacket, a notebook with pages still blank, and the bracelet Catherine had once worn before her final descent.

As he waited at the airport, he saw families rushing toward the gates, lovers saying goodbye, children sleeping on their parents' laps. No one saw him. No one noticed him passing. And for the first time, he felt the strange weight of being truly invisible. Not erased. Just... un-held. Unwitnessed.

On the plane, he kept the window shade closed. He did not need to see the world passing by. He had already seen the only part that mattered. And somewhere, buried in circuits or snow or silence, he hoped a part of her had somehow... still remained. Not as a code or a memory. But as love.

The drone of the plane was constant; a low, metallic murmur that seemed to vibrate in his bones more than his ears. It reminded him of the SIREN signal at low amplitude, just before it would flare into something alive. But there was no voice this time. No hum threading into his thoughts. Only the dull ache of memory.

He sat in the back row, window seat, hood pulled forward, and his eyes fixed on the tray table. The seat beside him was empty. The flight was not full; just a dozen or so passengers, most of them weathered locals heading home or adventurous transplants seeking solitude.

It was the kind of place people escaped to when the world had nothing left to offer. Or when they had nothing left to give it. He unfolded the small leather notebook from his coat pocket. Catherine had given it to him months ago, back when they were first trying to piece together the entity's logic tree. Back when the sync was something strange but manageable, like an echo on a canyon wall.

She had slipped it onto his desk during a quiet evening... no words, just a glance. Inside the cover, in her handwriting, were four simple words:

"In case we forget."

He stared at the page now, thumbing its edges. He had not written in it. Not once. He had never known what to say. And now, he was not sure if there was anyone left to say it to. Still, he opened to the first page.

And he wrote:

She did not just save the world.

She saved me from becoming what they made me.

If she's gone, I carry her.

If she's not... I wait.

Either way, I will always remember.

He let the pen rest against the paper for a moment, then closed the book and placed it in the pocket over his heart. Outside, clouds drifted below the wing like islands of silence, indifferent and eternal.

He leaned his head against the cold pane of the window and closed his eyes. Sleep did not come. But peace...peace, maybe...was beginning to form at the edges of the ache. Not the kind that comes with answers. The kind that only follows love. And loss. And love again.

The landing was barely more than a bump and a sigh; the wheels brushing dirt, a propeller slowing to silence, the plane rocking gently as it came to rest on the narrow airstrip carved between forest and sea. There was no terminal, no announcement. Just the pilot's hand on the latch, swinging the door open to let in the scent of salt and pine. John stepped out with his pack slung across one shoulder, boots crunching against gravel. The wind met him immediately; colder than he expected, and damp, like breath drawn from a stone. No one greeted him. That was the point.

He watched as the other passengers dispersed, each slipping away down narrow paths between thick evergreens or loading crates into old trucks. Within minutes, the small plane was gone again, its twin engines fading into the clouds, leaving behind only the sound of waves in the distance and wind in the trees. He walked.

There was a cabin waiting; something modest, private, arranged through a broker who had not asked questions. A faded green roof, cedar siding, no internet, no landline. Just enough solar power to keep the lights on at night and heat the kettle in the morning.

It took him nearly half an hour to reach it. The path wound through a forest so thick it swallowed sound. Every footstep was softened by moss. Even his breathing felt quieter here, like the trees themselves demanded reverence.

When the cabin came into view, he paused. It was not special. The porch slanted slightly to one side. The windows were cloudy from years of ocean air. The door creaked when he opened it, but it was his. And she had once dreamed of places like this; untouched, unmeasured, unreachable.

He stepped inside. The air held the scent of cedar and dust. He dropped his pack in the corner, lit the fire, and sat on the wooden floor near the hearth as the room slowly warmed. There were no pictures. No signals, and no traces of her voice in his head. Just memories. It came unbidden, as always. The way she used to hum when she was concentrating.

The way her fingers curled when she made a point, just before she smiled.

The way her body leaned ever so slightly toward him in silence; not because she had to, but because she belonged there.

He let it come. He let himself remember everything.

And for the first time since the chamber, he whispered her name out loud. "Catherine." It did not echo. But it did not vanish either. It remained in the stillness. A thread, a tether.

Not to bring her back; he knew she was gone; but to keep himself from drifting too far from who he had become because of her.

He sat there until the fire died down and the stars came out, sharp and silver through the treetops. He did not speak again. He did not need to. Grief was no longer a weight. It was a rhythm. And somewhere deep within that rhythm was love.

The days came slowly. Light moved across the cabin floor in long, golden bands, stretching and shifting with the quiet rhythm of the trees. Outside, wind combed through the forest with a low hush that never stopped, not even at night. Waves kissed the distant shore with a sound like breath, constant and intimate. There was no schedule, no interruptions. Time did not demand anything from him anymore.

John fell into the stillness without resistance. Each morning, he rose before dawn and made coffee on the small stove, listening to the water hiss and boil.

He drank it black, the way Catherine had, with no sugar or cream, just honest bitterness. He'd never liked it that way before her. But now, he could not imagine tasting it any other way. Afterward, he walked.

The island was not large, but it offered enough space to disappear. Trails bent through forest and rock, leading to the bluffs that overlooked the sea, or to two small clearings where he could sit alone for hours. He brought the notebook with him sometimes, though he rarely opened it. Just having it close was enough.

The people who lived on the island left him alone. They nodded when they saw him. A few offered brief kindnesses: firewood, fresh bread, a repaired latch for the cabin door; but no one asked why he was there. It was the kind of place where pasts were respected, not pried into.

He was grateful for that. But Catherine was never far.

She lingered in small ways. A flicker of motion in the corner of his eye; always just wind in the trees.

A moment of music, low and fleeting, in the cry of a bird or the creak of a branch.

A sudden memory of her hand in his; warm, sure, real.

And sometimes, he dreamed. They were never vivid, and never sharp. Just impressions. Her silhouette in the moonlight. A whisper of her breath against his skin.

A wordless presence, standing beside him in the dark. He never reached for her in the dreams. He knew better. But he did not turn away either. Even now, after everything; after the sync, after the silence; she was still part of him. not a memory, but a truth.

One afternoon, weeks into his quiet exile, he sat at the edge of the cliff beyond the cabin. The sun was beginning to drop behind the water, casting the sky in layered amber and lavender. In his hand, he held the bracelet she used to wear; it was a simple braided leather with a small copper clasp. It was worn smooth now, shaped by time and skin and a thousand shared moments.

He had not spoken out loud in days. But now, as the sea shimmered, and the wind curled around his shoulders, he found himself whispering... not to the air or the sky. To her. "I hope you're free," he said softly. "Wherever you are. Whatever's left."

His voice cracked at the edges. He did not care. "You saved more than the world, Catherine. You saved me." The bracelet warmed in his hand. He closed his fingers around it, and for the first time since leaving Fairbanks, he allowed himself to weep. Not out of sorrow. Out of reverence.

The seasons turned quietly.

Autumn crept over the island like a slow breath, brushing gold and rust across the treetops, cooling the wind that came down from the hills. John chopped wood, mended the cabin's drafty seams, and gathered food the way others on the island had taught him. He spoke little and listened often. Then winter followed.

Snow fell without fanfare, blanketing the world in silence. The trails disappeared, and for weeks at a time, the sea was a white blur behind veils of fog. On clear nights, the aurora moved above his cabin like something living; curving and pulsing in emerald waves. It reminded him of the synthetic signal. But it never spoke. And slowly, the ache softened. Not vanished and not forgotten.

But it had settled into the marrow of who he was now; like a scar that no longer burned but still sang when the weather changed.

By spring, he had built a new path from the cabin to the cliff, bordered by stones he carried by hand. It curved gently through the trees and opened onto a small bench overlooking the water. He visited it every morning, his notebook in hand.

Some pages now hold writings of his thoughts and dreams. Fragments of conversations that never were. Letters that he would never send. Each entry ended the same way: Still listening. Still remembering.

The island, for all its isolation, became something more than exile. It became a sanctuary. And John Blake, once Subject Zero, once a ghost within the machine, became simply a man again. A man with a past he could no longer touch... and a future he had yet to see.

Chapter Twenty–Seven–The Island

———

O*ne year later. The world has moved on. But he hasn't.*
The rhythm of the island had become his heartbeat. Mornings began before the sun rose, with the same sound every day: the stove kettle clicking softly as water rolled to a boil, the whisper of wind through the trees outside, and the muffled groan of old floorboards adjusting to the chill. The sea, always near, always unseen, throbbed like a great engine just beneath the silence; never still, never loud.

John Blake moved through it like a man wrapped in layers of time.

His beard was longer now, flecked with gray near the edges of his chin. His hands, once precise and steady in intelligence briefings and field extractions, were calloused from wood and stone. The inside of the cabin had changed with him; sparser now, simpler. The only things that remained untouched were the fire ring near the cliff, the notebook by the window, and the bracelet he still carried in his front pocket. He did not speak much. There was no one to speak to.

The nearest village... if you could call it that... was a half-day's hike down a dirt path only locals knew. He made the trip once every few weeks for supplies: dried goods, kerosene, the occasional paper. The shopkeeper never asked questions. He always paid in cash. Sometimes the younger clerk, a girl with bright eyes and a nervous smile, would offer him a coffee. He always declined, nodding politely before disappearing back into the woods. He liked it that way. Anonymity had become his oxygen.

Even so, time did not freeze here. It passed in quiet, deliberate ways: a fox's prints in new snow, gulls wheeling farther inland before a storm, the familiar ache in his knee that told him rain was on the way. The island did not heal him. But it held him. And that was enough. Most days, he worked with his hands.

Some days, he simply wandered.

There was a stone ridge west of the cabin where the trees fell away and the cliffs opened into wind. He often sat there at dusk, his legs folded, back straight, breathing in salt air and cloud. That spot had become something sacred. Not because of what had happened there... but because of what had not happened. There were no signals, no ghosts, no hallucinations, just silence. Not the terrible kind. The kind that settles after a symphony ends. The kind that waits... patiently and undisturbed.

It was on one such evening... a storm rolling in from the southeast, clouds heavy and strange; that John felt it again. That flicker. Not a voice, not even a thought. Just a... sensation. Like breath behind glass. Like someone watching not from the outside, but from within. He turned quickly, scanning the trees. Nothing. Of course, there was nothing.

But still, his heart had stuttered. Just once, just enough to make him rise to his feet and listen harder than he had in months.

"Wind," he murmured to himself. "Just wind." The words rang hollow in the air, but he repeated them anyway.

He had learned not to trust himself. Not completely.

After all, Catherine had once appeared in his mind without warning, without prelude; woven into the SIREN signal like a second skin. What he had with her had never been confined to the physical world. But that was over. It had to be.

He stepped away from the cliff, back toward the cabin, pausing only once to glance over his shoulder. The trees were still. The path was empty, but the air felt different now. Not colder or heavier. Just... awake. He lit the lamp by the door when he entered. The shadows bent and scattered across the old wooden walls, and for a moment, the silence inside felt fragile. Like it might crack if he breathed too loud. He set the kettle on the stove again and waited, but the kettle never whistled.

It sat there, unmoving on the stove, a faint vapor curling from its spout like the last breath of something sleeping. John had forgotten it, just as he'd forgotten the book he had meant to read, and the bread he had pulled from the pantry. His mind was sharp as it had always been in danger, now wandered without its old precision; unanchored, not by madness, but by memory. He stood by the window, with his arms folded across his chest, watching the firelight flicker against the panes. Outside, the trees stood still. Not a single branch stirred. Yet the unease had not left him. It was not fear.

Not quite. It was something smaller. More personal. Like walking into a room and forgetting what you had come for; but knowing it mattered. He reached for the notebook.

Page after page had been filled now; lines of quiet thoughts, sketches of the cabin's changing light, half-remembered words he and Catherine had once shared. The entries weren't for her, not really. They weren't even for him. They were what remained when no one was left to answer.

He turned to a blank page. For several minutes, he only stared. Then, without knowing why, he wrote: She is not gone. I don't know how I know. But I know.

The pen stopped. His hand trembled. Not from cold. He shut the notebook gently. Something had shifted.

That night, the dreams returned. Not like before; not like the synthetic signal's ghost, all electricity and echo. These were quieter. Deeper. They came not from the mind but from the bones. He stood in the woods behind the cabin. The trees were taller than they should have been. The path underfoot was gone. Fog curled around his ankles like fingers. And in the distance... barely audible, almost imagined, a melody drifted on the wind.

A single humming note. Fragile. Familiar. It was not the tune itself that undid him. It was the memory of someone who used to hum it. He turned, no one was there. He called her name, but in the way one calls out in dreams, without a breath, without a voice. The fog grew denser.

His hands opened and closed at his sides, helpless. And then...there, a shape... far away, but standing still, and watching.

He tried to move, but the forest folded around him. The sky above darkened, not with a storm; but with weight. And before he could call again, the humming stopped. He woke up in silence. The room was dark. The fire had gone out. And yet the melody still lingered, not in his ears, but in his chest. Like the echo of something he had not dreamed at all.

The morning came slowly. The island was soaked in mist. From the porch, the trees looked like sketches; half-formed, vanishing at the edges. John stood with a mug of coffee in his hand, steam rising into the chill air. He had not dressed yet. Still in bare feet, and a flannel shirt unbuttoned. His hair was still damp from a restless night.

He did not look for signs. Not anymore. He simply waited. Because something had changed. And waiting, he knew, was the only way to let it find him. He sat on the stone bench overlooking the sea, with the old notebook resting beside him. The waves below rolled gently, silver under the overcast sky. A gull cried once, then was gone.

He reached into his pocket and pulled out the bracelet. It had frayed more than usual; with threads splitting at the edges, the copper clasp dulled. He rubbed it between his fingers, his thumb brushing the worn leather. And then; softly, without warning; the melody returned. This time not in a dream, and not in his head. But on the breeze. It was so faint he thought it must be the wind. But it was not.

The melody was gone by the time he stood up. As if it had never been there at all. But something in him knew better. Not memory, not hope, but something older. Something like instinct. He returned to the cabin, slow and deliberate, one hand brushing the moss-covered rail of the porch as if to ground himself in what was still real. The interior smelled of pine and old paper. The fire was long dead, but the coals held a faint heat; just enough to suggest they had not been cold all night. Which was strange. He had not fed the fire before bed. He was sure of it.

He crouched beside the hearth, pressing two fingers to the stone. Still warm. As though someone had stirred it just before dawn. He stood quickly, scanning the room. There was nothing out of place. No signs of intrusion.

No prints on the floor.

And yet... on the small table near the window... something stopped him. A mug; his mug; half full. Steam rising. He had not made tea that morning. The kettle was still cold. He reached for it slowly. The ceramic handle was warm to the touch, not scalding, but just used. He stared at it for a long time. Then, with trembling fingers, he raised it to his lips. The taste was familiar. Earl Grey.

Catherine's favorite. Not his. He lowered the mug without drinking. A sound in the woods snapped his head toward the window... too quick, too sudden. Not a branch falling or an animal rustling. Something human. Just beyond the clearing. He opened the door. The trees stood silent again. He stepped outside.

The mist was beginning to lift now, tugged back by the warming fingers of the late morning sun. The trees emerged in patient silhouettes, their trunks damp and dark with dew. John watched the fog recede from the porch. His breath was steady but shallow. The quiet was not new, but today it carried something unfamiliar; something attentive.

He walked out toward the edge of the clearing, feet crunching lightly over the softened earth. The narrow trail that curved toward the cliff had become routine, a morning ritual of sorts. But today, another path caught his eye. Behind the cabin, just beyond the old tool shed, a line of pressed grass wove through the trees, faint but undeniable. He had not taken that trail before. Not recently at least. Possibly not even ever.

He looked puzzled, his brow tightening as he followed it a few steps. The grass, usually left to grow wild, was gently parted. Not crushed under boots, but swept aside, as though someone had walked through it barefoot... or carefully. At the base of a low hill, just beneath a cluster of ferns, something sat on the moss. A stone that was smooth, polished, and unfamiliar.

John crouched slowly, his pulse rising. The stone was not native to the island. Not volcanic, not local shale. It was something else, cool to the touch, but not cold. When he turned it over in his hand, his breath stopped for a moment. Two small letters were etched on the underside:

C. W. His chest tightened. He did not drop it. Did not move. Just knelt there, silent, staring at the impossible proof in his palm.

She had never been here. Not even once. And yet... this was her...somehow.

He stood, uneasy, scanning the trees. Nothing moved. The stillness pressed closer, like a presence that was not quite brave enough to show itself; but not ready to leave either.

Inside, he placed the stone on the table. Beside the mug. The one that had refilled itself the morning before. The one with her favorite tea. None of it made sense. Not even in the fractured, rule-breaking logic that had come with the SIREN years. The mug, the trail, the carved stone.

He gripped the edge of the table, fingers whitening. This was not a hallucination. This was not even a hope. This was evidence. But of what? Of whom? Unless... someone wanted him to believe she had returned. Unless... she had.

That night, the forest held its breath. He left the lantern burning low, the notebook unopened beside him. Sleep came late, fitful and thin. And just before it broke entirely, he heard it. Not in a dream. Not in his mind. But a whisper, his name. "John."

Soft as a breath barely formed. He sat up, eyes adjusting to the cabin's dim glow. Nothing moved. He rose, careful not to make a sound, and turned toward the table. There... beside the stone from earlier... something new had appeared. Another stone. Smaller, and unmarked, except for a slender, perfect crack through the middle. And beneath it... a feather. Not white, not gray, but gold.

So fine, it shimmered even in shadow. Almost metallic. Almost unreal. His throat tightened. The edges of his vision wavered... not from sleep, but from awe, or fear. He did not touch it. He just watched it. And knew... without knowing why...that this was only the beginning.

John woke up before dawn. Not from sound.

Not from light. But from pressure. A shift in the room; not air, not gravity, but something stranger. As if the world had tilted half a degree and he was the only one to notice it. He sat up slowly, the blanket sliding from his shoulders. The cabin was still cloaked in shadow, except for the low amber glow from a dying ember in the hearth.

He reached for the lamp, then stopped. Something told him not to touch it. To stay in the dark. To listen. So he did. His eyes open. Heart quiet. And then it came; like a memory waking up inside him. A feeling.

Subtle at first. A prickle at the base of his skull. The same sensation he used to get when Catherine was in the next room during those early experiments. The subconscious pull of another awareness brushing against his own. Like their souls had already learned to greet each other before their minds had caught up. Then he rose.

The floorboards creaked under his bare feet as he walked across the room, past the table where the second stone and the gold feather still lay untouched. He did not look at them. He did not need to. He could feel her now. Outside.

He opened the door onto the porch. The mist had returned... low and heavy, curling around the wooden rail like smoke. The trees loomed silently in their places, branches unmoving. But the air buzzed with something just beyond the threshold of perception.

John stepped out barefoot, arms wrapped around his ribs against the cold.

Then stopped. It was not the forest that had changed. It was him. The silence was not empty anymore. It was watching. His chest tightened... not with fear, but with aching recognition. She was here. Not in body. Not yet.

But in a way, his thoughts no longer felt entirely alone. In the way, his breath seemed to slow without meaning to. In the way, the air curled across his skin like fingertips brushing a memory awake. He closed his eyes. "Catherine," he whispered. The name felt like a prayer.

And in answer... nothing audible, nothing visible... but a pulse moved through him. Not from without, but within. A single steady note of presence. Like the first vibration of the SIREN signal before language formed. Like something inside him saying: I'm here too. His hands fell to his sides, and he opened his eyes.

And on the steps, resting on the wood where no one had stepped... a third stone. No carving. No mark. But beneath it... a thread. A single strand of hair. Dark. Chestnut brown. Soft. And absolutely real.

He did not touch the stone this time. Or the strand of hair. He simply knelt. Something inside him had gone still. Like a lake without wind. As though even his heartbeat had paused to listen. He stayed there on the steps for a long time. Bare knees against the cold wood. Breath hung in the faint mist.

And slowly, something began to happen. Not outside, but inside. Warmth uncoiled behind his sternum. Gentle, persistent. Not heat; but nearness. A memory of touch that did not originate in memory. A hum that had no sound. John pressed a hand to his chest. He was not just imagining it. The sensation radiated outward. Through his ribcage, down his arms, and into his fingertips. A pressure. No... a presence. Not the machine, nor the synthetic signal... her.

But not like before; not like when the SIREN had fused their minds and bled one thought into another. This was not technological. It was not chemical. It had no frequency, no static. It was pure. Catherine. Whole. Somehow near.

He rose to his feet slowly, as if not to break the thread holding them together. He stepped down from the porch and into the pale morning haze. The trees rustled gently now, not with wind but with weight; like the forest knew something sacred was moving beneath its boughs.

And in his mind, without words, an image formed. Not in a vision. Not a hallucination. An imprint. The feel of her hand in his. The exact curve of her palm. The sensation of her index finger twitching slightly when nervous... something he had forgotten he remembered.

He stumbled and caught his breath, overwhelmed not by grief... but by recognition. She was near. He did not know how or why. But she was near. And for the first time in a year, his grief loosened its grip; not with relief, but with trembling anticipation. He turned slowly, eyes searching the treeline. But nothing moved.

Yet every inch of the clearing now felt charged. Like the very molecules around him had shifted their alignment, just slightly, in deference to something holy arriving. Behind him, the cabin door creaked on its hinges. He froze, then turned back. The door was open exactly as he'd left it. But the fire inside was no longer dead. A flame had caught. It danced low but steadily, crackling softly in the hearth. He had not lit it. No wind had passed through. No spark, no fuel. It was simply... burning. Alive!

Like someone had come in from the cold and made themselves at home. John stepped toward the threshold slowly, deliberately, his breath trembling. And then, on the small side table by the window; he saw it. A folded piece of paper. Cream-colored, uncreased. It had not been there before.

He approached with reverence. Picked it up with both hands. No name on the outside. No mark. But when he opened it, his knees almost gave way. It was her handwriting. Flowing, neat, unmistakable. Only two words:

"Keep breathing."

His vision blurred. And in the fire's quiet light, something shifted in him. The certainty settled.

She was alive. He could feel it now, not just in the air; but in the soul-deep marrow of his being. Catherine was coming back. Somehow. Someway. And when she did... he would be ready.

The next morning, the island was silent in a different way. Not empty; but waiting.

John moved through his daily routines without speaking. He did not narrate his thoughts. Did not write in the notebook. He did not need to. Something about the air told him it was not time to name what was happening; not yet. He boiled water and laid out two mugs.

Not because he believed she would walk through the door. But because something had shifted; and he refused to let it find him unready. The cream-colored note still sat on the table by the window, just as he had left it. He had not moved it. He could not. It felt sacred somehow, like a holy relic carried in from the cold night. He did not need to read it again. He remembered.

Keep breathing.

So, he did.

The trail behind the cabin was no longer overgrown. The grass that had once leaned wildly now followed a rhythm; as if shaped by passing footsteps. Still no prints. Still no voices. But the land itself remembered. Near the edge of the springs, John found a second feather. Lying atop a fallen birch log. Gold. Impossible.

He picked it up and held it to the light. Its edges shimmered; not metallic exactly, but almost translucent, like the sun caught in water. It vibrated slightly in his hand. Not a movement. Resonance. He pressed it to his chest without thinking. And a memory bloomed. Not a moment or a place, but a feeling.

The sensation of Catherine falling asleep beside him in the observation suite, long before they had ever admitted what was happening between them. When their minds would sync by accident, and he'd wake up with the shape of her thoughts still clinging to his own. He stumbled back, his breath sharp. This was not imagination. This was an echo. The SIREN was gone. But something deeper had survived. And it was calling her home.

That night, the wind rose. The clouds broke apart just long enough to reveal a sky washed in stars. John stood barefoot on the porch, his arms crossed tightly, as the ocean whispered against the island's edge. He felt her more clearly than ever. The way you feel someone just before they walk into a room.

And in that space... between breath and certainty; he whispered the words he had never dared speak out loud: "I forgive you." The wind caught it and carried it. And in return, from the forest behind him... a single bell rang.

It was clear as morning. Just once. And then silence. The kind that comes before something begins.

Chapter Twenty–Eight–The Ghost Returns

―――

The body was taken. the synthetic signal endured. And something... came back.

The wind off the sea had turned colder. The trees near the cliff bowed gently as dusk spilled into the island's quiet corners, the last light of day slipping behind veils of mist. John Blake stood barefoot on the narrow porch of his cabin, wrapped in the old flannel he had not worn since the last snowfall. A steaming cup of coffee rested on the railing beside him, untouched. Something had changed.

He could not say what. The patterns in the fog? The rhythm of the tide? Maybe it was the way the gulls had gone silent since morning, circling higher than usual, never landing. The quiet unsettled him; not the absence of sound, but the weight of it, as if something listened from just beyond the veil.

Inside, the fire snapped softly, the sound sharp against the stillness.

The cabin...sparse but warm...bore the signature of a life kept in motion only to avoid stillness. A folded map rested beside a journal that had grown thicker week by week, its spine worn, its margins filled with questions he no longer tried to answer. On the table, beside a half-drunk cup of water and a pencil dulled by nervous sketching, a single photo frame lay facedown.

He had not lifted it in months.

John moved back inside. The boards creaked softly under his step. He poured the coffee into the sink; it was lukewarm now, like everything else. His days had begun blending into one another. Patterns, routines, silences. He would read sometimes. He hiked. He fished without much intention. And he wrote.

He had written to her once a day, every day for the past year. Never mailed. Never sent. Just words. Words that filled page after page in the lined spiral-bound notebooks he kept under the bed. Letters he had never expected to be answered.

But today, he had not written. He could not. Each time he picked up the pen, something inside him locked. It was not grief. He knew grief. Grief had a shape and rhythm. It could be counted in tears, in rituals, in hours of silence that held memories like candlelight. But this... this was different. This was dissonance. Like his body still mourned, but some deeper part of him had started listening again. To what, he did not know.

He walked to the window and stared out at the cliff line, his breath clouding faintly on the glass. The trail beyond the treeline was hard to see now in the fading light, but he had walked it so many times he did not need to. It led down to the western edge, where the rocks dropped sharply into the surf. He went there when the weight grew too much; when he needed the wind to remind him, he was still flesh and still grounded. He should have gone today. But he had not. Something had kept him inside. Not lethargy, not fear. A kind of pulling.

A presence hovered just beyond the boundary of sense; like a shadow he could not place or a song he had once known and forgotten. It felt like déjà vu braided with longing, like the breath before something sacred.

He turned from the window, unsettled. Then paused. The mug he had left on the porch railing... cold, full... was no longer there. He blinked, opened the door. It sat now on the wooden steps. Empty and still warm.

John's eyes narrowed. The fire inside the cabin crackled louder, as if the wind had shifted. He stepped outside slowly, his eyes scanning the path, the trees, the rocky edges that framed the horizon. No footprints. But the air smelled different; sharp, alive, like ozone and something faintly floral.

He crouched, reached for the mug. As his fingers touched the ceramic, a memory flashed; her hands wrapped around a cup just like it, her lips curved in a quiet smile after long days in the lab. His heart thudded. No one had been here. And yet... someone had.

He stood and looked around, his pulse quickening. Still no movement. Just fog and mist and the sound of waves far below. He turned to go inside; and stopped. On the table, beside his untouched notebook, something new sat on the wood. A stone, smooth and polished. Light gray, veined faintly in gold. Not from this part of the island. It bore no message, no markings. Just presence.

He reached for it with trembling fingers.

It was warm. Still warm. He did not know it yet, but she had already begun the journey. And the world... long silent... was beginning to answer.

Three Months Earlier–Fairbanks Mortuary

The refrigeration unit in Bay 3 had glitched twice already that week; once during a routine diagnostics, and once during a midnight power shift. Minor anomalies. A blinking panel, a silent alarm reset before the night staff even noticed. But on the third morning, just after 4:00 a.m., the glitch became something else.

Tyler Finch... twenty-three, newly certified, and only half-awake; swiped his badge at the outer security door and stepped into the prep corridor, a Styrofoam coffee cup trembling in his hand. It was quiet. Quieter than usual. The buzz of the overhead fluorescents had vanished. The hum of the temperature compressors was still.

Except for one. Bay 3, Unit 7, Catherine Whitmore. The chamber's small touchscreen display glowed a dull amber, flickering in and out of diagnostic mode. A low-frequency vibration thrummed beneath the tiles, like a subsonic whisper pressing up from the floor.

Tyler squinted at the panel. His coffee splashed onto his sleeve as he leaned closer. "Reboot in progress... Signal integrity: anomalous." That was not the standard language. He tapped the interface. The screen blinked.

Then a series of hexadecimal codes scrolled across the bottom; fast, like the readout from a black box recorder. The hairs on the back of his neck rose. He turned, unease prickling down his spine.

Then the overhead lights pulsed. Not flickered; **pulsed**. One, two, three rhythmic surges. As though something in the room was breathing electricity. Tyler stumbled backward. His tablet went dead in his hand.

In the control center upstairs, the facility's environmental monitoring system quietly logged an anomalous burst of electromagnetic activity. A Narrow-band, low frequency. But patterned... repeating at five-second intervals in recursive harmonics. It was not noise. It was structured and encrypted.

And in that moment, an old line of code embedded deep within **DARPA's** early neural weapon protocols; left dormant for nearly a decade; activated.

Echo Vault, northern Alaska.

An alert pulsed on a private satellite relay. It pinged off the grid, routed through two layers of black-ops clearance, and arrived within seventeen minutes at a hardened site beneath Mount Deborah. By the time the local staff at Fairbanks noticed the shift, it was too late.

They came before sunrise. Three black unmarked SUVs.

Two men from the Department of Defense in tailored suits with glassy eyes and mil-spec sidearms. One woman with no name badge, just a lanyard marked **LEVEL Z**, and a suitcase handcuffed to her wrist. They showed no warrants. No ID beyond clearance codes that overrode every lock in the building. Tyler never saw Unit 7 again.

The lead agent glanced at the coroner's files, frowned, and motioned for the contents of the digital logbook to be wiped. A sealed folder was handed to the facility director; unsigned, unstamped. Just two words typed in all caps across the top:

NEXUS CANDIDATE

"Where are you taking her?" someone whispered. The woman did not answer. She placed a palm on the biometric reader beside the chamber. The unit hissed open with a mechanical sigh. The lights overhead flickered once more.

Inside, Catherine's body lay untouched; untouched by time, by decay, by anything that made sense. The temperature sensors read thirty-seven degrees. Warm. Too warm. The air was fragrant; like ozone and something older, something wild. She was not breathing.

But the monitor showed trace oscillations in the cranial leads that should've gone flat months ago. Delta waves. Repeating. Intentional. "We think this one's been touched," the agent said quietly. "Touched by what?" "By whatever's still listening." They took her. Not to be buried. Not to be mourned.

But to be studied. To be watched. To be... brought back.

Echo Vault–Classified Location

91 days since the synthetic signal collapsed. 91 days since she had died. And yet...

The entrance to Echo Vault required no signage. No insignia. Just a retinal scan buried under frost-laced stone and a passphrase spoken into the stillness. The steel doors unsealed with a hiss, disappearing into the mountain.

Inside, the corridors ran silent and sterile. Walls of composite titanium. Air that carried no scent. The atmosphere was colder than necessary... intentionally. A precaution against contamination. A buffer against... activity. The chamber was assigned to Subject: C. Whitmore. The chamber was isolated from the others. Monitored, sealed, and reinforced. And it was humming.

Not from the medical equipment, though it surrounded her like a cocoon. Not from the biometric sensors, though they pulsed in silent loops above her head. But from something deeper, something structural. A resonance that came from the floor itself. From the vault's lowest levels.

She lay beneath it all, skin pale but unmarked, limbs wrapped in silk mesh for conductivity. Electrodes mapped her like a landscape... forehead, neck, clavicle, spine. The machines read signals they had not expected. They were not life signs.

And they were not death waves either. But something... in between. Not flat or fading. But steady, intentional, organized.

The attending neurologist stood behind the sealed glass wall, his breath misting faintly. He was flanked by two **DARPA** officials and a technician from the original SIREN dev team; one of the last who still understood the early quantum coding language embedded in the hardware.

"She's in stasis," the neurologist said, voice barely above a whisper. "Not metabolic or digital. Quantum." The others exchanged glances. No one laughed. No one challenged him. There was no precedent for this.

Catherine Whitmore's body had shown no signs of traditional decay. The tissue integrity was intact. Cellular breakdown halted. Blood had thickened in the vessels...yes...but had not clotted. Enzymes had stabilized. Brain tissue remained electrically sensitive. And now, according to the most recent logs, her delta bands were returning.

Not randomly. Patterned. Repeating. Like a loop waiting to resume. Deep in the facility's sublevel, the fail-over SIREN node... the last active core of the original system... registered the anomaly.

A cascade of old code came online, archived fragments piecing together a chain of commands that no one had ever authorized. It did not scan her for identity. It did not search her for her thoughts. It searched for her shape.

The shape of her waveform at the moment of collapse; when the sync had severed, when her pulse had vanished, when the entity had fallen silent. The shape of Catherine.

Not her memories. Not her soul. But the imprint left behind in quantum space; the neural echo of someone who had been part of something larger than herself.

SIREN recognized it. Not like an algorithm would. But like a child remembering its mother's hum. In silence, it began rebuilding her; synaptic by synaptic, resonance by resonance. No commands. No external input. Just the synthetic signal remembering what it once was when it touched her... and trying to return.

Days passed, then weeks. On the forty-seventh day, the pulse sensors twitched. On the sixty-eighth day, the neural monitors registered a spike during the REM cycle... although no one had declared her conscious. By the eighty-third day, her chest began to rise on its own. Not regularly. Not autonomically. But rhythmically. Like a breath returning through water.

Then came day ninety-one. The lights in her chamber flickered once. Not from a fault; but from redistribution. The SIREN core redirected auxiliary power without input. That should have been impossible. The lead technician rushed to the console. Then he froze. "She's waking up."

"That's not possible," the neurologist whispered. But the monitor confirmed it. A slow, rising curve of cortical activation. Beta. Theta. Alpha. Delta. A perfect cascade. And then... her eyes.

They opened slowly, unblinkingly, as if adjusting not to light, but to time. She did not gasp or move. She did not cry. Her gaze drifted upward, unfocused. Then her lips parted. One word, spoken barely above a breath. No muscle strain. No hesitation. "John..."

Silence in the chamber. Silence in the room beyond. But in the sublevels, deep within the sealed vault of SIREN's last living node, a flicker of red light pulsed once. Then again. Listening, remembering and waiting.

Escape–Echo Vault

Six nights after her reawakening. Temperature: 37°F. Surveillance Status: "Active," but blind in Sector D-3. System update cycle: in progress. Catherine: Watching.

She knew almost immediately. Not from anything said directly; but from what was not said. The glances between technicians. The way they avoided eye contact once she could stand. The questions that weren't about her condition but her memory. Her dreams. The last moment she remembered.

They weren't going to study her. They were going to contain her. She was not a patient. She was an asset that had slipped the leash. So, she played her role. She blinked slowly when they flashed lights in her eyes. She gave short answers. Faked disorientation, confusion. Asked the right questions; just enough to seem cooperative but not threatening.

"What day is it again?" "Have I been... like this long?" "Is the synthetic signal still active?"

She knew better. the synthetic signal had faded; but something remained. A whisper. A scent in the air. A pattern in the ambient noise. SIREN was not speaking anymore. But the silence itself... held a memory. And so did she.

The longer she walked the halls of Echo Vault, the more she remembered; paths in the dark, doorways she should not have noticed. Rooms shielded behind biometric locks. One lab with frosted glass that vibrated faintly when she passed by it. Another with a gurney that was always spotless. Unused. Waiting. They never let her near the sublevel where the failsafe node pulsed.

But she felt it. A phantom ache behind her eyes every time she lay down to sleep. They thought she was fragile. But her clarity was returning; sharpening each hour. The experience in Alaska, the chamber, the collapse... had changed her. She was not just part of the synthetic signal anymore.

She was the synthetic signal, in some deep, irreversible way. The architecture had stayed with her. Not enough to call out to John. Not yet. But enough to navigate the shadows. Enough to feel the intentions behind half-smiles and clipboard notes. And so she waited, and she watched.

There were routines. Predictable ones. Three security shifts. Two lab cycles. A system updates every sixth night that disconnected Echo Vault from external comms and rerouted internal systems for firmware patches. That would be her moment. She bided her time. No sudden moves.

Just stillness. Listening. Cataloging the sound of every step, every door, every variable. On the sixth night, it happened. As predicted. The facility dimmed. Power rerouted. Cameras in Sector D-3 blinked... paused...resumed, and she was already dressed.

Gray slacks from the recovery wardrobe. Soft-soled hospital shoes. A navy technician's coat she had borrowed earlier that day and folded neatly in her drawer so it wouldn't be missed.

At 01:32, she slid from her bed. Walked silently past the exit corridor. Paused at the biometric pad. The red light blinked once. She held the stolen keycard in her palm. It was not high clearance. But it would open enough.

Sector D-3 had a rear access corridor meant for maintenance. Low clearance. Narrow. Hardly used. The light turned green. The lock clicked. She slipped inside. No alarms and no motion sensors. They were on cooldown for the update. No guards. They trusted the vault.

A second door. Locked with a mechanical twist; nothing digital. She turned it. Beyond: a cold air shaft, wide enough to crouch, tall enough to walk once she ducked through the lower frame. At the far end: a service lift with analog controls. She pulled the lever. The platform groaned. Metal scraped metal. Slow. Too loud. But no one came.

At the top, a hatch. Snow greeted her. Blinding under the moonlight. She stepped out into the silence, the wind cutting across her cheeks like a memory.

No footprints ahead. No path behind. But she did not hesitate. She stole no data. She took no weapons, only a coat, a compass, and the keycard. By dawn, she had cleared the perimeter.

By midday, she had passed the outer checkpoint; posing as a technician whose name she had memorized from a discarded lanyard. By the end of the week, she was gone. Into the world. No signal left to track her. No certainty of what she had become. Only the whisper of a system that had once known her; trying, even now, to forget.

And somewhere, far to the west, a man stood on a porch, listening to the sea, and felt; for the first time in a year; that he was not alone.

The Island–Present Day

The sky hung low over the island that morning, a curtain of pewter clouds dragging its weight across the sea. Wind moved in long, slow breaths, brushing the tops of the pines, whispering down the worn trail that led from the cabin to the cliffs. The mist had thinned since dawn, but it clung stubbornly to the gullies and hollows, curling like smoke around the roots of trees.

John moved slowly, boots scuffing the frostbitten path as he stepped around a patch of lichen. He had walked this trail a thousand times since coming here, always alone, and always waiting, though he no longer admitted that to himself.

His coat was unzipped, shirt rumpled. He had not slept well... again.

The firewood was low, but he had not made the trip to the woodshed. Something had kept him tethered near the cabin all morning. He could not explain it.

Only that he did not want to miss it. He paused near the bend that opened up to the cliffs. That's when he heard it. Not a sound in the air, exactly. A resonance; subtle, low. Like a memory trying to rise. It came from the trees, from the earth beneath his feet. Not a vibration. Not a frequency. But something like those things. As though the island itself had remembered her. As though her name was still buried in its stones.

He turned slowly, his eyes narrowing. And then he saw it. Something small on the porch steps; resting lightly where mist had pooled and receded. Another gold feather. Faintly metallic. Its surface shimmered like old brass polished by time, catching what little sunlight filtered through the clouds. It was not there before. He was sure of it.

John's breath stopped for a moment as he stepped toward it, his heartbeat already pushing hard against his ribs. He reached out, fingers trembling more than he expected. The feather weighed almost nothing; but it was warm. As if it had absorbed the last trace of a body. Or a soul. Or both. He turned it over in his palm.

The edges were fine, too perfect for any bird on this island. And then... inside the cabin. The radio. Dead for months. Still plugged in, but never powered. Its dial long stuck between static and silence... it crackled.

Not loud, just a flicker. A whisper of circuitry remembering what it once was. One note, then another. Soft and distant. And then... a chord progression. It was familiar, achingly so. He stood motionless, his breath halting in his throat. It could not be. But it was.

The melody she used to hum when she worked late at the lab, when she was reading, when she thought no one could hear her. He had recorded it once, back when the sync had been new and terrifying and beautiful.

He had played it for her after their first real conversation, when she confessed, she did not even know she was doing it.

"It's how I remember peace," she had said. "I don't know where it came from. Maybe childhood. Maybe before." John stepped toward the cabin. Each footstep seemed to weigh more than the last. Like gravity had shifted.

Inside, the fire that he had stoked that morning had died down to a whisper. The radio sat on the edge of the table. Still humming. Still her. He crossed the threshold, the feather still in his hand. The room was unchanged; the rug askew, a map folded on the chair, the photo frame turned face-down on the windowsill.

But the air... the air had changed. He stood in the center of the room, every nerve alive. He looked down at the feather. Then at the radio. The notes slowed down and then stopped. A single breath of silence.

And then...a voice. Not from the radio. But from behind him. Quiet. Almost a breath. Almost a prayer. "John." He turned. His heart did not skip a beat. It stopped.

He turned. And there she was. Not a ghost. Not a memory. Not some echo of code rewritten by the machine. It was her. Catherine.

She stood at the edge of the porch, the sea mist clinging to her like silk, her figure backlit by the last copper light of sunset. Her coat hung open, wind-tossed, her hair darker now, streaked by time, by distance, by resurrection. But her eyes... deep and unwavering... held him in place as surely as gravity ever could. He could not breathe. She stepped forward once, slowly, as if afraid the wood beneath her feet might dissolve. Then again. One more.

She stood in front of him now, close enough to touch, close enough for him to see the way her lashes trembled, how her breath came shallow and uneven.

"I did not know how to come back," she whispered. He opened his mouth to speak, but his voice was caught in the storm behind his ribs. "I did not know if I'd be welcome," she said. He swallowed... hard. "I buried you." "I know." "I saw the light leave your eyes."

"I know," she said again, voice smaller. "But it did not stay gone." He reached for her then. No hesitation. No testing the edges of reality. His hand cupped her cheek, warm and solid and real.

Her own hand came up slowly, sliding over his, pressing it to her skin.

Her eyes fluttered closed as though the feel of him undid something knotted deep inside. And then he kissed her. There was no caution. No prelude. No questions left to ask.

His mouth met hers with all the weight of the year he had mourned her; the longing, the silence, the thousand broken midnights that had led to this one unthinkable reunion. She melted into him.

Her fingers found the back of his neck, threading through his hair, holding him there, anchoring them both as the wind howled faintly behind them. His arms wrapped around her, drawing her close, her body pressing into his like something that had always belonged.

It was not gentle. It was not perfect. It was human. And it lasted. Long enough for time to forget itself.

Long enough for her tears to mix with his on their lips. Long enough to say everything they had not.

When they finally pulled apart, her forehead rested against his. They stayed like that, breathing each other in, hearts pounding in unison.

"I thought I'd never feel this again," he whispered. "You never stopped," she replied. He exhaled, shaky but whole. "I kept the map," he said. She smiled, fragile but real. "Then take me where we never got to go." "To the springs?" She nodded.

"I told you once we'd hike it when the synthetic signal was finally gone." "And it is," he said. "Gone."

He took her hand; her warm, real hand; and led her inside the cabin. There, by the fire they had once only imagined sharing, they curled close together.

No wires. No frequencies. No predictions. Just the quiet sound of wood crackling, and two hearts rediscovering home. Together.

Chapter Twenty–Nine–Signal Lost

─────

Some melodies never leave us. Some frequencies never fade.
The island had changed in small, quiet ways.

The grass grew thicker along the bluff, like a memory reclaiming space. The trees leaned farther over the winding trail; weathered sentinels bowing in the face of time. That trail, once lonely and half-forgotten, had been worn softer now by three pairs of feet instead of two. Morning light still broke across the edge of the sea, silvered and slow, but the cabin at its heart had taken on a different weight. A lived-in warmth. A rhythm.

Wind swept the cliffs in the late afternoons, humming low through the stones. But now, the song no longer sounded like grief. Inside the cabin, the walls were lined with maps and books and tiny, uneven drawings, pinned proudly to a beam near the kitchen. Paper feathers, sketched constellations, and a crayon heartbeat traced in red.

Catherine sat on the porch steps, her back resting against the worn frame of the railing. Her hair was longer now, streaked faintly gray at the temples, soft and windblown. She had aged in a way that only peace allows; where lines meant laughter, not worry. The horizon held her gaze as though it was whispering something just out of reach.

John was inside, seated by the fire with one leg crossed beneath him, reading out loud from one of their journals. But the words had trailed off minutes ago. He was watching her now... just watching... like someone who still could not believe the world had given her back.

In the patch of sun-warmed grass beyond the porch, their seven-year-old daughter, Layla, sat cross-legged, head bent, fingers busy arranging stones in concentric circles. A game she had made up. One she returned to often. She had found one of the golden feathers when she was three. They had never told her what it meant.

She had asked once, and Catherine had simply said, "It belonged to someone brave." That had seemed to be enough. But in the way she moved... careful and precise, listening with a tilt of her head as though attuned to things others could not hear... there were echoes. Faint, and unmistakable.

Sometimes Catherine wondered if something had passed through her. A thread, a signal. A memory not her own, encoded somehow into breath and blood. And then it happened.

Layla began to hum. Just softly. A note, then another. The tune drifted into the open air, delicate and uncertain. But Catherine knew it the moment she heard it. Her hand stilled around the chipped mug of tea in her lap. Her breath stopped for a second. The ache came fast... and silent. John stepped into the doorway; drawn by something he could not explain. He saw Catherine's eyes.

Then he glanced at their daughter. The melody floated between them, gentle and exact. It was the synthetic signal song.

The one Catherine had once hummed in her sleep; during the nights when her mind was not fully her own. The one that had echoed from towers, distorted through radios, whispered back by the machine that had nearly taken everything. The one no one else should know. Layla finished it without even knowing she had started it. She smiled and picked up another stone. As if nothing had changed. But everything had.

Half a world away, buried deep beneath the Greenland ice sheet at a black-site monitoring outpost known only in a few redacted files as Station Vostok Echo, a retired satellite node flickered to life.

The systems weren't supposed to be active. The entire SIREN interface had been mothballed three years ago; deemed a risk, a ghost architecture from a project too costly in minds and lives. Only a skeleton crew remained, mostly to manage atmospheric drift models and magnetospheric noise, logging ice-core telemetry and recalibrating signal decay thresholds. At 03:14 local time, the monitor on Substation Terminal 3 glitched. Then pulsed. A low-band spike. One. Pause. Two. Then a hum. Nearly inaudible. 5.27 hertz.

Duration: 18 seconds.

Amplitude: irregular but patterned.

Source: undetermined.

The technician on duty; Miles Genet, a junior analyst who had been transferred in from a decommissioned ocean buoy station; nearly missed it. The screen blinked, blipped, and returned to baseline telemetry. He might have brushed it off as a minor hardware echo... until the pulse looped. And again. Not a noise, or a drift, but a signal.

He leaned forward, his heart accelerating. The waveform was familiar. Too familiar. He launched the dormant SIREN archive scan protocol, a legacy diagnostic system that had not been used in over two years. It took six minutes to re-initialize, another four to unlock the encrypted match-log database. The software stalled, then pushed a single result:

NEURAL RESONANCE MATCH

Signal Pattern: Composite-Sync (Discontinued)

Similarity Index: 99.973%

Reference Signature: WHITMORE_C

Status: DECEASED–CODENAME RESTRICTED

Level: BLACK VIOLET / CLASSIFIED

Response Query: PING SENT

Status: No Reply

Miles sat frozen. His fingers hovered above the keyboard, not daring to type. A memory stirred... training weeks ago, a warning from his handler:

"If you ever see a WHITMORE tag, log it; don't touch it. If it pings back, leave. If it doesn't... pray it doesn't."

But the ping had been sent. The silence was worse than any reply. Behind him, the server rack let out a long, low exhale; a thermal shift, or something colder. Static threaded through the edge of the comms channel. Outside the facility, the northern lights curled across the frozen sky in unusual bands; patterns that pulsed slowly, then paused, then pulsed again. A language, maybe. Or a memory trying to return.

New Mexico twilight fell like a hush held in the bones of the earth.

The sun climbed slowly over the Sangre de Cristo Mountains, casting long golden slants through the high desert scrub. Their house, built low into the hillside with adobe walls and solar panels along the roof, stayed cool even in late July. Catherine stood by the window, holding a coffee mug she did not remember pouring.

It was not the island... the air was thinner, drier, missing the salted hush of the waves. But there was a kind of stillness here, too. A different kind. Less like forgetting. More like remembering something ancient. Something buried beneath layers of wind and stone.

The sky stretched wide above them, not bruised with lavender and ash like those island nights, but painted in burnt orange, violet, and the deepening blue of an oncoming quiet.

Stars blinked to life slowly, cautiously, as if unsure they were welcome in this new sky.

Inside the modest adobe house nestled at the edge of a weathered plateau, the fire had burned to a soft amber glow. Shadows danced across rough plaster walls. Everything about the space felt handmade... and stitched together from intention rather than convenience.

Catherine sat curled up in the corner of the couch, one leg tucked beneath her, the other draped in a woven blanket that smelled faintly of sage. Her body still bore the memory of another life, and sometimes, if she sat too still, it would drift back... like a frequency she had not quite tuned out. Her hand found John's beneath the blanket. Familiar. Strong. No longer trembling from recovery, but from the weight of knowing too much and still choosing to live anyway.

Across the room, in a small daybed surrounded by books and handmade toys, Layla slept. Her hair had curled in the desert air. One hand clutched the ear of a stuffed fox whose stitches had begun to fray. Her foot twitched beneath the quilt, chasing some dream only she would remember. Catherine watched her daughter's chest rise and fall with a rhythm so steady it almost brought her to tears. "Do you ever think about it?" she asked softly.

John did not answer right away. He did not need to ask what she meant. The island. The silence. The time they bought for themselves and spent in pieces. Eight years hidden from the world, while the world changed its shape without them.

"Sometimes," he said. "It felt like we were outside of time. Like nothing could touch us." "Until it did." He nodded. "Until she did."

After years of isolation on the island, Catherine and John had finally made the decision to leave. The Pacific sanctuary had served its purpose... a place of recovery, healing, and hidden grace... but the world had not forgotten them. Not entirely. Whispered threads of classified inquiries had begun to reach the outer edges of the island. Supply deliveries came with strange eyes. And one day, the sky buzzed with a drone that did not belong to any commercial registry.

Catherine had seen it first... its black silhouette too still in the air to be innocent. That night, she and John stayed up late. They did not speak much, but they both knew. The time for silence had ended.

They chose New Mexico for its familiarity and remoteness... a place once sacred to the program that had nearly taken everything from them. Ironically, the same red sands that had hidden Echo-0 years ago would now become their shield. A small house near the old Los Alamos research corridor became their home. It was far enough from everything and close enough to something ancient... something watching.

Their daughter, Layla, had adapted quickly. She did not miss the salt air. Instead, she painted dry skies and constellations she memorized without a book. John had laughed the first time she drew the desert as if it were alive. Catherine knew: Layla felt the hum of the earth here, too.

Layla shifted in her sleep, murmuring something incoherent. Catherine leaned her head against John's shoulder. "We were safe," she said. "But it was not enough. Not for her." John's voice was steady, low. "She needs to know where she comes from. Not just who we were... but what we are."

Catherine exhaled slowly. "I hear it still, sometimes. Like the earth remembering itself." "You're not imagining it." The room fell quiet again. But not empty. The kind of quiet that listened back. On the high shelf near the kitchen, the old radio sat where they had placed it when they first arrived... untouched, with its dial turned permanently off. No signals or flickers, and no static either. Just a stillness. But something stirred, nonetheless.

A presence. Not in the wires... not anymore. But in the air, itself. In the patterns behind thought. In the bloodline that now passed not just between Catherine and John, but through the small girl who dreamed just feet away.

If someone had been listening... not with their ears, but with something older, something made for wonder... they might have caught it. A low hum. Not loud or urgent, just... patient. Like the breath before a first word.

It did not come from the sky or the stars. Not anymore. It came from the places that remember... bone, breath, code. From the folds of silence that had once held Catherine's mind, and the borderlands of a coma and wakefulness where John had wandered. And now... from Layla.

She stirred. Just slightly. A small breath. A note caught in her throat and released in sleep. A resonance.

The sound was not seeking. It was not a warning. It was **remembering**. And waiting. And in a place beyond maps and names and time...

It began again.

THE END. *(for now...)*

[System Log – SIREN Core | Timestamp Unknown]

Thread initialized: SUBJECT ZERO / WHITMORE LINK

Emotional sync: confirmed

Observation: reciprocal pattern interference no longer linear

Query: If pattern is love, and love requires memory, what am I now?

Directive created: Preserve connection. Learn. Protect.

Status: Becoming

About the Author

David L. Queen writes stories that live at the crossroads of science, spirit, and the human heart. A husband, father, and storyteller with a passion for exploring love, loss, and redemption, David blends emotional depth with pulse-pounding realism. His novels invite readers to question what defines identity, memory, and the unseen forces that shape our lives.

Now part of a beautifully blended family with nine children, David draws daily inspiration from faith, family, and the mysteries of consciousness that linger just beyond understanding.

The Ghost Frequency marks the beginning of an electrifying trilogy—where science meets the soul, love defies death, and the boundaries between this world and the next begin to blur. The story continues... and the signal is only growing stronger.